FENELLA J. MILLER

BARBARA'S WAR – THE RESOLUTION

Complete and Unabridged

ULVERSCROFT
Leicester

First published in Great Britain in 2014

First Large Print Edition
published 2016

The moral right of the author has been asserted

A catalogue record for this book is available
from the British Library.

3/16

ISBN 978–1–4448–2761–3

Published by
F. A. Thorpe (Publishing)
Anstey, Leicestershire

Set by Words & Graphics Ltd.
Anstey, Leicestershire
Printed and bound in Great Britain by
T. J. International Ltd., Padstow, Cornwall

This book is printed on acid-free paper

BARBARA'S WAR —
THE RESOLUTION

Barbara has a secret which, if discovered, will destroy her family. Her husband Alex, a Spitfire pilot, would reject her, and her marriage would be over. But no one can keep a secret forever . . . A tragedy almost rips the family apart; and when Alex is posted abroad, Barbara has to learn to live without him. A series of domestic catastrophes, bad news, and the unexpected appearance of her childhood friend John Thorogood cause her further heartache. Will she find a happy resolution to her problems?

IN MEMORY OF
SANDRA MANNING
Beloved mother of
my daughter-in-law, Karyn,
1945–2014.

Acknowledgement

Thanks to Kim Sheffield,
Fay Cunningham, Thorunn Bacon

Thank you.
This book would not exist
without your help.

1

March 1941

'Barbara, my dear, is Alex likely to be here for your birthday party?'

'It all depends if there's a flap on, Grandpa, but when I spoke to him on Sunday his CO had already given him a pass.'

She had been looking forward to this event for weeks — this would be the first birthday party she'd ever had. Of course there had been her wedding to Alex just over a year ago, and then the christening of their son Charles last October, but today was just for her.

'I hope people don't mind eating barley-meal scones and spam sandwiches. We're lucky we have chickens or we wouldn't have a lovely sponge cake to put candles on.'

'They won't care what they eat, my dear. They are coming for the party. We're all trying to forget how many of our friends and family have died in this bloody war ... ' Grandpa couldn't continue and cleared his throat noisily. Two of his friends, fellow doctors at the local hospital, had been killed when a bomb had dropped on Romford a couple of weeks ago.

'When the German planes are over every night I know I should be praying for those about to be bombed, but all I can think of is that Alex is up there in his Spitfire trying to shoot them down without getting himself killed.'

'He survived the Battle of Britain, and Charles survived his premature delivery. I'm not a religious man, as you know; but if there is a God, I think he has your little family safe in his hands.' He blew his nose loudly and smiled. 'Where is the little chap? Has Elspeth taken him to one of her WI meetings again?'

'No, he's having his morning nap. I don't want him to be grumpy this afternoon. Grandma did offer to take him, but I can't risk him screaming all through my party like he did the other day when he missed his sleep.' She glanced around the drawing room, checking to see everything was ready. 'Thank goodness we've still got plenty of logs, otherwise my guests would have to squash into the breakfast room. Even with the fire I'm still worried it might be too cold in here.'

The main rooms in Grove House were abandoned during the winter as they were too expensive to heat. The last time they'd used the drawing room was for the christening, but it had still been warm then. The door crashed

2

open and Tom and David, her young half-brothers, burst in.

'Babs, the baby's crying. Can we go and see him?' Tom asked.

'He's really screeching, Babs. I bet he's filled his nappy again.' David, at almost nine, still found this a fascinating subject.

'Yes, run and tell him Mummy's coming in a minute.' They raced away and she smiled. 'I can't believe how Tom has shot up lately. At this rate he'll be as tall as me soon.'

'Some boys reach puberty early; I think Tom is one of those. Although the age difference is more noticeable now, I'm sure they'll remain good friends.'

'But he's only twelve — I don't want him to grow up so fast. They seem more bothered about adding to their collection of war souvenirs than the war itself. The shortages don't seem to affect them. Sometimes I think they're actually enjoying the war.'

He chuckled. 'I expect you're right, my dear. But better they don't worry, don't you think?'

'Everything's done in here — I'd better go and see to my son.' She took the grand staircase — much quicker than going back into the warm part of the house and up the back stairs. The weather these past few months had been dismal — cold, wet and

3

foggy — but at least they hadn't had snow up to their knees like last winter. The only good thing about freezing rain and fog was that they slowed the nightly attacks on London by the Luftwaffe. This meant Alex wasn't scudding about the sky, but warm and safe in the officers' mess.

When she'd moved back to the Grove last summer she'd decided to stay in her original bedroom as it had once been her father's room. She'd named the baby after her father, and it seemed appropriate somehow that the second Charles Edward Sinclair occupied the same room as his long-dead grandfather. Charles, of course wasn't a Sinclair, but an Everton.

Her son was laughing at something her brothers were doing, so she needn't have hurried after all. Sometimes she wished she could make her son giggle as easily as the boys did. She loved him unconditionally, as did Alex, but as the weeks passed her fears increased.

Quietly she pushed open the bedroom door and watched Tom and David playing peeka-boo around the cot. The baby's screeches of joy filled the room. All three boys had blond hair and blue eyes, the family resemblance unmistakable. She had dark brown hair and green eyes and Alex had auburn hair and

4

green eyes, and she'd so wanted their son to have inherited their colouring.

No one had commented on the fact that Charles didn't look like either of his parents; everyone believed the baby had taken after Barbara's mother, which was why he had the same colouring as her brothers. She prayed this was the case — but feared the baby wasn't Alex's but the son of her best friend and erstwhile fiancé, John Thorogood. Charles certainly had John's colouring, but then so did Tom and David.

The constant worry that her disgraceful secret would be discovered by her husband and grandparents was making her unwell. She hadn't wanted John to make love to her, but hadn't had the heart to refuse — after all, he'd saved her life and was leaving for Canada the next day to train as a pilot. John had been her best friend but she'd never been in love with him. Since she'd broken their engagement and married Alex, he must hate her.

Nor had she expected to meet Alex at a no-holds-barred New Year's Eve party the following week and discover he returned her love. What had happened between them had been inevitable — Grandpa had warned her that too much alcohol often led to poor decisions.

She rarely slept for more than a few fitful hours and her appetite was nonexistent. She weighed less than she had before she'd got pregnant and it could only be a matter of time before Alex commented. He would be devastated if the baby turned out not to be his son — he adored the little boy, and his brief visits were spent mainly with Charles. Barbara loved seeing them together and was happy to share the precious time with her son. Maybe her twentieth birthday wasn't the best day to panic about something that might never happen.

Her son spotted her lurking in the doorway and held his arms out and babbled something that sounded like 'mama'.

'Hello, little man. Are you having fun with your uncles?' She lowered the cot side and scooped him up. Her nose wrinkled. 'What a smelly boy! Let's get you clean and dry before you come down for lunch.'

Tom made a dash for the door. 'Yuck! Come on David, we don't want to stay in here for that.'

'Shall we take the dogs out for another game?' David pressed his nose against the steamed-up window pane. 'It's not raining now — should be all right with boots and macs on.'

'Off you go, boys, but please don't get

muddy. Remember you're wearing your party clothes.'

They vanished and she turned her attention to Charles, who was waving his arms about and struggling to be put down. 'Not yet, young man. Clean bottom first, then you can crawl.'

She was sitting on the carpet watching her son play with his bricks when the door flew open. 'Darling, I got away early and I can stay the night. Isn't that fantastic?' Alex dropped to the floor and snatched up the baby. 'Hello, little man. Are you pleased to see your daddy?' Charles cooed and grabbed for Alex's cap, which was tucked under his greatcoat epaulette. 'No you don't, sweetheart.' He kissed him and replaced him on the carpet. The baby immediately scuttled off to investigate something interesting on the far side of the room.

'Alex, how wonderful. We'll have a whole evening and night together.'

He pulled Barbara onto his lap and for a blissful minute they kissed. His lips were cold and his chin rasped her cheek. Too soon he raised his head, his eyes dark. 'I'm sorry, but I'm absolutely knackered, darling. Any chance I can get a quick kip before the festivities start this afternoon? It was bloody awful last night. I'll have a shave when I get up.' He grinned and as always her stomach flipped. 'I'll make it up to you tonight.'

She didn't ask why he was so tired — he no longer talked about the excitement of being a flyer. Two of his closest friends had died recently, so every time she heard the Spitfires overhead she feared he would be next.

'We'll have to wait until young sir's asleep — but he's always off by seven nowadays. He had his nap so I won't have to disturb you. I'll send one of the boys to wake you when people start to arrive.'

Alex yawned and his jaw cracked. 'I'll chuck my coat and jacket on the sofa, Babs, and crash out as I am, if you don't mind.' He kicked off his shoes and fell back on the bed. He was asleep before she could answer.

She flipped a rug over him and leant down to pick up her son, who was trying to wriggle under the bed. 'Silly boy! Let's leave your daddy to sleep and go downstairs and see your grandma and grandpa, shall we?'

When her grandparents had suggested having a party to mark her birthday, she'd been unsure — being twenty wasn't anything special — and she suggested they wait until next year. She'd been persuaded to go ahead because Alex wasn't going to be based in Hornchurch for much longer, as his command was being slowly re-equipped with the

Submarine Spitfires, and when all the squadron had new planes they would be transferring to Castletown on the Isle of Man.

'We don't want your daddy to go overseas, do we, darling? If he does, we might not see him for years.' She used the back stairs as they led directly to the part of the house the family used every day, but carrying a wriggling baby made negotiating the twists and turns more difficult.

Tom was waiting for her in the passageway when she emerged. 'Isn't Alex coming down? Grandma says lunch will be ready in a minute.'

'He's catching up on his sleep; I expect he was flying all night. He wants one of you to wake him up at three o'clock so he's got time to shave before the guests start arriving.'

'Mrs Brown has made potato and vegetable pie for firsts and apple crumble for seconds. It smells yummy.'

'He'll have to make do with my party tea. Have you washed your hands?' He waved them in the air and the baby copied him, gurgling with laughter. 'What a clever boy you are, Charlie. Can you clap hands too?'

The kitchen was warm and welcoming and David was already at the table. Joe, the cook-housekeeper's son, who worked outside and looked after her mare, was also waiting. 'Sorry, Mrs Brown, but Alex isn't coming to lunch. Sit down, Tom, and then you can eat.'

She hurried into the breakfast room to join her grandparents. Grandma had put the highchair next to her. 'Are you quite sure you want to feed him? I'm quite happy to do it.'

'If you don't mind, my dear, I love giving him his lunch even if he is a bit messy. Edward is making a phone call — some emergency at the hospital again. I do wish he'd retire. He's too old to be working so hard. Sit down, Barbara. I'll put the harness on Charles.'

Lunch was delicious and her son ate almost as much as he threw on the floor. By the time she'd cleaned him and the surrounding area, her brothers had finished their meal.

'Is there anything else you want us to do, Grandma, or can we go upstairs for a bit?'

'No — run along, boys,' Grandma said. 'Thank you for your help this morning; it was invaluable. What time are your friends coming?'

David answered, 'Mr Everton said they could cycle over after lunch so they should be here soon. We won't get dirty, so don't worry about our best clothes being spoilt.'

They vanished and Grandpa smiled fondly. 'Marrying Alex was the best thing you could have done, my dear. It makes those delightful Everton boys also seem like part of our family.' He swallowed and dabbed his eyes with a handkerchief. 'Every time I see your baby and hear him called Charles I'm thrilled. When your father died we never thought we'd hear his name in this house again. Even though this bloody war shows no sign of being over, I'm a remarkably happy old man at the moment.'

'We're lucky living in the country; the bombing and food shortages aren't such a problem.' Barbara shuddered as she remembered her narrow escape last year when Radcliffe Hall had been bombed and she'd been trapped underneath the rubble in the shelter. 'By the way, the boys are calling this little chap Charlie instead of Charles. I think I might do the same. Charles seems a bit grown-up for a baby.'

Deciding not to disturb the boys but wake Alex herself, she left her son playing happily with his grandparents and dashed upstairs. She stepped into her bedroom, but it was empty. Alex must be in the playroom with his brothers. He hadn't had time to visit his parents on his last short pass and hadn't seen them since Christmas. He must be looking forward to catching up with the rest of his family this afternoon. His sister Valerie and

Peter, her husband, were coming with their baby Judith, who had been born the week after Charlie.

The four boys were sprawled on the floor playing Monopoly. 'Have you seen Alex? I thought he must be upstairs with you.'

Jim shook his head. 'He's not been up here, Babs. We were rather hoping he'd come up before the party. We've not seen him for ages, have we, Ned?'

'Did you check your bathroom, Babs? If he was in the bath you wouldn't see him 'cause it's so big.'

'Actually, Ned, I didn't look in there. How silly of me! Don't worry about putting this away; as you two are staying the night, you can finish it this evening.'

She left them to their game and hurried back to check if he was correct. There were signs in the bathroom that Alex had shaved, but he certainly wasn't there now. She checked her hair was neat and her lipstick unsmudged and then went in search of her missing husband.

She poked her head into the study, which was now their sitting room. Grandma and Charlie were there. 'Is Alex with Grandpa? I can't find him anywhere.'

'I think he must be, my dear. The wretched telephone hasn't stopped ringing. I'm glad

Edward had it moved into the library. I always felt as if I was eavesdropping when he was talking about his patients.'

'If you're happy to hang on to the baby for a bit longer, I'll go and see what's keeping them.'

Barbara pushed open the library door and laughed. Alex and Grandpa were standing by an open window, smoking cigars and drinking whiskey. 'Good heavens! I didn't know you smoked, Alex. Is it the thought of my birthday party driving you both to drink?'

Alex grinned and put his cigar and glass down hastily. 'Sorry, darling. I've taken to having the odd cigarette; it seems to settle the nerves after a big op. As for the whiskey, I couldn't let Edward drink on his own, now, could I?'

When had Grandpa stopped being Dr Sinclair and started being Edward? Why hadn't she noticed how close the two had become?

'It's not the idea of your party, my dear, but the very sad news I've just had. You'd better sit down; this is going to be rather upsetting.'

Alex joined her on the battered Chesterfield and held her hand. 'Go on, Grandpa, what is it?'

'Mrs Williams crashed her car yesterday

and died in hospital this morning. I don't think she ever got over her daughter's death last year.'

Barbara blinked back tears. 'Clarissa dying whilst with me in the air-raid shelter must have been a horrible shock. Also, when her house was bombed it left her with nothing. I've written to her more than once but she didn't answer. I should have made more of an effort . . . '

'None of this is your fault, my dear. Mrs Williams is another casualty of this bloody war. There was nothing you could have done about it; your priority was to your premature son. You were in hospital taking care of your baby when Clarissa was buried.' He carefully stubbed out his half-smoked cigar and did the same with the one Alex had been puffing on. 'Would you like to join us in a small toast to the dear departed?'

She managed a watery smile. 'No thank you, Grandpa. You know I don't like strong drinks.' She squeezed Alex's hand and stood up. 'You stay here and finish yours, darling. I'll give Grandma the news. I expect everyone will be talking about it; bad news travels fast.'

'We've got about half an hour before the first of your guests arrive, Babs, so I'll finish this drink and then perhaps we could take our son for a walk in his pram?'

14

Grandpa shook his head. 'No, this malt is too good to gulp down, my boy. I'll keep it for you and you can have it after dinner tonight. Much better you spend some time together. Precious little of it lately.'

They wasted several valuable minutes putting on coats and getting the baby snugly into his smart coach-built pram. This must have cost Barbara's grandparents a small fortune, and she was the envy of the young mothers in Ingatestone when she walked into the village.

Although cold, the sun was bright and what remained of the garden was bursting with spring flowers. 'Shall we go around to the stables first, Alex? I haven't seen Silver today, and Patch and Buttons will be roaming about somewhere too. Charlie loves them.'

'Those puppies have grown into super dogs, but I still can't believe they came from the same litter. Do you manage to steal your mare and get out for a ride occasionally?'

'Fortunately there's not much to do at the moment, so Joe doesn't need her to pull the cart. I exercise her most days. It's just today, with all the party things to do, that I've not had time.'

The dogs greeted her with enthusiasm and the baby clapped his hands and tried to scramble out of the pram in order to reach them. 'Sit still, Charlie. You're going to fall out if you're not careful.'

Alex deftly tightened the harness. 'There, you little imp. Shall we pick your mummy some daffodils for her birthday?'

'I think Grandma counts them. There used to be thousands all over the park before your dad and his Land Girls ploughed it up and planted wheat.'

'Better to have bread than daffodils, I suppose. Do you still hanker to join the Land Army?'

'Sometimes, but now I've passed my first-aid certificate at least I've got a useful skill. I'd love to become a doctor, but that's not going to happen.'

'Don't see why not. You've got the necessary qualifications, you can afford to pay for your training . . . '

'You wouldn't mind me leaving Charlie to be looked after by someone else?'

He stopped so abruptly the baby was thrown backwards, but he thought this was part of a new game and chortled with laughter. 'Good God, Babs, I wasn't suggesting you did it now. No, after the war when I'm home to help out. Mind you, I was rather hoping our son won't remain an only child.'

'I'm sure he won't, but I don't want to be

pregnant again for a while. I really didn't enjoy the experience.' She reached into the pram and tickled the baby. 'Anyway, I'm sure there's a rule somewhere that forbids married women doing a medical degree. Don't worry, it's just a pipe dream. I'm very happy being a wife and mother at the moment.'

★   ★   ★

Alex looked away, hiding his dismay. He didn't like the sound of those words 'at the moment'. Since the dramatic events of last year she'd seemed withdrawn. Not surprising, really, that such a dreadful experience had made her subdued. In fact, he and Edward had been talking about the possibility Babs had got some sort of depression caused by the birth of the baby, as well as everything else.

She was certainly not the happy, vivacious girl he'd married last year; it was as though her youth had vanished overnight. Nowadays she rarely laughed; if he was honest she seemed on the verge of tears most of the time. God knew how she'd be when his squadron moved to the Isle of Man in a few weeks. They were just waiting for the last of his bods to get the new Spitfires and they would be ready to go. Time for another squadron to take the brunt of the fighting, and give his blokes a bit of a breather.

Maybe it would be a good idea for her to get out of the house, take her mind off things and find out if she qualified for a place at medical school even though she was married with a small child. He didn't know much about depression, but from what Edward had told him it sounded bloody horrible.

At least in bed together things were good — making love was something they both enjoyed. He caught her eye and she blushed, obviously recognising the signals. 'Darling, do you think that we could move Charlie into the dressing room tonight?'

'It's a bit small and claustrophobic in there, but I don't see why he can't go into the room we've got ready for him. He's getting on for eight months and it's high time he learned to sleep on his own. If we leave both bedroom doors ajar we'll be able to hear him if he wakes up.'

Her eyes sparkled and she looked like the girl he'd fallen in love with. 'If we go back immediately we can do that before your party starts. I can get the boys to move the cot with me whilst you keep young sir occupied.'

He grabbed hold of the handle of the pram, spun it round, and raced for the back door. The baby squealed and waved his hands

18

around as he bumped over the cobbled yard. 'Come along, Charlie Bear, your mummy and daddy are going to move you into your very own bedroom.'

'It's a good thing he had his lunch a couple of hours ago; all that jolting would probably have brought it up again. Next time he gets grouchy I'll dash up and down over the cobbles with him. He seemed to find that really exciting.'

Alex unbuckled the harness and scooped his son up. 'He's a bit pongy, sweetheart. Must have shaken it out the other end.'

She giggled and aimed an affectionate punch at his shoulder. 'In which case, my love, you can have the pleasure of changing his nappy whilst I go and fetch the boys from the playroom.'

'Fair enough, but for God's sake don't tell anyone. I'd be the laughing stock of the mess if the boys found out I'm changing nappies.'

She ruffled his hair and ran lightly up the stairs in front of him, leaving him to what was really a woman's job. He kissed his wriggling baby and smiled. Women flew the new planes from the factories to the airfields — not just the single-seater fighter planes, but also the bombers — and the idea that women should stay in the home doing the chores didn't really make sense anymore.

Tom looked up as Barbara came into the playroom. 'Do you need us downstairs already? Thought we had another half hour.'

'No, not downstairs, but I do need your help, boys. We want to move the cot into Charlie's room and Alex can't carry it on his own. Would you mind leaving your Meccano for five minutes?' She looked at what the four of them were making. 'They look interesting, Ned. Are they cranes?'

'Yes, Babs, it's a competition to see whose crane can lift the heaviest object. I reckon Jim and I will win.'

David, who was nearest, gave Ned a hearty shove. 'You won't. We're the best at building aren't we, Tom?'

'That's enough of that horseplay. No fighting allowed on my birthday.'

They scrambled up immediately. 'Sorry, we keep forgetting. And we're not fighting, just messing about.' Jim, the oldest by a year, looked exactly like Alex. His shock of auburn hair and bright green eyes would turn the girls' heads when he was older, but that was no compensation at the moment. His nickname was 'carrot top' and he hated it. Ned, a year older than David, had mouse-brown hair and hazel eyes — more like Mrs

20

Everton than his father.

'Right, if you're quick you can come back and play for a bit longer. Alex and I will come and watch when you're ready to start the competition.'

'Good show. You can be the judges,' Tom said.

Alex had changed the baby and even managed to button up his romper suit and replace his bootees. 'Come along, you lot, there's work to do. Here, little man, you go to your mummy now.'

With Alex directing the operation, the cot was transferred without knocking anything over or damaging the freshly painted woodwork in the new nursery.

'Why doesn't Charlie sleep upstairs with us, Babs? That's where babies and children should be.'

'When he's older, David, I'm sure he'll love to be up there with you big boys, but he needs to be near me at the moment.'

'Does that mean you're going to be living at the Grove forever?'

'Nobody lives forever, stupid.' Tom scowled at his brother. 'Babs and Alex and Charlie will want their own house when the war's over. You know that, Grandpa's told you loads of times.'

'We're going to be here for ages, so don't

21

let's worry about it at the moment, David.' Alex threw his arm around the boy and hugged him.

'I'm not worried, Alex. I just like having Babs living here. I didn't like it when she was at Radcliffe Hall.'

Charlie was wriggling to be put down, so Barbara placed him on the rug before taking David to one side. Both her brothers had been with her grandfather when the bomb had dropped on Radcliffe Hall and the building had collapsed. Although Grandpa had turned the car round and taken the boys straight home before driving back to help with the rescue, David had taken weeks to recover from the shock of nearly losing her.

'David, darling, even when we do move it will only be nearby, so you can come and see us whenever you want. I'm not going to live near the base again as it's a bit too noisy.'

'I heard Grandpa say Alex is going to be posted a long way away. Do you promise you won't go with him?'

'I promise. Charlie and I will stay here with you and Tom until the war's over — and that doesn't look as though it's going to be any time soon.'

2

The boys dashed back upstairs to continue building their cranes, leaving Barbara and Alex to move the remainder of the baby's belongings into his new room.

'Do you like your nursery, Charlie? Are you going to be a good boy and sleep in here tonight and give your daddy and me some time alone?'

'Put him in the cot, darling, then we can get things sorted out without having to watch him every second.'

By the time his toys and clothes were put away, it was three o'clock and the first guests were arriving. Grandma had invited all the young mothers from the village, which meant there would be almost a dozen infants and toddlers. Luckily Barbara's birthday was on a Saturday this year, so all the school-age children could be there as well.

'This is going to be more like a children's tea party than an adult event. I think the little ones will outnumber the grown-ups.' Barbara was sure Grandpa would find some excuse to vanish halfway through the afternoon, and she thought that any husband unfortunate enough to be on leave would do the same. No doubt they would retreat to the billiard room for a bit of peace and quiet.

'Let me take Charlie; you go and greet your guests.' Alex strolled off to show his son the balloons tied in colourful bunches around the drawing room. Barbara had decided there would be party games, not just for the children but also for the adults.

After a riotous afternoon of pin the tail on the donkey, musical chairs, and pass the parcel, she was exhausted. The sandwiches, cakes and scones had been devoured and the raspberry cordial drunk without complaint. Tom insisted on taking far too many photographs with his box Brownie. He said that all family occasions should be recorded. The last guests, Alex's parents, were ready to leave at six o'clock — no one wanted to drive in the blackout.

'I can't tell you how much I enjoyed today, Babs. Having both my grandchildren and my children under the same roof was something special. I doubt it will happen again now Peter has got his papers and Alex is going overseas.' Mrs Everton adjusted her hat and smiled. 'Thank your grandparents for me, won't you? We'll collect the boys after church tomorrow as usual.'

Barbara and Alex escorted them to the

door and waved them off. 'Wasn't it a good party?' Barbara said. 'Judith and Charlie are so sweet together. It's going to be wonderful seeing them grow up as friends, as well as cousins.'

'With any luck we'll both have more children. Mum and Dad didn't have any brothers or sisters and their parents died a long time ago. I'm really enjoying being part of two families now.' Alex gestured to the empty room. 'What's happened to Edward and Elspeth? I've not seen either of them for some time.'

'Grandma is making a pot of tea. The boys are upstairs, and you can tell Grandpa he can come out of hiding. He's in the library reading the paper.'

'Okay. I don't want any supper tonight; I'm still full after that enormous spread.'

Mrs Brown and Joe were busy clearing up. With luck, Barbara and Alex would have the evening to themselves. 'Charlie's exhausted after all the excitement. I'm going to give him his bath and bottle and put him to bed early.'

'I'll give you a hand. I want to spend as much time with my son as I can before I go to the Isle of Man. God knows when we'll see each other again.'

Barbara swallowed a lump in her throat. 'I don't want to think about it tonight, darling.

Let's pretend you're going to be in Hornchurch until all this beastliness is over.'

'You go up, Babs. I'll just say goodnight to the old folks in case they are expecting us to come down again.'

The baby fell asleep before he'd finished his evening bottle, and Alex gently lifted him from Barbara's arms and put him in his cot. 'He looks as if he's settled for the night. Do you think he'll be all right to leave whilst we pop upstairs to see the boys and their constructions?'

'Once he's sound asleep he rarely wakes until dawn; he'll be fine.'

When they went into the playroom it was deserted. The Meccano had been abandoned all over the floor. Barbara began to pick it up but Alex stopped her. 'Leave it, sweetheart. You've done more than enough today. I suppose we'd better go down. We can't leave your grandparents in charge.' He stopped and his expression was serious. 'Have you noticed that your grandfather looks tired? Is he overdoing it at the hospital? A man of his age should be sitting at home with his feet up reading the paper, not working full-time in something as stressful as medicine.'

'He was working part-time before the war, but now most of the younger doctors have been conscripted or volunteered there's nobody else to do the work. He's not the only semi-retired doctor now working full-time; he told me there were two others at the hospital like him.'

'Did I tell you my brother-in-law, Peter, has lost his reserved occupation status? Everyone from eighteen to fifty is now expected to do some sort of war work, and that includes women.'

'I wish I could do more, but until Charlie's older I can't really leave him with Grandma; he's too heavy for her to carry about. Once he's out of nappies and running about I'm definitely going to volunteer to work at the hospital.'

'Good idea, Babs. That way you'll know for sure if you want to train to be a doctor later on. The more experience you get, the more likely it is you'll get a place one day — although the rules will have to change to allow you to take a place at a teaching hospital.'

'With women flying planes, driving buses and ambulances and so on, surely things will have to change after the war ends. I'd better come with you — I really should say goodnight and thank my grandparents for my splendid party.'

They found everyone in the kitchen finishing up the remains of the party food.

'We wondered where you boys had got to,' Barbara said.

'Jim was hungry, so we came down to find what there was to eat, Babs. We toasted the old sandwiches and they're scrummy. Shall I do one for you and Alex?' Tom waved his burnt offering in the air.

'Thanks, but I've had more than enough to eat. We just wanted to say goodnight and to check that you four can put yourselves to bed without any fuss.'

'Course we can, Babs. We're not babies,' David insisted. 'Did you know, Babs, that when the bomb dropped yesterday, Mr Purvis's poor old milk horse was blown up?' David told her. 'Rotten luck, don't you think?'

'Very sad. That's the fourth bomb to drop in Ingatestone this year. The raids seem to be getting worse; I can't imagine how horrible it is for those living in the East End.'

'No wonder you need new Spitfires, Alex. The old ones must be worn out,' Ned said between mouthfuls of burnt spam sandwich.

'Let's not talk about the war, boys. I'm trying to forget about it today.'

'Sorry,' Ned said, his happy smile vanishing.

Grandpa, who was eating the last of the scones with obvious enjoyment, quickly changed the subject. 'Go up, my dear. Spend some time with your young man. Elspeth and I can oversee the bedtime routine. We're going to have a game of billiards after we've finished — about time these young men learned how to play.'

Barbara kissed her grandmother and squeezed her grandfather's shoulder but didn't make the mistake of attempting to kiss her brothers. Even David didn't want to be kissed in public anymore.

'Thank you. Be good, boys. We'll see you at breakfast. Alex doesn't have to be back at base until after lunch, so we can go to church tomorrow morning.'

'Mum and Dad are going to collect us after morning service, so they'll see you again, Alex. Joe said we can take Silver out for a drive, if that's all right with you, Babs?'

'Yes, please do. Then I won't have to worry about riding her tomorrow. Tom and David know how to put the harness on, but you might need help getting her between the shafts. As Joe and Mrs Brown have the rest of the weekend free, Alex and I can give you a hand.'

She didn't want to stay any longer, just in case Charlie woke up. You couldn't hear him downstairs so for the past few months, since he'd moved into his cot, she'd had to run up and down the stairs every ten minutes to check he was still asleep. Now he was in his own room, she could take a book upstairs and read, which would make life a lot easier.

'If you want to use the bathroom first, darling, I'll check he's still asleep.' Alex kissed her and her pulse skipped. It seemed truly decadent to be tumbling into bed so early, but as her grandparents had suggested it, it couldn't be as daring as she thought.

'Once Charlie's settled in his nursery, Alex, I thought I'd ask the boys to baby-sit so I can spend an evening downstairs occasionally. They could play cards or something in our room just as easily as in the playroom.'

'Good idea. It's ridiculous having to keep dashing about the way you've been doing. No wonder the rich people had nannies.'

'I'm sure my father didn't see very much of his parents, and it took Grandma a long while to get used to handling Charlie. Have you noticed that Grandpa is still a bit wary? Such a shame; I'm sure if they'd been closer my father wouldn't have left the way he did.'

'If he hadn't run off he would never have met your mother and we wouldn't be sitting here now, would we?'

'I suppose not. Anyway, there's a second Charles Edward Sinclair living here now, so everything has come full circle.' Alex nodded, but his smile had gone. What had she said to upset him? Then she realised she'd forgotten to add Everton to Charlie's name. Was this because she was beginning to think the baby wasn't his?

If only there was some way of proving it one way or the other. Of course, she had some photographs of John taken the Christmas before last. When she and Alex had got together she'd put them away at the back of the walk-in closet. She would find them when she was alone; there wasn't time tonight. Comparing Charlie with the photos might give her an answer — but it might not be the one she wanted.

Wouldn't the boys have remarked on the resemblance if there was one? Tom and David had known John since they were babies but had never suggested Charlie looked like him. Barbara's stomach lurched. She swallowed and breathed through her nose, praying her nausea would settle. This might be the last night she and Alex had before his squadron left Hornchurch, and having a bout of biliousness would ruin it for both of them.

* * *

Alex slipped into the nursery and closed the door behind him. It would take a few minutes

31

for his eyes to adjust to the darkness and whilst he waited, he listened to the gentle sound of his son breathing. He swiped his eyes with his sleeve. Why the hell did he mind so much when Babs called his son a Sinclair and not an Everton?

He moved quietly to the cot and could just make out the shape of the baby. As usual he was on his tummy with his knees tucked under him. It didn't look very comfortable, but he supposed babies were different. The blankets had been kicked to the end of the mattress, so he carefully pulled them back and tucked in the edges.

The baby didn't stir. Hopefully, now he was sound asleep, the covers would stay over him. He stretched down and stroked Charlie's head, loving the feel of the soft hair under his fingertips. He was a lucky sod — an intelligent, beautiful wife and the best son in the world. Mum had said his life would change when he was a father, that he would view things differently, and she was right. Being a father made the bloody horrible job he had to do so much easier. He had something real to fight for. Some of the blokes were risking their necks every day just for king and country, but he had a wife and son to protect and this made it seem more worthwhile.

Babs didn't mean to upset him; she loved him as much as he loved her. He wasn't going to say anything; tonight was going to be special for both of them. He hardened at the thought of being able to make love to her all night. His mouth curved. With luck the baby would sleep in and they would have a few hours in the morning as well.

She must have finished in the bathroom by now, so he'd better get moving. He was reluctant to leave his son, as he didn't spend nearly enough time with the baby the way things were. He shouldn't complain, as he'd been based at home for the past two years, and a lot of blokes were overseas with no chance of getting home for the duration.

He left the doors ajar so they could hear Charlie if he woke during the night. The bathroom door was closed — strange, as Babs usually left it open. He hesitated, wondering if he should knock, then decided to walk straight in.

She was standing with her back to him in the bath, using a trickle of water from the geyser to wash herself. She glanced over her shoulder and her smile twisted his guts. Maybe he wasn't so lucky after all — the blokes with no family would find it less painful to move to the Isle of Man next month. Leaving her was going to tear him apart.

'Hang on, darling, I'll wash your back for you.'

'Lovely, thank you. When I'm done, do you want me to do the same for you?'

Alex's expression changed and in two strides he was beside the bath and had his arms around her. She was still a bit damp but he didn't seem to mind. He lifted her over the high side of the bath and walked backwards down the steps. He didn't have any intention of washing her back when there were more interesting things to do together.

He swung round and almost ran into the bedroom. Fortunately, she'd already turned the blankets down so when he tumbled them onto the bed she didn't have to wriggle in order to get between the sheets. She watched him tear off his uniform as if it was on fire. His eyes never left her. She was pinned by the intensity of his stare.

Her mouth was dry, her heart pounding. She was as eager as he to make love. Thank God she was at the end of her cycle and was unlikely to get pregnant, because there was no time to remind him about taking precautions.

★ ★ ★

Charlie slept in until seven o'clock and Alex volunteered to go down and fetch his morning bottle whilst Barbara changed him and brought him into their bed. She decided to pull the bedclothes over the sheets — she didn't like the idea of their baby scrambling about where she and Alex had made passionate love.

When she walked into the nursery, Charlie was on his knees holding the cot bars and making a determined effort to stand up. 'Well done, darling. I think you'll be walking before you're a year old at this rate.'

The baby waved his arms around and smiled, revealing his two bottom teeth. Barbara was back in her bedroom with a sweet-smelling baby just as Alex returned with the glass bottle full of warm milk.

'Can I feed him, Babs?' His eyes glittered. She didn't need to ask why — the thought of him leaving in a the few weeks, possibly for years, hung between them.

'I'll have a quick wash and get dressed; I think Mrs Brown has planned a special breakfast for you. We mustn't be down late. Were the boys downstairs?'

'No, only Joe and his mother. He told me we were having eggs, sausages *and* bacon. We don't even get bacon on the base very often nowadays. I hope you're not using up your monthly ration just for me.'

'We probably are, but we want this breakfast to be special. You probably won't have any more twenty-four-hour passes before you go.'

She couldn't continue, so handed the baby over and dashed into the bathroom before he could see her tears. She must save the crying until he'd gone, as she wanted only happy memories on what might be his last morning at the Grove.

When she emerged Alex and Charlie had gone — presumably into the nursery. She grabbed clean underwear and walked into the closet to find something suitable to wear for church. She grabbed the nearest skirt, blouse and cardigan, not caring whether she was colour-coordinated today. As she turned to leave, the shoebox in which she'd put the photographs of John caught her eye on a shelf at the far end.

With her clothes draped over one arm, she tucked the box under the other and carried it into the bedroom before carefully hiding it under the bed. As she was putting on her cardigan Alex came back, swinging Charlie around like an aeroplane.

'The boys have just gone past, so I'll go down with this little man. I'll see you there, darling.'

'I won't be too long, but I haven't found a pair of stockings without holes so far. I might have to do a bit of rapid mending.'

'Don't worry about your stockings; you can mend them after breakfast.' He laughed and, still jiggling the baby, headed for the kitchen. Barbara hoped all the bouncing didn't make Charlie sick so soon after his milk.

She couldn't go until she'd found the photographs. There was a picture of Alex, Charlie and herself standing in pride of place on her dressing table. This would do to compare her son's image with John's.

Her hands were shaking as she withdrew the box from its hiding place. She put it beside her on the eiderdown and flicked off the lid. The first few photographs were grainy and blurred, not sharp enough for comparison. Then, at the very bottom of the box, was a photograph taken in Hastings when John had just returned from university.

Her world stood still. She put the pictures side by side. There could be no doubt at all — Charlie was the image of John. She squeezed her eyes shut and opened them again, hoping what she saw would somehow be different.

No — the black-and-white images remained the same. What should she do? Surely it was only a matter of time before someone else noticed the resemblance. Her brothers had grown up with John — what if they blurted out her shameful secret in front of her grandparents?

Her chest was tight, as if an iron band had somehow fastened itself around her, making breathing all but impossible. She wanted to put the incriminating photo back in the box and hide it in her closet where no one would ever see it, but for some reason she couldn't move. She wanted to get up, but her body wasn't responding to her commands.

★ ★ ★

'Where's Babs? Isn't she coming down for breakfast?' David asked. 'I'm starving, and the eggs will get all hard and horrible.'

Alex put the baby in his high chair and did up the harness. 'Keep an eye on Charlie for me and I'll nip up and get her. I thought she was right behind me.' He turned to the housekeeper poised over the Aga, spatula in hand. 'Don't let this delicious food spoil, Mrs Brown. Babs and I will be down in a minute, but everyone else should tuck in.'

Babs had looked a bit pale; he hoped she wasn't coming down with something. He threw open the bedroom door and froze. She was sitting on the bed, tears streaming down her face, clutching what looked like photo-graphs against her chest.

Something was dreadfully wrong. He grabbed the door frame, unable to move forward for a moment. Then he was beside her. 'Darling, what's happened? I can't bear to see you so upset.'

She shook her head and turned away from him. 'I'm sorry, I'm sorry . . . ' She couldn't continue.

He tried again to embrace her but she flinched away and scrambled to her feet. 'For Christ's sake, Babs, you're frightening me. What are you sorry about?'

She pushed the photo from the dressing table into his hands, along with a snap of somebody else, and then bolted to the bathroom. The key turned in the lock behind her. Whatever it was, it had something to do with these pictures. He held the snap in one hand and the framed photograph in the other. The small picture was of a man he didn't recognise, but he looked familiar. Who the hell was it?

He frowned — of course, this was that John fellow, the one Babs had been engaged to. Bloody hell! Had he gone for a Burton? That must be why she was so upset. The bloke had been her best friend since she was small; losing him would be like losing a brother. He dropped the photographs on the bed and went over to the bathroom door.

He was about to knock when he realised she couldn't have received news of the bloke's death because she hadn't been downstairs this morning. He returned to the bed and picked up the family photograph as well as the other picture and held them side by side. Bile rose in his throat. Seeing the photo of Thorogood next to the image of Charlie, he could see that the resemblance between the two was unmistakable. He wasn't the father — she must have slept with that bastard before she'd slept with him.

His dreams, his happiness, his life, collapsed around him. He'd got up this morning thinking he was happily married to a wonderful woman and the father of a beautiful son. Now that was all gone. Barbara was a slut and a liar, and Charlie was another man's child.

The marriage was over. He couldn't forgive such a betrayal by the woman he'd trusted. He stood up. His hands were shaking and his eyes blurred. In two strides he reached the bathroom door and raising his foot, smashed it open.

★ ★ ★

Barbara slid down the wall opposite the bath and dropped her head on her knees. She couldn't face him, not now. She would hide in here until he left. He wouldn't remain at the Grove once he knew the baby he adored wasn't his real son. If only she'd told him at the New Year's Eve party that she wasn't a virgin, none of this would have happened.

Suddenly the lock splintered and the door flew back. Alex towered over her, his face twisted by fury and his fists clenched. She cringed into the corner, convinced he was going to strike her. Memories of the physical abuse she'd suffered at the hands of her mother flooded back.

'You bitch! I wish I'd never set eyes on you. First you ruined Thorogood's life, and now mine. This marriage is over. You'll never see me again. With any luck I'll get shot down and won't have to divorce you.'

'Please, don't hit me. I'm sorry — '

His expression changed and he lowered his hands. 'Bloody hell! Is that what you think of me? I don't hit women or children. I'm going now. I don't care what you tell your grandparents — but I'm going to tell my mum and dad that the marriage is over because you've done something unforgivable.' He wiped his arm across his eyes. 'Don't worry, I won't tell them the truth. It's not

Charlie's fault he's got a slut for a mother. I don't intend to ruin his life as well.'

He shook his head, half-raised his hand, and vanished. He banged about for a few minutes and then the bedroom door slammed. Slowly she pushed herself upright and stumbled to the sink. She didn't need to look at her reflection to know how awful she looked. She soaked a flannel in cold water and held it to her face.

Her stupidity had torn their family apart. If she'd had the sense to leave the photograph where it was until Alex had gone, none of this would have happened. He would have left happy, and by the time he returned the war would be over and Charlie's parentage would no longer matter so much.

The Evertons would hate her and probably stop Ned and Jim from playing with her brothers — four more innocent victims made miserable because of her. She couldn't face going to church this morning. What was she going to tell Grandpa and Grandma? The family would be waiting downstairs for her and Alex to join them for his special breakfast.

The last thing she wanted was bacon and eggs, but there was no reason for everyone else to have their treat spoiled. She ran her fingers through her hair and risked a glance in the mirror. Her eyes were a bit pink, her face paler than usual, but she didn't look like someone whose husband had just walked out.

She'd no idea what she was going to say when she got to the kitchen, and was hoping inspiration would come on the way down. The sound of knives and forks and laughter drifted down the passageway from the kitchen — good, the boys were eating; they hadn't waited. This meant she could go straight into the dining room and speak to her grandparents.

This door was also open. She hesitated, waiting for the wave of nausea to subside.

'Is that you, Barbara, my dear? Mrs Brown has put your breakfasts in the warmer.' Grandma had sharp hearing.

Barbara swallowed nervously and walked into the breakfast room. 'Sorry, I think I've picked up a tummy bug. I'm feeling really sick. Alex sends his apologies; he's decided to go back without breakfast, as I'm not going to be able to share it with him.' It sounded a feeble excuse but she couldn't think of anything else.

Grandpa dropped his cutlery and pushed his chair back. 'You look very unwell, Barbara. I suggest you go back to bed. Elspeth and I can take care of Charlie.'

'Someone has to take Ned and Jim to

church — their parents will be waiting for them.'

He nodded. 'Of course, I'd forgotten. Elspeth, if you can look after the baby on your own for a couple of hours, I'll do church parade with the boys.'

They looked so worried, so loving, but when they found out the truth would they look at her the way Alex had? Would they reject Charlie because of his parentage?

She swayed and put out a hand to steady herself. Immediately her grandfather was beside her. 'Come along, young lady. I'm taking you back to bed.' Despite being almost seventy, Grandpa's arm was strong around her waist.

She didn't protest, allowing him to guide her through the house and into her bedroom. He pushed her gently onto the bed. 'I'll fetch you a basin in case you vomit.' He stared hard at her. 'Is there any possibility, my dear, that you could be pregnant again?'

'I don't think so. We've been really careful.' The last thing she wanted was another baby. She fell back on the pillows and curled into a ball. She should tell Grandpa the truth, but couldn't face talking about it at the moment. Her grief was too fresh, too raw. Maybe tomorrow she'd have the courage to explain.

'Get into bed, Barbara. You can't stay where you are.'

He came back with the promised china basin and, seeing her struggling to remove her clothes, took over the task. When he'd finished and her nightdress was back on, he pulled back the sheets and she crawled in.

'Sleep is what's needed here, my dear girl. I'll come and see you as soon as I get back from church.'

He patted her shoulder and then closed the door quietly behind him. Her head was heavy, her eyes gritty, and she didn't want to think about anything just now. As she was drifting into welcome darkness she remembered the splintered lock on the bathroom door.

She jerked upright, wide awake. Grandpa knew she wasn't unwell, but grief-stricken. She had two hours to wait before he rejected her too. Grandma had sent her father away when she'd discovered he was marrying someone beneath him — would the same thing happen to her and Charlie? They would think 'like mother like daughter' and wish she had never come into their lives.

She might as well get dressed again and start packing. At least she wouldn't be short of money; her trust fund was enormous. Since she and Alex had got married last year she had full access to the principal as well as the interest. She would move somewhere no one knew her, say she was a widow, and start a new life.

What about Tom and David? If she ran away she would be abandoning them. She seemed to stagger from one disaster to another, most of them her fault. Perhaps she wouldn't start packing right away; she would wait and see what her grandparents wanted her to do. If they thought her appalling behaviour would bring disgrace to the Sinclair name then she would leave without protest; but for her brothers' sake she was prepared to remain at the Grove, however painful that might be.

Mr and Mrs Everton would know the split was her fault even if they didn't know the real cause. They would blame her for breaking their son's heart and wouldn't want to speak to her again. Valerie wouldn't want her coming round anymore either. Spending time with another new mother had made the weeks when she couldn't see Alex more bearable. Baby Judith was adorable, and she had the Everton red hair. Was it only a matter of time before they put two and two together and realised Charlie wasn't actually an Everton?

Almost certainly word would spread

around the congregation, and next time Barbara went to church there would be pointing fingers and sly looks behind her back. In future she would go to the eight o'clock communion service with Charlie. That way Tom and David and her grandparents wouldn't be embarrassed.

She swung her legs over the bed and slowly stood up, feeling like someone three times her age. Grandpa had neatly folded her clothes on a chair and she didn't have to find anything else to put on. The room she had shared with her husband whenever he got leave already felt different. Charlie had his own nursery, and she would be sleeping alone in here as she had done for six months before she had married Alex.

He had left several drawers open in his hurry to reclaim his belongings. She hoped she'd find the odd sock or handkerchief, possibly a civilian shirt or jumper on the rail in the closet, but he'd left nothing. She shot into the bathroom. Yes — he hadn't been able to collect his wash bag. Not much to remember him by, but at least she had something of his.

The photograph of Alex, Charlie and herself was face down on the carpet, the pictures of John beside it. She replaced the portrait on the dressing table, put the scattered snaps of her erstwhile fiancé in the old shoebox, then returned it to the closet and shoved it behind a stack of old books. She never wanted to see them again. One day she would have to explain to her son why he had grown up fatherless, but until then she would try and forget.

She was supposed to be too unwell to look after her own child or attend church so could hardly go downstairs. She decided to change the bed. She didn't remove the pillowslip *he* had used, just the sheets. She hugged the pillow and buried her nose in the feathers. His aroma lingered in the fabric and her eyes filled. He'd walked out saying he hoped he would be killed, and that was her fault too.

Crying wasn't going to bring him back — nothing ever would. She'd always known this day might come, and had to learn to live without him. She must pretend she was coping, but the thought of being without the man she loved for the rest of her life was tearing her apart. The boys and her baby didn't deserve to be miserable because of her mistakes. Somehow she would get on with her life and be the best mother, sister and granddaughter she could be. She would never be a wife again. If she couldn't have Alex, she would have no one.

3

Barbara listened at the foot of the stairs several times in case the baby was crying, but he was quiet. She tidied the nursery and dusted furniture that was perfectly clean and then did the same to her bedroom. Keeping busy was the answer — if she didn't give herself time to think maybe she wouldn't break down.

She stood at the long windows in her room gazing out at the park, which was no longer a park really, as there were acres of wheat growing where once there had been grass. Grandma had put Charlie in the pram and was walking up and down on the terrace, pointing out the daffodils.

Should she go downstairs and explain what had happened, or wait until Grandpa came up to her? The boys would know something was wrong. She would have to think of what to tell them that would make sense. As she was dithering about in the passageway the back door opened and David, Tom and Grandpa came in. Was she imagining they were all subdued? There was a murmur of voices and then the boys went out again

— presumably to join Grandma and Charlie on the terrace whilst Grandpa came up to see her. The phone rang and Grandpa answered it.

Barbara retreated to her bedroom and stood with her back to the window as far away from the door as possible. At least ten minutes passed before she heard him approaching. He didn't knock, but walked straight in. She'd expected him to look withdrawn, disgusted, angry even, but he just looked incredibly sad and seemed to have aged ten years since this morning.

She forgot her own misery and rushed to his side. 'Grandpa, come and sit down. I suppose Mr and Mrs Everton have already spoken to you.'

'It's the most dreadful news, my dear. What happened between you and Alex is trivial in comparison.' She took his elbow and guided him the padded armchair.

'What is it? Has someone died? Please tell me what's happened.'

'The Evertons weren't at church today so I had to take the boys back to the farm, but there was no one there. They've come back with me. I just received a phone call from Alex.' He sighed and wiped his eyes on his handkerchief. 'Little Judith has died. When Valerie put her to bed last night the baby was

50

fine, but when she went in this morning Judith was dead.'

'How awful! I can't believe it — she's the same age as Charlie. They must be devastated.'

'Alex asked us to keep the boys for the moment, but not to tell them. He's got compassionate leave so is going to stay with his sister and brother-in-law. There will have to be some sort of post-mortem examination at the hospital because the baby died so unexpectedly.'

Barbara dropped to her knees beside him and put her arms around his shoulders, shocked to feel how frail he was. Her split with Alex, however awful it seemed, was trivial compared to the loss of a baby and the health of her beloved grandfather. 'They had a miscarriage a couple of years ago, which made Judith even more special . . . ' She couldn't continue; could only imagine the agony Valerie and Peter were in. If anything happened to Charlie she wouldn't be able to carry on.

They cried together for a while, then Grandpa cleared his throat and hugged her briefly. 'I won't ask what happened between you and your young man. I saw the state of the bathroom door, so realise it must have been serious. Is this a permanent rift, do you think?'

'Yes, I'm afraid it is. It's nothing to do with him; it's me. I'll tell you what happened, but not now.' She used the arm of the chair to push herself upright. She'd never enjoy a birthday again knowing that Judith had died on the same day. 'I don't know how we're going to keep this news from Ned and Jim. I can't stop crying, and you're not much better.'

'You can stay in your room, as everybody thinks you've got a bilious attack. I'll give my face a quick splash of cold water and then I'll be perfectly fine.'

Whilst he was in the bathroom, Barbara heard the telephone ringing again. She had to go down; she couldn't leave it unanswered. She snatched the receiver from the cradle.

'The Grove, Barbara Everton speaking.'

There was a silence and then Alex replied. 'You know about the baby?' His voice was gruff.

'I do. I can't tell you how sorry I am. Is there anything we can do, apart from keep the boys here for the moment?'

'No, it's too bloody for words. Valerie and Peter are in pieces, Mum and Dad not much better. They want me to tell the boys . . . ' He didn't need to state the obvious. Coming back under the circumstances was going to be incredibly difficult for him.

'Why don't you let me do it? You don't want to come here, not now.'

There was a long, painful silence. So long she thought he'd put the phone down. 'I couldn't tell them about Charlie even if I wanted to. That would mean they had lost both grandchildren today. I'll never be able to forgive you, but for everyone's sake we have to pretend nothing's happened.'

'I'm not sure what you mean. Are you saying you will continue to recognise Charlie as your son? That our marriage isn't over?'

'I love Charlie. It's not fair on him if I disappear. He deserves better than that. Mum and Dad will need to spend time with him; he'll be doubly precious now. I can't take that away from them. But our marriage is effectively over. As long as I don't have to see you, I can keep up appearances until the squadron moves at the end of the month.'

'Thank you. I don't deserve — '

'It's not about you. I don't give a damn how you feel. If it wasn't for this tragedy you'd never see me again. I warn you, Barbara, it won't take much to push me over the edge. I'm coming over now; make sure Ned and Jim are ready. Mum and Dad want them here. Fortunately they agreed with me when I said it would be better if Charlie wasn't around at the moment, because I couldn't stand to be in the same room as you.'

'What do you want me to tell the boys?'

'Just say I'm coming to get them. I'll tell them myself. I won't be coming in. Send them out when you hear the car.'

There was no goodbye; he just replaced the receiver with a click. He would be here in about half an hour; she'd spend the time packing the boys' things. Wouldn't everyone expect her to comfort Alex? But why was she thinking about this? All that mattered was doing what she could to help the Evertons cope with this appalling tragedy.

When one heard that someone's brother, husband or father had been killed, it was sad — of course it was — but servicemen and women expected to be killed in a war. Even civilians knew they were at risk if they lived in a city. But a beautiful nine-month-old baby girl dying for no apparent reason was just too sad for words.

Like an automaton, Barbara headed upstairs and collected the boys' scattered possessions and rammed them into their suitcase. She was fairly sure she'd shoved some of her brothers' belongings in as well, but couldn't find the energy to do anything about it. She wanted to rush downstairs and snatch Charlie from her grandmother but forced herself to remain upstairs. One thing was certain: she was going to move his cot back into the bedroom. From now on she would be checking on him every hour just in case he succumbed to whatever had taken Judith.

Once Ned and Jim had gone, she would get her brothers to help move everything. She collapsed on the bed in despair. It didn't really matter if her baby stayed in here for the next few years — the need for privacy was over.

Her head was fuzzy, as if she were coming down with a nasty cold. Her throat was raw and she ached all over. She pressed her hand to her forehead, expecting to find she was running a temperature, but her skin was clammy; the very opposite of feverish. Could grief make her feel as if she were actually ill?

Alex would be here in a minute, so she'd better go downstairs with the suitcase and then find their coats and so on. They must know something was wrong, but nothing could prepare them for the news they were going to receive. They were laughing and messing about on the terrace. How long would it be before they smiled again?

Barbara dumped the case outside the back door and wandered into the kitchen. Mrs

Brown and Joe had the day off, so she had the place to herself. Would Grandpa tell the boys, or would she have to do it? They'd had so much to cope with in the last two years, being abandoned deliberately by their father (her stepfather) and inadvertently by their mother when she was incarcerated in a lunatic asylum. How would they cope with this news?

David was the more vulnerable; she'd have to make sure he coped. Sometimes he was rather withdrawn and could only be coaxed out of a bad mood by extra attention from all of them. Both the boys loved Alex and were already upset about his going overseas. At least they wouldn't know the marriage was over — and maybe by the time Alex returned he would have changed his mind and be able to forgive her.

The sound of a car interrupted her thoughts. She ran through the house and out onto the terrace. 'Ned, Jim, Alex is here for you. Hurry up, he's waiting.'

They bundled in, followed by David and Tom. Grandma walked slowly behind them, pushing the pram. Grandpa was nowhere in sight.

'Do you know why Mum and Dad didn't come to church today, Babs?' Jim asked.

'Alex will explain it to you. Your suitcase is on the doorstep.' She was about to hug them when she remembered they no longer liked to be embraced.

'Bye, Tom, David. I expect we'll see you at school tomorrow.' Jim pushed his brother through the door before he could change his mind about going home. The four boys were never happier than when they were together.

'Goodbye, Uncles. It's been fun having you here all weekend,' Tom said.

The door closed behind them and the boys looked at Barbara curiously.

'Come into the kitchen. I'm afraid I have some dreadful news to give you.'

★ ★ ★

Charlie got more than his usual amount of fussing and kissing that afternoon. Tom and David didn't leave his side for a second, and even Grandpa spent the remainder of the day in the sitting room watching his great-grandson playing with his adopted sons.

'Charlie has to have his bath and go to bed now, but you can help if you want to, boys.' The baby was getting fractious, as he was usually in bed by this time.

'Can we all get in together, Babs? Your bath is big enough to swim in,' David said. Tom looked horrified.

Grandpa ruffled David's hair. 'If you put

on your swimming trunks, my boy, I don't see why not.'

'It would be fun, if you don't mind, Babs,' Tom said eagerly, obviously relieved he wouldn't have to be seen in his birthday suit by his big sister.

'As long as I don't have to get in my swimsuit and join you, I think Charlie would love it. You do realise, don't you, that the water can't be very hot?'

'We don't care, do we, Tom? It'll be jolly good fun splashing about in your bath. Ours is titchy by comparison.'

'I'll get the bath filled whilst you two go and change. As there are three people going in, I'm going to run a bit more water in tonight. Five inches seems a bit mean.'

'An extra inch would be fine,' Grandma said, 'but more than that wouldn't be safe for the baby.'

The boys shot off and their laughter lifted the sombre mood. 'I don't want to leave Charlie on his own tonight, so I won't come down even when Tom and David are settled.' She was at the door when she remembered about moving the cot. 'I'm having Charlie in with me again. I'll get the boys to help me with the cot.'

Grandpa stood up. 'Absolutely not. Moving him will just make the boys more fearful. I can promise you, my dear girl, these sorts of tragedies are very rare indeed. Leave both your bedroom door and the baby's door open — you'll be able to hear him perfectly well.'

'You're right, better to keep things as they are, at least for the moment.'

'Don't worry about coming down again; we'll come up and join you in your room. That's another reason for leaving young sir where he is. Elspeth and I rather thought we could get Joe to move a couple of chairs in there tomorrow, then we can sit together in the evening again.'

'My wireless works perfectly well. I don't know why we didn't think of this before. I can run up and down stairs to fetch whatever we need from the kitchen.'

'Excellent. Don't worry about us, my dear; we'll make ourselves comfortable whilst you're upstairs with the boys. That way we can listen out for Charlie at the same time.'

'I'm just going to make his bottle — '

'Let me do that for you, Barbara. I'll bring it upstairs in twenty minutes.'

'Thank you, Grandma. I'd better get a move on or they'll be down before the bath's ready.'

That was something she had to do before the boys arrived — remove the wood splinters and smashed lock. If she hung a towel on the doorknob, with any luck they wouldn't notice. She put the baby on the lino and gave him something to play with whilst she collected the bits in an old flannel and dropped them in the waste paper bin.

She turned on the cold-water tap before turning her attention to the hot. The geyser protested as usual, but hot water gushed from the tap and the enormous bath was soon filling up nicely. She had just wrapped Charlie in a large towel when her brothers burst in. 'We're ready for you, aren't we, Charlie Bear?'

The baby wriggled and pointed at his rubber ducks, which were still standing in a row on the windowsill. 'Du du.'

Tom grinned. 'Look at that, Babs, he's saying 'duck'. Clever little boy, aren't you, Charlie? Shall I put them in for you?'

'Is it all right to get in?' David asked. He had already climbed the three steps and had one leg over the side of the bath with his toes dipping the water.

'Of course. Jump in.'

He took her words literally, and the resulting splash sent water cascading over the side of the bath. The baby screamed with glee and Tom dived in after his younger brother.

'I'm absolutely drenched, David. I hope you're going to mop the bathroom, as you've caused all the mess.' She was laughing, not something she'd expected to do today. 'Are you ready? I'm going to put Charlie in the bath now. Can you grab his ducks, David?'

The bath was so huge, both boys and the baby had ample room to splash about and enjoy themselves. Barbara didn't hear her grandmother come in.

'My goodness, I think there's more water on the floor than there is in the bath.'

Barbara looked round. 'I just hope it doesn't escape and go through the ceiling before we have time to mop it up.'

Tom had the baby sitting between his legs and David was opposite. They were playing a riotous game of 'Row, Row, Row Your Boat.'

'Charlie's had such fun, and so have the boys. This was just what we needed this afternoon. The water's getting cold, so I'm going to take him out. I expect he'll scream, but you'll have to ignore that.'

Immediately Tom knelt and gripped the baby firmly around the waist. 'Up you come, baby. Go to Mummy.'

Barbara reached over and enveloped her son in a warm towel, ignoring his wails of protest. 'Bottle and bedtime for you, Charlie.'

'Jump out, boys, and get dry. I'll tidy up in here. You run along and get into your pyjamas, and your sister will be along shortly to read your story.'

'There's no need, Grandma, I can do it as soon as I have this little man in bed.' Barbara stood well back as the boys scrambled out of the bath. 'Is the bottle in the nursery?'

'On the chest of drawers, my dear.' Grandma handed Tom and David a towel but they didn't stop to dry themselves, and vanished in high spirits. 'Just what they needed. I don't want them to grieve for the little girl.'

'It's going to be very difficult for the family over the next few days. Bad enough to lose a baby like that, but then having to go through the horror of an autopsy as well — it doesn't bear thinking of.' Barbara buried her face in Charlie's towel, and he reached out a slippery wet hand and patted her cheek. 'Let's get you into your nightclothes, darling.'

As expected, he was asleep before he'd finished his bottle, and she gently put him in the cot and pulled the covers over him. The bathroom was pristine; Grandma had mopped the floor and taken away the wet towels.

Barbara put a match to the newspaper and kindling and waited for the fire to catch before she went upstairs to tuck the boys in and say goodnight. Tom was too old for bedtime stories, but David still enjoyed being read to.

They were a bit quieter than usual, but seemed to have adjusted to the tragedy. Barbara left them propped up in bed reading. 'Lights out in half an hour — it's school tomorrow.'

'We will, Babs,' Tom said. As she was leaving the room he stopped her. 'Will Ned and Jim come to school, do you think?'

'I shouldn't think so, Tom, but if they do they might not want to talk about it. Just be kind to them.'

'They will have to share Charlie with us, otherwise they won't be uncles anymore.' David sniffed and rubbed his eyes on his pyjama sleeve.

Barbara sat next to him on the bed and hugged him. 'They probably won't want to be around him for a little while, David. Seeing Charlie will just make their loss so much harder to cope with. But I'm sure they'll be happy to come over again in a few weeks' time.' The boys seemed happy enough with this explanation, and she left them reading with the promise that she'd return later to check the light was off.

Although she'd only been upstairs for a few minutes, she couldn't stop herself going in and checking Charlie was sleeping safely. He had already rolled over onto his tummy and kicked off his blankets. She re-covered him and crept out.

The fire was well alight and she threw on a few logs — coal was in short supply, but fortunately there was plenty of wood available on the estate. If they were going to use this room as a sitting room in the evenings, then she needed to make it look less like a bedroom. Fortunately the room was large enough to be divided into a sitting and sleeping area. All she had to do was rearrange the furniture a bit and they could be really cosy.

She turned on the radio, and after a few hisses and crackles the sound of Jimmy Dorsey's band filled the room. She dragged the daybed from under the window and moved it closer to the fire and then put the two small armchairs opposite. The matching hexagonal tables were perfect; a table lamp could go on one, and the other could be used as a coffee table.

She stood back to view her changes. A few more cushions would improve the daybed, as Grandpa sometimes complained about his back. He could put his feet up if he wanted to — not that he would — and she and Grandma could use the armchairs. There were several footstools downstairs; she would ask Joe to bring them up tomorrow.

It was almost eight o'clock — she'd better check the boys were asleep, and then nip down and tell her grandparents everything was ready for them. The boys were fast asleep, but the light was on and she switched it off. As she was about to go downstairs she heard the distinctive rattle of crockery on a tray.

'Grandma, I said I would come for the cocoa. Let me take it from you.'

'I'm perfectly capable of carrying a tray up a flight of stairs, Barbara. I'm not in my dotage yet.'

'Unlike me, my dear. I'm totally decrepit.' Her grandfather chuckled but his words sent a chill down her spine.

'I've checked Charlie and the boys and they're all sound asleep.' She stepped aside so they could see the changes she'd made. 'What you think? I've made it as comfortable as possible.'

Her grandmother put the tray of cocoa on one of the tables. 'It looks lovely, Barbara, especially with the fire alight and just the table lamp on.'

'Let's sit down, my dear,' said Grandpa. 'We would like an explanation of what happened this morning between you and Alex.'

Barbara closed her eyes and took several deep breaths. Should she lie or tell them the truth? Alex had said that in the circumstances he couldn't tell his parents — but what other explanation would make any sense? Last night her grandparents had watched them, seen how in love they were; only the truth would do. Telling them could mean losing not only their respect, but their love. Wouldn't it be better to lie?

'I did something truly dreadful and Alex found out.' She risked a glance at them, expecting to see shock or disapproval, but they just looked as they always did — interested and loving. 'I can't bear to tell you this — I hoped I would never have to — but I want to try and make you understand. John came to my room the night before he left and I couldn't say no to him.'

'Oh my dear, how unfortunate,' said Grandma. 'Now you mention it, I can see that Charlie is the image of John. Poor Alex, to have learnt this on the same day that his niece died.'

Grandpa smiled sadly. 'Elspeth is right, my dear. It makes no difference to us or to you, but the news will have devastated your young man. I'm not surprised he kicked the door in. Is he going to tell his parents?'

Barbara couldn't understand how they

could be so accepting. She ignored his question and asked one of her own. 'Why aren't you disgusted? I slept with two men in less than a week. Doesn't that make me a — '

'Don't you dare say that word, young lady. You are still our precious granddaughter, and Charlie is still our great-grandson.' Her grandmother was a constant surprise. 'Edward, I'm sure Alex will keep this information to himself. Telling his parents would mean they will have lost both grandchildren, and that would be too cruel.'

'Alex will never forgive me, but he said he will keep up appearances until he leaves. I don't see how this will work, as the Evertons and the boys will see at once that we're not speaking — especially at the funeral.'

Grandpa handed her a mug of cocoa. 'Drink this, Barbara, and let's listen to the radio. Plenty of time to consider your options tomorrow; we don't have to make any decisions tonight.'

★ ★ ★

The next morning Tom and David were rather subdued, but they made no mention of the events of yesterday and left for school as usual. Mrs Brown and Joe had been horrified, and the atmosphere in the kitchen was oppressive. Barbara put Charlie down for his mid-morning nap in the pram and wheeled it to the far end of the study so she and her grandparents could talk without disturbing him.

Grandpa opened the discussion without preamble. 'This is a very tricky situation, my dear. We must go to Home Farm and offer the Evertons our support. I've not been able to contact them as they are still with their daughter and son-in-law. However, they'll be home soon and will expect to see you. They are your in-laws; they will want you to be there. But if you come with us you might bump into Alex, which would be unpleasant for both of you.'

'I hardly slept last night, but I couldn't cry; I just felt numb, as if my head was full of cotton wool. What's happened between Alex and me seems unreal, and I'm not sure I've even taken in the fact that Judith is dead. How can she be when she was here on my birthday, crawling around the floor and giggling and laughing with Charlie? How can a perfectly healthy baby just die like that?'

'I've no idea, Barbara, and sometimes the post-mortem doesn't come up with anything concrete either. I'm afraid this isn't the first case I've come across. A few years ago the same thing happened to a couple in

Mountnessing — a healthy little boy just died in his sleep. They never did discover the cause. Tragic for the parents never to know — but it was established that they'd done everything parents should do.'

Barbara jumped up and ran to the side of the pram to check her own child was sleeping peacefully. She'd never leave him on his own again just in case the same thing happened to him. Grandpa joined her and put his arm around her waist, holding her tight. He wasn't usually given to outward displays of affection.

'My dear girl, that was incredibly stupid of me. This sort of tragedy happens very rarely. Remember, I'm an old man and have only come across two cases in my career. Nothing is going to happen to your baby.'

'Don't forget he was born five weeks early in an air-raid shelter and could have suffered some sort of damage from the dust in the air,' Barbara said. 'I know he's been fine, not even a winter cold, but after what happened I'm going to worry, whatever you say.'

'All young mothers worry, but you mustn't become obsessive about it. I'm a reasonably proficient doctor, and I give you my word as a professional that your son suffered no damage from his unusual arrival and is absolutely healthy.'

She rested her head against his tweedy jacket for a moment, letting his strength and confidence flow into her. Her panic subsided. 'You're right, but it's going to be difficult not being overprotective in the next few weeks.'

'Come and sit down, you two. Your drink is getting cold.' Grandma sniffed the brown liquid suspiciously. 'This is supposed to be coffee, but it certainly doesn't smell or taste like it. The addition of chicory just makes it bitter.'

'Actually, Elspeth, I'm beginning to quite like it.'

'I'm with you, Grandma. I think I might prefer to drink hot water.'

They regrouped around the coffee table. 'Mrs Brown has given us the last of the Jacobs assorted biscuits,' said Grandma. 'I don't suppose even Harrods will have any more.'

Talking about trivialities was postponing the difficult decision that had to be made. Should Barbara go with her grandparents and offer her sympathies and risk meeting Alex, or remain behind and possibly cause her in-laws even more upset?

When the disgusting coffee was finished and the biscuits eaten, she was still no nearer a solution. The telephone rang in the library, the shrill tones quite audible through the wall. She leapt to her feet, glad to have the excuse to leave the room.

'The Grove, Barbara Everton speaking.' There was no answer and she guessed it must be Alex. 'Hang on a minute, Alex, I'll get Grandpa.' She was about to put the phone down when he spoke. She almost didn't recognise his voice. It was hoarse, his words almost slurred.

'No, don't go. Christ almighty, this is a bloody nightmare. My sister has had to be sedated, and Peter has been given a postponement for his call-up. My parents are walking around in a daze, and they all want me to make things better.'

'Is there something I can do to help? I'll do anything — '

'I need you, Babs. I can't cope with losing you and Charlie on top of everything else. It's going to be difficult, but I don't think I'll get through this without both of you with me.'

She was speechless. Whatever she'd expected him to say, it hadn't been this. 'Where are you? Grandpa can bring us straightaway.'

'I'll come to you. I want to see Charlie, but I don't think it would be a good idea to bring him here, not so soon . . . ' He couldn't go on, and she heard him swallowing and wiping his eyes. 'I'll be there in half an hour.' The phone went dead and it was several seconds before she replaced the receiver on the cradle.

Her legs were wobbly and she collapsed onto the nearest chair. She couldn't take this in — he was coming back to her and he was prepared to give her another chance. Tears dripped through her fingers. He wouldn't be coming back if his niece hadn't died. She couldn't think of this as a silver lining — she would rather have lost Alex than for Valerie and Peter to have lost their precious baby.

'My dear girl, don't cry like that. Who was that on the phone? Here, use my handkerchief and blow your nose and dry your eyes, and try and tell to me what happened.' Grandpa pushed it into her hands.

She snuffled and gulped and gradually regained control. 'Alex is coming back. He said he can't lose us as well as the baby.' A spasm of grief shook her. 'I don't want him back because of this tragedy. I want Judith to be alive, I — '

'Of course you do, child, but getting through these awful days will be so much easier for both of you if you're together.' He squeezed her arm affectionately. 'At least we don't have to make that decision. We can all do what we can to help the Evertons.'

'I suppose it would have been better if I hadn't told you and Grandma, but I'm glad I did. Ever since I knew I was pregnant I was

72

worried the baby might not be Alex's. I so wanted to tell you both, I hated having this secret between us.' She blew her nose a second time and stood up. 'Alex just assumed he was the first, and I can't tell you how much I wished I'd told him the truth then.'

'Better that you didn't, my dear, because then you would be an unmarried mother and you would be obliged to marry John when he came back. For all the complications and deceit, I'm glad you said nothing and married Alex. You love each other. You'll get through this somehow.'

'Grandma, I'm going to make up a bed for him in a spare room and then he can choose where he wants to sleep.'

'I think that's a good idea, Barbara, and will save embarrassment all round. I'll watch Charlie, if you want to go and do that now. Alex will be here soon.'

4

'Will you be all right on your own with Valerie and Peter, Mum? I'm going to get Babs — she'll stay for a couple of days, so you can go home and sort things out for the boys and Dad.' Alex put his arms around his mother and for a moment she rested her head on his shoulder. 'Charlie won't be coming.'

'Is Mrs Sinclair all right with looking after the baby overnight?'

'Mrs Brown and Doctor Sinclair will help. I've got to be back at the base tonight, but the adjutant has promised I can get some more time off before we leave at the end of the month.' They couldn't set a date for the funeral until the coroner had got his report, but someone at the hospital had promised to hurry things up.

'I don't understand why this happened. I've always been a God-fearing woman, but after this, I'm just not sure.' She stepped away and wiped her eyes. 'You go and fetch your wife. She's a good girl and will know what to say to Valerie. Someone's got to clear out the nursery — but I don't think Valerie is ready for that.'

The vicar had visited his sister and her husband and offered them what comfort he could. Alex didn't have much time for religion; he'd seen too much death and destruction recently to believe there was a benevolent power taking care of the world. But if the platitudes and mumbo-jumbo made Valerie feel better, then he'd keep his mouth shut.

Dad had had to go back to the farm with his younger brothers — the Land Girls couldn't be expected to take care of the livestock and everything else on their own. Ned and Jim hadn't wanted to go, but his parents had decided the boys would be better off at school with something to take their minds off the tragedy.

Outside the sun was shining, the chickens clucking and pecking as usual. The world seemed the same, but it wasn't. How could his sister and brother-in-law recover from this? He squeezed his eyes shut. He'd done more than enough crying; he needed to be strong to face Barbara after what she'd done to him.

How could the innocent girl he thought he'd married turn out to be little better than a slut? If he'd known she'd already gone to bed with Thorogood, he'd never have asked her to marry him. He would have been miserable knowing she would be marrying someone else, but he wouldn't be feeling as bloody awful as he was now — and wouldn't love a baby that wasn't even his.

He stumbled into his car and slammed the door. He couldn't be bothered to struggle with the roof — this had been a bugger to put up since he'd ripped a hole in it last year. One of the blokes at the base had patched it up so it was waterproof, but he only bothered to use it when it was actually raining.

The raids on London by the Germans meant he and his command were busy every night trying to shoot down the bastards before they dropped their bombs. He hadn't had even a few hours free for a month, and he'd been counting the minutes to his twenty-four-hour pass. Instead of a relaxing time spent with his wife and child, he'd fallen headfirst into a nightmare.

The Sinclairs must know he and Barbara had had a major bust-up. They couldn't have failed to notice the smashed lock in her bathroom. But had she told them why he'd left? Would it make any difference if they knew?

He swallowed a lump in his throat. If anything happened to Charlie, he'd be as devastated as Peter and Valerie. He didn't care if he wasn't his biological father; as far as he was concerned, the baby was his son and would always be so. His parentage must remain a secret — if her grandparents were aware of the true facts, they must never reveal them. Mum and Dad mustn't find out.

He arrived at the Grove without having been aware of the journey. As he headed for the back door, he realised he hadn't actually asked Barbara if she was prepared to stay with Valerie and Peter for a couple of days. She would be expecting him to stay with her, but he had to be back at the base tonight — he couldn't expect his second in command to carry the responsibility for more than one night's sorties.

He wasn't sure what he was going to say to her, or if he even wanted to talk about her revelation, or just pretend it hadn't happened. He vaulted out of the car without bothering to open the door, and headed for the back door. Usually he walked in without knocking, but he wasn't sure what his reception would be this time. He didn't have to make a decision as the door opened and both Edward and Elspeth came out to greet him.

'My dear boy, I can't tell you how sorry we are for your loss. If there's anything we can do, please don't hesitate to ask.' Edward patted his shoulder.

'We can only imagine the pain all your

family must be suffering right now. Come in, Alex. Barbara is upstairs somewhere making up the spare room.' Elspeth took his hands in hers and squeezed them.

'I'm hoping that Barbara will take over from Mum for a couple of days — she needs to go home and get things organised for Dad and the boys.' He'd noted the tactful reference to the spare room; Barbara had obviously told them everything. 'Knowing about Charlie doesn't change how I feel, and I don't want my family to ever know . . . ' His voice faltered; he needed to say something about his marriage, but didn't know what he'd decided.

'Goes without saying, my dear chap,' Edward said. 'There's no need for anyone else to know. Go and speak to Barbara; things might be a bit clearer then. Whatever you decide, you'll always be welcome here.'

Alex couldn't respond. He raised his hand in acknowledgement and shot through the door that led to the back stairs. He wasn't sure what he was going to say to Barbara, or if he could ever forgive her; but he knew he had to see her — that she was the only one who could help him get through this.

* * *

Barbara transferred Alex's forgotten toiletries and a couple of towels to the bathroom that adjoined the spare room. She'd just finished when she heard footsteps approaching. She didn't want to speak to him in here, as it was too claustrophobic, so she moved into the spacious corridor to see him vanish into the bedroom.

She walked to the window seat at the far end and waited for him to re-emerge, not sure if she should call out and let him know where she was. Her heart was pounding, her mouth dry; she wasn't ready for this confrontation. He'd been so angry, had said such horrible things, and she didn't blame him one bit.

She flopped back against the window and closed her eyes, wanting the next few minutes to be over. She must have dozed because suddenly he was beside her and put his arms around her.

'Darling, I'm sorry for what I said. I didn't mean it. I don't care what happened before we were together. I love you and I love Charlie, and as far as I'm concerned he's my son. It says so on the birth certificate and that's all I care about.'

For a few wonderful minutes she relaxed into his embrace and they cried together. Eventually she pushed him away. 'Alex, you have nothing to be sorry about. Please, will you let me explain?'

'I don't think talking about it is a good idea, Babs. The only way this will work is if I pretend I don't know.'

'Our marriage will fail if we leave things as they are. This secret has been between us from the start — I need to tell you everything if we're to have any chance of making this work.'

He moved away, his expression closed and distant, and folded his arms across his chest. 'If you insist, go ahead. But I warn you, unburdening yourself is going to make things harder for me. Do you really want to push me even further away?'

'Of course I don't. I love you — I've never loved anyone else. But I have to do this.' She scrambled to her feet and stood in front of him. 'Have you really looked at me lately? Have you noticed how much weight I've lost? How unhappy I've been?'

'We thought you were suffering from some sort of baby blues — it's what Edward and I were talking about the other day.'

'I'm not depressed, but this secret was destroying me. You need to know how it happened.'

'Go ahead, but spare me the gory details if you don't mind.'

She couldn't look at him whilst she told him how Charlie had been conceived or why she hadn't said anything to him at the New Year's Eve party. It didn't take long; there wasn't very much to tell, after all. 'You need to know that even if I had told you and we hadn't got married, I wouldn't have married John. I don't believe that marrying someone you don't love can ever work.'

The silence stretched and she didn't dare look at him, knowing what she would see there. He was right, she should never have made him hear the sordid details. She turned her back and tried to stem the tears with an already wet handkerchief.

'Bloody hell, sweetheart, don't cry any more.' His hands slid around her waist and he pulled her backwards until she was sitting on his lap. 'You're right, I wouldn't have married you if I'd known, so I'm glad you didn't tell me. I don't regret marrying you, and I understand why you couldn't say anything. I love you, and in the end our marriage will be stronger because of this.'

'My grandparents know the truth.'

'But nobody else needs to. It's a good thing your brothers have blue eyes and blond hair — I shouldn't think anyone else will suspect he's not mine.'

She settled into his arms, scarcely able to

comprehend that he'd forgiven her. She didn't want to make love, just to be held and hold him in return. He stirred first.

'I can't stay here, Babs. I have to be back at the base this evening.' He tipped her face with one finger and kissed her. 'And if I could, I'd not be staying in the spare room.'

'Good — I just thought I'd better get it ready just in case. Is there any chance you'll get any leave before you go?'

'God knows. I bloody well hope so. There are several family men in my flight and we all want to spend time at home before we go overseas.' He stroked her hair, and she half-smiled. 'I've come to ask you a huge favour, sweetheart. I've squared it with the old folk. Mum needs to go home for a day or two, and we want you to stay with Valerie and Peter until she gets back.'

Her stomach clenched. 'Of course I'll come. Are you sure Valerie wants to see me? Won't it just make her feel worse?'

'As long as we leave Charlie here it'll be okay. There are baby things all over the house — if you could put everything in the nursery it would make things easier for them.'

'Do you know when the funeral's going to be?'

'Next week sometime; they're waiting to hear from the hospital.' He crushed her close and then took her hand and pulled her to her feet. 'I want to see Charlie before I go. If you pack your bag I'll nip down and spend a few minutes with him.'

He walked out, his shoulders slumped. He'd aged ten years in the past two days. She probably didn't look any better; but she was sure, now Alex and her grandparents knew the truth and had forgiven her, that she would begin to recover her looks and her spirits. Once the funeral was over things would be a bit easier for Valerie and Peter, but she doubted they would ever fully recover from the loss of their beautiful daughter.

Her friend was going to need all the support she could give her over the next few months — especially when Peter was finally drafted. He'd applied to join the RAF, too; he was a skilled mechanic and was hopeful he would be trained as ground crew and be based at Hornchurch.

Barbara threw a change of clothes and her overnight things into a suitcase and then dashed into the nursery to check her grandmother would be able to find what she needed for Charlie whilst she was away. It didn't seem fair that her future now seemed bright, the nightmares about her secret gone forever, when Valerie had nothing to look forward to but misery and loneliness.

Her family was in the sitting room and the baby was wide awake and in Alex's arms. His smile was heartbreaking and she swallowed. 'I expect he's a bit smelly, he always is after a nap. I'll change him before we go.'

'I'll bring him up, but I'll leave the nappy to you. I've not recovered from the last time I did it.'

'Are you sure you can manage for a couple of nights, Grandma?'

'I'm looking forward to it, my dear. Don't forget I've got a medical man to help me out, as well as Mrs Brown and the boys.'

'Run along, Barbara, and get that little chap clean and dry for us. We're going to take him for another walk in his perambulator when he comes back.'

'He likes being pushed over the cobbles in the backyard, Grandpa, but it's jolly hard work and you might be better going through the house and out of the French windows in the drawing room.'

Alex was already in the passageway so she hurried to join him. She grabbed a clean towel and dropped it on the floor in the nursery and then knelt beside it. 'Right, little one, let Mummy sort you out. Then Daddy and I have got to go away for a while. I hope you're going to be good for your grandpa and grandma.'

The baby waved his arms and blew bubbles at her. Alex handed her the box with all the necessary bits and pieces and then joined her on the floor. He reached out and began to tickle Charlie under the chin, distracting the baby whilst she quickly changed his nappy.

'I wasn't sure how I'd feel when I held him again,' he said quietly. 'I don't feel any different. He's my son, and I hope you won't feel you've got to tell him the truth when he's older.'

She closed the second safety pin, pulled up his rubber pants and deftly rebuttoned the rompers. 'There you are, all clean and dry for the moment.' She was about to pick him up but Alex got there first. This gave her time to consider her answer. She wasn't sure if she could promise never to reveal the baby's parentage, so she chose her words carefully. 'I don't see any need for him to know. The best thing we can do is carry on as if nothing's changed.' She hesitated, not sure if she should finish her sentence. 'But if he ever asks me a direct question, I won't lie to him.'

'Fair enough.' He looked incredibly sad. 'If I go for a Burton you might feel differently. Better for Charlie if you contact Thorogood — and at least he'll still have a father. Do you know, Babs, I'm actually glad I know. At least you'll both have somebody to take care of you.'

She sprung to her feet and flung her arms around them. 'Don't say things like that. You're going to come back to us and we'll have more children and everything's going to be fine. In fact, I'm sure that Valerie and Peter will have more children eventually as well.'

He rested his chin on her head with the baby sandwiched between them. 'I hope so. At the moment Valerie's saying she'll never go through it again. She'd rather be childless than lose another baby.'

'I'll talk to her in a few weeks, when things have settled down a bit. Grandpa says it's rare for a baby to die so suddenly, so the chances of it happening again must be tiny.'

'We'd better get a move on; I promised Mum I wouldn't be long. Grab your bag and I'll bring this little monkey.'

Leaving Charlie for the first time since he'd been born was made even more heart-rending by the fact that her son seemed to sense his parents were abandoning him. He struggled to escape from Grandma, stretching out his arms in a desperate attempt to reach Barbara.

Alex bundled her out of the back door and into the car. 'He'll be fine, Babs. He's upset because we are. Please don't cry, or you'll set me off again.'

She huddled in the bucket seat of his ancient MG, her throat raw with tears. He reversed the car with his usual panache, but instead of roaring off down the gravel drive he stopped and switched the engine off again.

'Listen, he's stopped crying already.'

'He has, thank goodness for that. I was upset for my grandparents. They would hate having to look after a miserable baby.' She turned on the seat and kissed him, his cheek rough beneath her lips. 'Thank you, I feel better now.'

The closer they got to their destination the more worried she felt. She wasn't sure she would be able to give Valerie and Peter the support they needed; she wasn't much good at this sort of thing. But if Alex believed she could do it, then she'd give it a go.

He pointed to a cloud of black smoke off to the right of them. 'Romford took a hammering last night; we lost two blokes over the channel. I hope someone picked up the poor buggers; they won't survive long when the sea's so cold.' He had to shout to make himself heard.

'I'll be glad when your squadron moves to the Isle of Man. I'm going to miss you terribly, but at least you'll be safer away from London.'

He took her hand and squeezed it tightly. 'All my chaps have done more than thirty missions, so we're due for an easier posting. I pity the poor blighters taking over — most of them are inexperienced.'

'Don't think about it. You've done your bit; you flyers helped save Britain from Hitler last year. If the Luftwaffe had destroyed the RAF, Churchill said, we would have been invaded.' Her words were blown away by the wind and the noise of the engine. She wasn't going to shout them again; they were approaching the farm and her mouth was suddenly too dry to speak.

He slowed and turned in through the gate. A Land Girl was wheeling a barrow of muck across the yard and paused to raise a hand in greeting. She didn't smile — Barbara thought she might never smile again. Nobody came out to greet them from the house, and the place had a neglected look as if the occupants had moved away. The curtains were drawn and even the birds were quiet.

Neither of them made any move to get out of the car. Alex gripped Barbara's hand, but she didn't dare look at him. 'Right, let's get this over with. I can't stay long, Babs; I've got to run Mum home and get back to the base.

I'm on duty the next three nights, but should have a few hours free on Thursday.'

Her heart sunk to her shoes. She didn't want to be away from Charlie for so long, but couldn't tell him. She flung open the car door and jumped out, grabbing her bag from the miniscule back seat.

'God, darling, don't look so worried. You won't have to stay until Thursday, Mum will be back tomorrow or the next day and Dad will run you home. I'll call in here on the way past and then come straight to the Grove.'

She managed a wan smile. 'We'd better go in; the longer we hang about out here the harder it's going to be.' He put his arm around her shoulders and they walked slowly to the back door.

Somehow Barbara expected to hear Valerie crying, but the house was eerily silent. The quiet brought home, as nothing else could, that there was no longer a baby living here. Where was everybody? The kitchen was deserted, no kettle steaming on the range, and dirty crockery on the table and draining board.

'Alex, I'm not going to see them right away. I'll tidy up and make some tea, soup and sandwiches and then take that in to them. Can you hang on for an hour whilst I do it? Your mother needs to eat before she goes.'

He nodded. 'Good idea. They've been sitting in the front room since it happened. Mum said Judith had never been in there, so it's easier than the rest of the house. I'll be back to help you take it in.'

They embraced and he strode off, leaving her to the chaotic kitchen. Having something concrete to do made being here a bit easier. In less than the hour the place was sparkling and lunch was ready. She found two large wooden trays and put the tea and sandwiches on one and the bowls of soup and cutlery on the other.

There was time to make potato pastry for cheese pasties for tonight. She'd just finished and was putting them in the pantry when Alex returned. His face was colourless, his eyes sunk into his head. She shoved the baking tray on a slate shelf and ran to him. He clung to her and she rubbed his back and murmured words of comfort as she did to her brothers when they were upset.

After several minutes he recovered. 'I feel so helpless. There's nothing anyone can say or do to make things better for them. I just don't know what to do.'

'You can't do anything. You just have to offer love and support and pray that they can hold things together until they get used to the idea.'

'Pray? I wish I could, but I just don't believe any of that claptrap anymore. Valerie told the vicar not to call anymore; telling her that her baby was in a happier place wasn't especially helpful.'

'What an idiot! How could their daughter have been any happier than she was with them? I just think dreadful things happen to good people and there's nothing anyone can do about it. I heard on the news last night over a thousand people were killed in the last raid on London.'

'Not much comfort to them, is it? I think it would be easier to bear if she'd died in an air raid. Then at least they would have someone to blame. Now they're blaming themselves.'

'I'll tell them what Grandpa said; maybe I can help them after all. If I can convince them there was nothing they could have done about this, they might feel a bit better.' She pointed to the heavier tray. 'You carry this in and I'll take the soup.'

'Might as well, as you've already done it. Can't say I've got much appetite, but we all need to eat. I hope you can persuade my sister to have something.'

The front room was dark, the curtains drawn, and Mrs Everton and Valerie were sitting slumped on the sofa whilst Peter stared at the wall. Barbara placed the tray on the sideboard and marched over to the window and flung back the curtains.

'I've brought you some lunch and you can't eat it in the dark.' She didn't wait for a response but handed the two women a napkin and spoon. Listlessly they took them, but didn't speak. 'Peter, why don't you sit down?'

He did as she asked and accepted his cutlery without protest. Alex poured the tea and put sandwiches on the side plates. 'The soup smells delicious, Babs. I didn't realise I was hungry,' he said loudly.

'Here you are, Mrs Everton, Valerie. I've only given you a little but I'm sure you can manage that.' She took a third bowl to Peter and then sat next to Alex at a small table by the window and began to eat. She ignored the others but was aware they'd followed suit. She glanced at Alex and he smiled and pressed his foot against her calf.

Nobody spoke; there was just the sound of spoons against china. Without being asked, Alex replaced his empty bowl on the tray and started pouring out the tea. Barbara collected the empty dishes and handed round the sandwiches.

These were also accepted without comment, and the atmosphere in the room lifted a little. Being hungry made everything harder to deal with. Barbara returned to the table with her own sandwich and Alex gave her a cup of tea. He tapped his watch and looked at the door. She understood immediately and nodded. He swallowed the last of his drink and put the cup in the saucer noisily.

'Mum, I have to be back at base by three o'clock, so if you've finished your lunch we need to get a move on.'

Mrs Everton briefly hugged her daughter and stood up. Barbara was shocked at her mother-in-law's appearance: her hair was unkempt and she looked as though she'd been sleeping in the clothes she was wearing. She probably had, as Alex said she'd not been home to collect anything fresh.

'I'm ready; thank you for coming, Barbara, and for making this lunch. Just the ticket. I'll be back tomorrow, Valerie love. I have to do a bit of cooking and laundry for your dad and the boys.'

Valerie didn't answer, just nodded listlessly. Peter had his arm around her and he managed a small smile, but he didn't speak either. Both of them looked dreadful, dark-eyed and haggard. They would both feel better if Barbara could persuade them to have a bath and go to bed for a few hours.

'I'll see you in a few days, Alex. Take care, darling.' He raised a hand and guided his mother from the room. The oppressive silence returned.

'I'll take this into the kitchen,' said Barbara. 'Is there anything else you'd like?'

'No, thanks,' Peter replied, his voice almost inaudible.

She gathered up the remains of the lunch and put the empty tray underneath the one full of crockery, then carried it back to the kitchen and quickly washed up. There wasn't any point in asking them any questions; they were in no state to make decisions. She would check their bedroom was free of baby things and then run them a bath. If she just gave them instructions she was pretty sure they would do as she asked. At least she had a plan, and her stay would accomplish something useful.

5

By Wednesday Barbara was desperate to go home. She'd cleaned the house from top to bottom, done the laundry and the ironing, removed all traces of the baby from the rooms, and put everything in the nursery. As she folded the little matinee jackets and nightdresses her cheeks were wet, and this made her even more eager to return to Charlie. However when Mrs Everton had asked her to stay on for an extra night, she couldn't refuse.

She'd heard nothing from Alex, but no news was good news, so she was certain he was unhurt. She'd spoken to Tom and David and they seemed remarkably cheerful considering the circumstances. Mr Everton was expected later this morning and she already had her overnight bag packed and waiting by the back door. She'd prepared lunch and made a vegetable stew for the evening meal, and Peter had insisted she take a large ham.

'Please have it, Barbara. After all you've done for us these past two days we want to say thank you.'

'Won't you need it next week? I expect

there'll be a lot of people coming back after the service.'

'We're not having anyone back, Valerie doesn't want to. It's going to be hard enough having folk offering their sympathies at the church without them being here.'

'I know what you mean. It's different when it's an old person, but . . . ' She couldn't go on and he turned away, embarrassed by his tears. 'You just need to get through the next few weeks. Anything I can do to help, you only have to ask.'

'Actually, we were wondering if you might offer to have Ned and Jim live with you at the Grove for a bit? Mr Everton can't look after the farm and the boys, and we really need Valerie's mum here at the moment.'

'We'd love to have them; they're part of the family already. I'll give Mrs Everton a ring and ask her to pack their clothes before she comes. If she telephones Brentwood School, your boys can come home with ours this afternoon.'

Her mother-in-law picked the phone up immediately. When Barbara made the offer she accepted without demur. 'I didn't like to ask, but not having to worry about them will make things a bit easier all round. Mary, one of the Land Girls, is happy to make my Fred's meals.'

Barbara checked she wasn't being over-heard. 'Did you know Valerie doesn't want anyone back after the funeral? Peter just told me.'

'I'm not surprised. She's not coping very well.' She sniffed and blew her nose. 'Mind you, none of us are finding it easy. It's just not fair, taking that little baby away from them.'

'She doesn't cry, just sits there looking defeated. She eats when I ask her to, but I think if I didn't insist she wouldn't bother.'

'It doesn't do to bottle it up. She'll be better after a good cry. Seeing that little coffin next week will make it seem real. I'll need to be here for at least a couple of weeks, which will bring us to the Easter holidays. Are you sure Doctor and Mrs Sinclair don't mind having my two for so long?'

'Of course not. There's plenty for them to do, and if you can let us have their ration books, I'll give them to Mrs Brown.'

'I'll be over in about an hour. I'll leave the boys' things in the back of the car. Didn't Alex say he was getting a few hours off today?'

'I'm hoping so. He said he'd call in on his way past and then spend the rest of the time with us. Peter told me he's been accepted as ground crew but doesn't have to report to

Hornchurch until after the funeral.'

'I don't know how our Valerie will manage when he's not there all the time. I can't stay with her indefinitely, and she's got to run the farm with just the Land Girls when Peter's gone.'

Barbara replaced the receiver and wandered into the kitchen to make yet another pot of tea. Fortunately there was always a plentiful supply of milk, as well as eggs and vegetables. Sitting with Valerie and her husband was exhausting and she was running out of small talk.

They used to have plenty to say — they had become really close over the past eighteen months — but now Barbara's friend was so withdrawn, weighed down with grief, that she couldn't reach her. She'd said that things would get easier with time, but had got no response. Not surprising, really, as this was the silly thing everyone said when someone died. Most bad things hurt less as time passed; her own miserable childhood now seemed as if it had happened to someone else.

The postman peddled into the yard and raised a hand in greeting. She went out to meet him.

'Morning, Mrs Everton. Another lot of cards. How are they holding up? It ain't right,

98

a little scrap like that. Bad enough when it's an adult.' He handed her a dozen or more envelopes.

'Thank you. They've not opened anything yet.'

'I reckon it's not sunk in. It'll be the funeral that'll bring it home.' He shook his head and wobbled off to deliver the rest of his post.

She took the pile of sympathy cards and put them with the others on the kitchen table. There were more than thirty already. The phone rang in the hall and she hurried to answer it.

'Barbara, is that you?'

'Yes, Grandpa. I was just going to ring you. I'm really worried about Valerie. I'm not sure if it's the sedative her doctor has given her that's making her so withdrawn, or if she's really unwell.'

'Shock and grief are like a physical illness, my dear. It might well be a week or two before she is able to function normally.'

'That's what I thought. Is Charlie all right?'

'Charlie is very well, but we'll all be glad to have you back.'

'I can't wait to return. Why did you call?'

'I was just ringing to tell you that Mrs Williams's funeral is this afternoon — it's in the church where the baby will be buried next week. Elspeth thought you might like to go. No, stupid thing to say. Nobody *wants* to go to a funeral. I'm not working today, so I could come over and collect you and we could go together.'

'I'd forgotten all about it. You're right, I should go. Alex is coming here later. What time is the service?'

'Three o'clock. I don't suppose there'll be a wake, so you should be back at the same time as the boys.'

'Golly, I was supposed to ring and tell you that Ned and Jim are coming to stay for the next few weeks. Mrs Everton asked if we'd look after them until things improved over here.'

'Excellent idea. Best to keep them busy.'

Barbara hung up and turned to see Valerie standing behind her. 'Was that my mum?'

'No, it was my grandfather giving me some news.' She didn't think it would be tactful to mention the funeral.

'Is she going to be here soon?'

'She will be here in about half an hour. I'm going to wait until Alex comes after lunch and not go back with Mr Everton, if that's all right with you.'

'Was that the postman just now?'

'Yes, I've put the letters and things on the kitchen table. Do you want to open them?'

Valerie didn't answer but drifted into the front room, closing the door behind her. Her friend couldn't make it plainer that she wasn't welcome anymore. Valerie must have heard her talking about Charlie when *she* no longer had a daughter.

Barbara decided not to stay, but return as originally planned with Mr Everton. She didn't think anyone would notice she and Alex were absent from the funeral. If Clarissa Williams was still alive it would be different.

She was about to ring her grandparents again but thought she'd better not. She would be home in an hour and could explain then. She put her ear against the front room door and could hear voices inside. That was a good sign — at least they were talking, not sitting in silence as they had been up till now.

The car eventually arrived and her mother-in-law rushed in and hugged her. 'Thank you, Babs, for looking after things here. I'll let you get off. I've rung the school, so my boys will know to get off the bus with Tom and David.'

'Anything else I can do, just let me know. But I must tell you, I don't think Valerie wants me here anymore. I'm just a constant reminder of what she's lost.'

Mr Everton staggered in with two heavy suitcases. 'I'll just take these upstairs, love, and then we can be off.'

'There's no hurry. I'm sure you want to spend a bit of time with Valerie.'

He shook his head. 'No, too much going on at the farm. I'm not good with this sort of thing — best leave it to the missus.'

'He's taking it hard, Babs,' said Mrs Everton. 'He can't bear to see his little girl in such pain. Looking after Ned and Jim is how you can help us. Don't worry about our Valerie; she hasn't accepted the fact that her lovely baby is gone.' She dabbed her eyes and Barbara put her arms around her.

'I'd be exactly the same. I won't come round until you think she's ready to see me.' They hugged briefly and then Mr Everton clumped down the stairs.

'Give us a ring, Ida, if you need anything. Are you ready, Babs?'

The drive back was completed in silence and Barbara was relieved to clamber out of the car. 'Don't get out, Mr Everton. I'll grab the cases from the back seat.' He drove away without saying goodbye.

The cases were too heavy for her to carry — heaven knew what was in them. Joe could get them; they wouldn't come to any harm where they were for a while. She ran inside and headed for the kitchen, where she could hear Charlie babbling and chuckling.

He saw her come in and immediately beamed and held out his arms. She didn't stop to speak to her grandparents but tried to pick him out of the high chair, forgetting he was strapped in. By the time the reins were removed everyone was laughing.

'Darling baby, have you missed your mummy? Have you been a good boy?'

'He's been absolutely splendid, my dear,' said Grandpa. 'Slept through the night, and Elspeth didn't have to go in to him yesterday or today until seven o'clock.'

'I'm so glad. He's teething and could have woken up a couple of times. Did you sleep in my bedroom or move him into yours?'

'Used your room, Barbara. Mrs Brown and I have changed the sheets.'

'Thanks, Grandma. I don't know if Alex will be able to stay, but I hope so. By the way, I'm sorry to arrive when you didn't expect me until later this afternoon, but I couldn't stay there any longer. I was upsetting Valerie.'

'Not going to the funeral then, my dear?' Grandpa asked.

'No, I'd rather spend time with my family. I'm hoping that there won't be anyone there who actually knows we lived at Radcliffe Hall last year.'

★　★　★

103

'Alex, old bean, when are we off to the jolly old Isle of Man?' one of his squadron asked as he was heading for the door.

'Not the foggiest, but not until all the bods have got a brand-new Spitfire. There's some hold-up at the factory and I don't reckon we'll get the last four planes until April at the earliest.'

'Good show! Although it's non-stop bloody action at Hornchurch, I don't fancy patrolling over the Irish Sea. At least we've got a chance of being picked up if we bail out over the Channel — nobody's going to find us out there.'

'True enough, but far less chance of being shot down. We won't be there long, just time enough for us to recuperate. We'll be back in the thick of it by the autumn, I guarantee it.'

Alex mimed drinking a pint and headed for the bar. They weren't on call until dawn, so he might as well have a beer before he turned in. He opened the door and the blue fug of the mess caught at the back of his throat. Everybody on the base now seemed to be a heavy smoker. He decided to give the bar a miss and go to his quarters.

He didn't bother to undress. His orderly would be calling him in a few hours, so there was no point getting comfortable. Normally he was unconscious the moment his head hit the pillow, but since his niece had died and Barbara had dropped her bombshell, he'd found it difficult to sleep. Flyers like him expected to die every time they took off — tragedy was part of the war — but not an innocent baby.

Things like this made a chap think. After his initial fury that Charlie wasn't his actual son, he'd realised what was important to him. He couldn't love the baby any more than he already did, even if he had been his natural child. Once Barbara had explained to him how she'd come to sleep with Thorogood, he couldn't really blame her. She'd been put in an impossible position and had made the best of it.

He loved her and as he hadn't been on the scene when Charlie was conceived, he didn't have the right to complain. He was going to tell her that if anything happened to him, and Thorogood survived, she should marry him so Charlie had a father. The thought of his wife in the arms of someone else screwed him up, but he'd rather she was with a bloke who loved her as much as he did than be on her own.

Decision made, he switched on the light and got out the Basildon Bond and his fountain pen. He would write her a letter and get the adjutant to hang on to it for him and give it to her if he kicked the bucket. Best to get his affairs in order whilst he could. If a beautiful, healthy baby could die so suddenly, then nobody was safe from the Grim Reaper.

He finished the letter and scribbled his name. He read it through again and his eyes filled. Imagining Babs reading this made his death seem closer than ever before. There were only two other pilots on the base who'd flown as many missions as him. The mortality rate was sickeningly high; he must be living on borrowed time. He had so much to live for, and wallowing in what might happen wasn't going to help anyone, especially his fellow pilots. Once a bloke started anticipating his own death, he was less effective and more vulnerable.

He folded the three sheets of flimsy paper and pushed them into the matching envelope and then wrote Barbara's name on the front. He'd ask his orderly give it to the adjutant tomorrow. He turned off the light and this time was asleep instantly.

When he was woken at three he didn't feel too bad. He shaved quickly and had finished dressing and drunk his tea in less than ten minutes. 'Can you give this to the adjutant for me? You know the drill,' he asked his orderly.

The man nodded. 'Right-o, sir. It's been a quiet night; them bleeders ain't been so busy.

Reckon you'll have a nice restful time on your watch.'

'Good show. I better be off — don't want to miss the lorry and have to cycle in the dark.'

For the first time in weeks they weren't scrambled, and he spent the intervening hours playing brag and drinking tea. When they were relieved at lunchtime his mood was more optimistic and his doom-laden fears seemed childish.

He reminded his flight that he wasn't going to be on base. 'I won't be around until our next shift, lads, but if I'm needed they know where to reach me and I can be back in half an hour.'

Nobody complained that he was having preferential treatment. They knew the reason he was getting time off when they weren't.

★　★　★

Charlie had just fallen asleep in his nursery, and Barbara was stretched out on the daybed in her room reading, when she heard Alex in the passageway. The print had danced in front of her eyes and she hadn't taken much of the story in; even a cracking good yarn couldn't hold her attention. She tossed the book aside and stood up. Her heart was hammering and she clenched her fists to stop them trembling. Whatever he'd said, she still couldn't believe he'd accepted her betrayal so easily.

The door opened and he stepped in. His smile made her toes curl. He opened his arms and she flung herself in. He kicked the door shut with his heel. 'Do we have time before he wakes up?'

'He's only just gone down so we've got an hour.' She tipped her head back and pulled his down. His lips were icy but his tongue was hot as it entered her mouth. This is what they both needed — to lose themselves in passion and forget everything else for a few precious minutes.

They barely made it to the bed and their lovemaking was fierce and wonderful. Afterwards they lay side by side, delightfully hot and sweaty. Her skirt was around her waist and the only item of clothing he'd removed were her knickers.

'You've still got your shoes on, Alex. I can't believe we've just made love fully clothed and in the middle of the afternoon.'

He chuckled and gently pushed her hair out of her eyes. 'Shocking behaviour, Mrs Everton.' He rolled sideways and kicked his trousers and underpants off the end of his legs. 'Hang on a minute, darling, and I'll take everything else off.'

Whilst he was busy undressing she wriggled out of her skirt and almost ripped the buttons off her blouse and cardigan in her hurry to remove them. He helped with her brassiere and petticoat so they were naked.

'I love you so much, Babs. I just want to stay alive for the rest of this bloody war so we can buy our own house and be a proper family.'

'And I love you, my darling Alex, and I don't care if I get pregnant today.'

'God, I didn't think of that. I'd love another baby — maybe next time you'll have a girl. I've always wanted a daughter to spoil.'

She stroked his shoulder and then her fingers moved across his torso and she touched his chest hair. She loved the roughness beneath her fingers, quite different to the hair that grew on his face or his head, but it was all the same vibrant chestnut colour. 'I don't care what we have, as long as he or she's healthy.'

They spent a further glorious hour in a determined effort to increase the size of their family. Charlie eventually called a halt to their lovemaking. Barbara scrambled up and tugged on her dressing gown. 'I'll change him and then bring him in. You use the bathroom now and then I can get dressed afterwards.'

He grinned, swung his legs out of bed and

stood up, unashamedly naked. 'I hope you don't meet your folks — Charlie is making enough racket to raise the dead. Although they probably realise that we've been in bed, they can pretend they don't know, as long as we don't mention it.'

The baby was getting cross; his wails would be heard all over the house. 'Don't worry about it. They might be old, but they're not stupid. However much he screams they won't come up here.'

Half an hour later they were all decent again and heading for the kitchen. 'I'll give this young man his tea, if you want to go and say hello to Grandpa and Grandma. I expect they're hiding in the sitting room until they're quite sure we're downstairs.'

Mrs Brown was talking to someone. 'Now then, naughty boys. I don't care if your mummy gave it to you, you're not going to eat it in here.'

Barbara pushed open the door and laughed. The housekeeper was scolding the two dogs, who were sitting wagging their tails with a large, very dead rabbit between them. 'Goodness me, did Lavender catch that? It's huge.'

'She's a clever cat, and this one's nice and fresh and will make a tasty meal for us tomorrow. I reckon there'll be a regular supply now the weather's better. Good thing the dogs had the sense to bring it in and didn't try and eat it.'

'Horrible thought! Is there any chance of some tea and something to eat, Mrs Brown? Alex has to go fairly soon and he missed his lunch.'

'How about scrambled eggs on toast? Shall I do one for the baby as well?'

'That would be wonderful, thank you. The chickens must be laying again.'

'I've got a dozen cracked eggs and we've got to eat them up ourselves.'

Barbara smiled, sure the regular supply of cracked eggs had nothing to do with the chickens. 'I'll go and find Alex.'

'No need to do that, sweetheart. I'm here,' Alex said. 'Let me put Charlie Bear in his high chair and then you can make the toast.' He winked at her. 'I'm absolutely ravenous.'

He wolfed down his food and drank two mugs of tea with total concentration, then glanced up and grinned. 'Sorry, appalling table manners. We all gobble down our food, as we never know if we're going to be scrambled . . . '

She laughed and the baby banged the tray of his high chair and pointed at Alex. 'Dada. Dada.'

Alex stretched out and grabbed a waving

hand. 'Clever boy. I'm your daddy and that's your mummy. Can you say 'mummy'?'

'Muma, Muma,' Charlie said and clapped his hands.

'I suppose he's too small to start saying 'grandpa' or 'grandma'?' Grandpa had wandered in to join them.

'He's only nine months old, Edward,' said Grandma. 'I think he's incredibly clever to be saying anything at all. I believe our great-grandson is highly intelligent as well as the most beautiful baby in the county.'

'Elspeth my dear, I think you might be a trifle biased. However, I am forced to admit that in my experience it's very unusual for a child so young to begin talking.' He stroked the baby's head and Charlie beamed at him.

Alex returned to his meal and Barbara continued to spoon eggs into her son. When he finished the last mouthful he screwed up his face and prepared to scream his disapproval. 'No, Charlie, we don't want any of that.' She put two Marmite soldiers on his tray and his face relaxed as he investigated this new food. 'Now he's got teeth at the top and bottom, I think he's ready to try a bit of toast.'

All five of them watched to see how he reacted. 'Good grief!' Alex said. 'Look at us — no wonder he's so advanced with so many adults taking an interest.'

'I'm surprised he's not becoming spoilt, but you're very good with him, Barbara, and don't stand any nonsense.' Her grandmother nodded approvingly. 'I think we can safely say that he likes Marmite on toast.'

Alex nodded towards the door and Barbara stood up. 'Can you keep an eye on him for a minute, please?'

'Of course. You need to spend as much time as you can together. We understand how important this is.'

'Thank you, Grandma. We won't be long.'

As soon as she was outside the door, Alex grabbed her hand and almost dragged her into the library. She shivered, not just from the cold. He closed the door before she could ask what was wrong and he pulled her almost roughly into his arms.

'I love you so much, and each time I leave you and Charlie it gets harder.' He kissed her and she responded, wishing there was something she could say that would make things easier. There was more desperation than passion in his kiss.

'Darling, things won't seem so bleak in a few weeks,' she said. 'You'll be going somewhere safe. I know it's going to be hard, but I'd much rather you were not in the thick of it.'

He ignored her comment. 'How soon will you know if you're pregnant?'

'My cycle has been more regular since I had Charlie, so we should know before you leave. Not for certain, but if I miss my next period it will be a pretty good sign.'

'I'd better say goodbye and get going. I need to get some shut-eye before I'm on duty again.'

'Will I see you again before next week?'

'I shouldn't think so. I've got to have the afternoon off for the funeral, so I can't ask for any more leave. The CO says when the new squadron arrives we'll get a forty-eight-hour pass before we go.'

'If you have time, will you ring me when you get back to the base? I know someone would get in touch, but I need to hear your voice to be sure you're safe.'

He hugged her and for a moment they stood silent, knowing as always that this could be the last time they saw each other.

★　★　★

That night Barbara didn't have time to worry, as there were four lively boys to organise as well as the baby. Fortunately none of them had much homework and they were able to go upstairs and play for a couple of hours before she had to supervise their bedtime preparations. Once the baby was asleep, her grandparents joined her in her bedroom and they settled down to listen to the evening concert on the wireless.

'I'm just going up to get the boys into bed, then I'll go down and make us some cocoa,' said Barbara. 'Hopefully I'll be back before the news.'

'Don't worry about that, my dear, unless you desperately want some. I've locked up and switched off the lights as neither Elspeth nor I want anything else tonight.'

'In which case, I won't bother. I shan't be long.'

The boys were already in their pyjamas and sitting on Tom's bed playing cards. 'I'll just check your school things are ready and then leave you to it, boys. Make sure you turn out the light by nine o'clock.'

She left them to their game, noticing that the Everton boys now slept in Tom's bed and her brothers in David's. When they first started staying overnight, David and Ned had shared. Both the beds were small doubles, so there was plenty of room, but she would ask Joe to find single beds. Jim and Tom were too big to share.

She called goodnight and after a chorus of replies, switched off the playroom light and left them to their own devices. She checked the baby was asleep and joined her grandparents.

'Everything's fine upstairs. They've promised to go to sleep when they've finished their card game. Aren't you listening to the concert tonight?' The wireless was barely audible.

'We wanted to talk to you, Barbara, about how things are with you and Alex after your unfortunate revelation.' Grandpa waited for her to sit down before continuing. 'We've not had the opportunity to discover how things have been resolved.' He smiled and raised an eyebrow. 'We rather think that everything is fine after this afternoon?'

She blushed. 'Yes, after his initial anger he decided he didn't care. As far as he's concerned Charlie's his son and he doesn't want anyone else to ever know the truth. I know I shouldn't, but I keep thinking that if Judith hadn't died we wouldn't still be together. I feel absolutely dreadful about this — as if somehow I profited from her tragedy.'

Her grandparents exchanged glances. 'We thought the same, my dear, but don't dwell on it. As long as you and Alex are on course, that's all that matters. I'm sure eventually you would have sorted things out, but far better now than later.' He reached out and threw a couple of logs on the fire.

'Was it very difficult with Valerie and her husband?' Grandma asked. 'I gather from Edward that she's not coping. I've seen it before, my dear. Sometimes it takes a young mother much longer to accept her loss than it does for an older woman. Maybe after the funeral she'll be able to grieve — but only time can heal her.'

'There are families in the village who have lost children, but the parents appear to be coping far better than your friends,' Grandpa said. 'I think losing a baby is so much more difficult than losing an adult offspring.' He sighed and shook his head sadly. 'Somehow knowing that other families are sharing a similar loss seems to make things easier.'

'I don't think the boys should go to the funeral; has Mrs Everton said anything about this?'

'No, Grandma, but I agree. Unless they ask to attend I think they should go to school as usual. By the way, Alex thinks they won't have the last few planes until the middle of April. Although it will be wonderful having him here for an extra couple of weeks, I'd rather he left as planned and wasn't flying every night.'

Grandpa glanced at his watch. 'Soon be time for the news. Then we're going to retire, my dear. I've got an early start tomorrow.'

'I don't think you should be doing as many shifts as you are, Grandpa. I don't care how short-staffed they are, you're looking very tired lately.'

He shrugged. 'Not much I can do about it, Barbara. Our little hospital and surgery is essential to the war effort. Mind you, I've noticed there are far fewer people coming than before the war. Money is tight for families, with only the pathetic amount the War Office pay.'

'It isn't fair people like us can pay for our healthcare — '

'Life isn't fair, Barbara. Just be grateful you've been born into a wealthy family and don't have to worry about money.' He stood and turned up the volume on the radio, preventing any further conversation about politics.

6

Barbara didn't want to hear the news; she was depressed enough. Judging by the amount of activity overhead, it was obvious there was a major raid over London tonight. She didn't need to be told about the hundreds of casualties.

She checked the boys were asleep and then slipped into the nursery and sat in the darkness, listening to her son breathing softly in his cot. She waited until she heard her bedroom door open before getting up.

'Goodnight. Don't worry about the boys getting off to school, Grandma; I'll do that.'

She curled up with a book and read for a while before getting ready for bed. She made sure both the nursery door and her own were open and then turned her light out. Could she be pregnant again? She'd conceived the first time, so must be pretty fertile. She counted the days from her last period and was fairly sure she was in the middle of her cycle. This was supposed to be the best time, so she could be having another baby in nine months.

Alex had been so eager to add to their

family that she'd gone along with him when really the very last thing she wanted was to be pregnant again so soon after having Charlie. Would the baby, if there was one, have red hair like his father?

Her stomach plummeted. Was that why Alex was so keen? Did he want a baby that was his own flesh and blood and not somebody else's child? This wasn't the only problem. They hadn't thought this through. Wouldn't Valerie be even more distraught when she heard?

Barbara rolled over to hug her pillow. Alex's scent lingered on the sheets, and this added to her distress. She hoped she was wrong, but she had a horrible feeling he wanted to replace not only Judith, but Charlie, with a baby that was actually his. He might think he'd accepted John's son, but his sudden wish to have another baby pointed to a different reason.

Yet again she'd done something she didn't want to, just to please a man. First she hadn't had the heart to refuse John when he climbed into her bed, and now she'd let Alex persuade her to try for another baby when he knew perfectly well she wanted to wait until Charlie was older. She'd not enjoyed her pregnancy, and the thought of waddling about like a barrage balloon whilst taking care of a baby filled her with horror. Of course, she'd cope like any other young woman would have to, but no one could convince her that having another child would be good for anyone — and especially not for Valerie.

When Charlie woke up at dawn she was relieved to have something to do. She'd had precious little sleep and was sure she'd be grumpy today. She got him up and took him downstairs while she made his morning milk. Life was a lot easier now he could have cow's milk; it had to be diluted with boiled water, but that didn't present any problems. National Dried Milk had been made available for infants since last year, and she'd used it until Charlie was old enough to digest the real stuff; but it was fiddly to mix, and she was never sure if she'd made it too thick or too thin despite having instructions on the tin.

At least women could stop breastfeeding earlier and help the war effort by working in factories and so on. No doubt the nation's grannies and aunties were looking after the babies whilst the younger women worked. Why shouldn't she do the same? She wasn't sure if Alex would approve, but he wasn't going to be in England to comment. Although he said he would be on the Isle of

Man for six months, he was unlikely to return to Hornchurch; he could be sent anywhere in the world where Spitfires were needed.

If Barbara wasn't pregnant then she'd ask Grandma if she and Mrs Brown between them would be prepared to take over Charlie's care during the day so Barbara could work as a volunteer nursing orderly at the hospital. Even if Grandpa wasn't going in to Brentwood every day, she could cycle the five miles quite easily.

Making this decision made her feel as if she was finally taking charge of her life, not allowing herself to be influenced by other people. She would never regret for one instant the birth of her son — he was her world, and meant everything to her — but if she'd said no to John as she'd wanted to, her life would be so different.

She hadn't been in the kitchen long when Mrs Brown appeared. 'Morning, Mrs Everton. You're down early today. Do you want your breakfast, or will you wait until the boys are here?'

'I'm not hungry, thank you. I'll have a bit of toast later. It's such a lovely morning, I'm going to take Charlie to see Silver and the chickens.'

'That little mare of yours is a godsend. My Joe thinks she's smashing. He couldn't do so much on the estate if he didn't have her to pull the cart.'

'I don't get to ride her nearly enough nowadays, but she's getting plenty of exercise so I don't feel guilty.'

When she came back the boys were sitting round the table smartly dressed in their school uniforms. She thought the Eton collars silly, but Brentwood School liked to think of itself as top-rank, and so the boys had to dress as if they were at the famous public school. Jim and Tom were still wearing short trousers like the other two, which was also ridiculous. Jim wouldn't be allowed to go into long for another year and he was already taller than her.

'I'll walk to the bus stop with you this morning, if you don't mind,' she said. 'It's far too nice to stay indoors.'

'Can you meet us with Charlie this afternoon as well?' David asked.

'I'd be delighted to, if you're sure I won't embarrass you.' Her remark was addressed to the older boys but they smiled, obviously not bothered by being accompanied by an adult. They shot off to collect their satchels and put on blazers whilst she got the baby into his coat and in the pram.

Grandma appeared through the door from the stairs and kissed both her and the baby.

'Good morning, my dears. Are you walking to the bus?'

'We are, Grandma, I can't understand why they seem happy to have me there. They don't let you or Grandpa meet them.'

'They don't want to be seen with us, but I'm sure being associated with a beautiful young woman like yourself will give them status with their friends.' She smiled. 'Tom and Jim are growing up, Barbara; of course they notice pretty girls.'

'Good grief! I should have thought of that myself. I rather like the idea of being a pin-up girl.'

On the way to the bus stop Jim let the others go ahead and walked beside her. 'Babs, how long are we going to be staying with you? We like it here, but . . . well, we'd rather be at home so we can help Dad on the farm.'

'Your mother asked us to take you until the end of the Easter holidays.' She hesitated, not sure if she should explain why. If Jim was adult enough to ask the question, he deserved an answer. 'Your sister isn't coping well and your mother needs to be with her for the next few weeks, especially as Peter has been called up. She doesn't want to worry about you two as well.'

He didn't look convinced. 'I'm old enough

to leave school next Christmas; I'm not a child. Dad needs us; we ought to be there.'

This wasn't going well. 'What about a compromise, Jim? You could live with us but go and work on the farm after school, at weekends and during the holidays. That way your mother would know you're both eating properly and not falling behind with your schoolwork. Also, she wouldn't have to worry about your laundry and so on.'

He nodded and grinned. For a second he looked just like Alex. 'Okay, Babs, I'm happy with that. We'll come back here as planned, change and cycle over right after school. We'll be back before it gets dark and there'll be plenty of time to do our prep.' He dashed after his brother, and Ned turned around and waved.

Her brothers ran back to her. 'Can we go over with them after school, Babs? There's lots we can do for Mr Everton. The work will be done quicker and they can come back earlier,' Tom said.

'If he's happy for you to go, then I don't see why not.'

The bus stop was a hundred yards ahead and a small group of similarly uniformed boys turned to stare. There were several older boys in the group. 'I'll leave you here. I won't come down this afternoon. You'll need to run home if you're going to get off to the farm promptly.'

She waved and immediately turned the pram and headed home. Knowing she was being admired by the sixth-formers shouldn't make her feel uncomfortable, but it did. After all, they were only a couple of years younger than her and quite capable of making embarrassing comments. She supposed she should really have discussed this new plan with her grandparents. Too late to worry about that; she'd given her word.

Alex didn't have time to come and see them on Thursday, but he did ring a couple of times. They wouldn't meet now until the funeral the following Monday. The hospital had released the baby without being able to find the cause of death.

The new arrangement with the Everton boys was working well, and the Grove was surprisingly jolly considering the reason for their guests staying. Two extra beds had been put up in the playroom, and Tom and Jim now slept there whilst the younger boys remained in the bedroom. Surprisingly, there had been no argument about this, for which Barbara was grateful.

The funeral was at midday and Barbara was dreading it. None of the boys had expressed any wish to attend, and had left for school without complaint that morning.

'Mrs Brown, are you sure you're going to be all right with Charlie? He can have his morning nap in the pram and we should be back before he has his afternoon rest.'

'We'll be fine, Mrs Everton. He's a good little boy, and me and Joe will enjoy looking after him. Don't you worry about a thing.'

'There isn't going to be a wake, as far as I know, so we should be back before two o'clock. I've put everything you need in that basket.'

Her grandfather came in, looking frighteningly old in his black suit. 'Come along, my dear. Charlie will be absolutely splendid with Mrs Brown. Let's get this over with. Elspeth is already in the car.'

She slipped her arm through his and he patted her hand. 'I've never been to a funeral, Grandpa, and I really don't want to go to this one.'

'None of us do. I'm afraid there have been far too many these past few months. Sometimes I believe it's easier for the parents of the young men who have died overseas who can't have a funeral.'

Barbara scrambled into the back seat of the small black car and Grandpa slammed the door behind her. Grandma turned, the black veil on her hat partially obscuring her face and making her look rather mysterious. 'Are you all right, Barbara? This is going to be difficult, especially for you. It's a pity you can't sit with Alex.'

'We both thought it better not to. I'm just a reminder to Valerie and Peter that I still have my baby.'

Grandpa snorted. 'Utter nonsense, my dear. You should be with him. I can't believe it's anything to do with Charlie. As far as they're concerned, he's Alex's son too.'

'I can't think of anything else, Grandpa. Anyway, unless Alex asks me to sit with him, I shall stay with you.'

The drive to the church was too short. The group of black-garbed mourners hovering around outside the church entrance stared at them as they approached, but there was nobody Barbara recognised. 'Do we go in, or wait outside?' she asked, hoping she wouldn't have to stand with the strangers.

'Go in, my dear,' said Grandpa. 'No point in hanging about out here. The hearse will be here shortly, and we don't want to be in the way.' He put his arms around Grandma and herself and ushered them into the darkness of the church.

An organ was playing softly and there was a quiet murmur from the assembled congregation. The church was packed; Barbara hadn't realised Valerie and Peter were so well thought of in the area. There weren't enough spaces on the crowded pews for them to sit together.

'Doctor Sinclair, Mrs Sinclair, Mrs Everton, there are seats for you at the front with the family.' An elderly man, presumably some sort of church official, prepared to lead them down the central aisle and pointed to the second pew on the right.

'I'm going to wait for Alex, Grandpa. I don't think Valerie will notice I'm there, and I need to be with him today.'

He nodded. 'We'll see you afterwards. Don't worry about us.'

She stood to one side in order to allow the sidesman to escort her grandparents to the correct pew, and then went to wait outside. A middle-aged lady, her face blotchy and red, moved across to speak to her.

'You'll be Alex's wife, then? I'm Peter's mum, and that's his dad over there. Dreadful business; don't expect to have little ones die like that.' She sniffed and dabbed her eyes. 'Valerie's coming back with us. Neither of them want to be in the house at the moment.'

'I can imagine how difficult it is for you all. I'm so sorry for your loss.'

'We should have been in the car with them. Not right, only one set of grandparents being allowed to follow the hearse.'

Barbara didn't know how to reply to this; whatever she said might be misconstrued. But Mrs Rigby was waiting for her answer. 'Maybe they could only have one car, what with the petrol shortage and everything.'

'Maybe you're right, Mrs Everton. Anyway, water under the bridge now. Valerie and Peter will be better off with us; we don't have any other grandchildren to remind them of their little Judith.'

There was no time to reply, even if she'd known what to say, as the hearse was approaching. It glided to a halt and her throat closed as she saw the tiny white coffin in the back of the car. It was so small, and looked lost in the large space meant for an adult. Although surrounded by wreaths and sprays of spring flowers, nothing could disguise the fact that someone's darling baby had died.

The second black car was stationary behind the hearse, and a passenger door opened and Alex tumbled out. In two strides he was beside Barbara, and she fell into his arms. He was shaking. She held him tightly and they cried together. Through blurred eyes she saw Mr and Mrs Everton emerge, supporting Valerie between them. Her friend was barely able to stand, her face distorted by grief. Where was Peter? Why wasn't he beside his wife? The sound of the hearse being opened caught her attention. 'Surely Peter isn't going to carry the coffin himself? How can he bear to do that?'

Alex's voice was hoarse. 'Valerie insisted. She would have done it herself if he'd let her.'

The undertakers formed up on either side of Peter and his tragic burden. Valerie and her parents were next, with Mr and Mrs Rigby behind them. Barbara and Alex moved after them, and then the group of other relatives got into position at the back.

The vicar led the sombre procession, reading from his Bible as they walked slowly into the church. The congregation were on their feet. The organ was silent, the minister's voice echoing hollowly. Apart from the chanted words, the only sounds were the sobs and snuffles coming from the majority of those present.

Barbara didn't bother to wipe her eyes; she had her arm around Alex's waist and he had his around hers. Without this support they wouldn't have managed the long walk from one end of the aisle to the other.

Peter continued on his own and tenderly laid the body of his baby on the central table. Only a single spray of flowers had been brought in; the rest must have been left in the hearse. He stood there with an arm braced on either side of the tiny coffin, his shoulders bowed. Alex released his hold and moved forward to gently guide his brother-in-law to his place beside his wife.

There was no comfort in the service; nothing that the vicar could say about the glory of the afterlife would make any difference. Barbara's faith wasn't strong, and the banalities spoken by this priest pushed her further away from a belief in a divine and loving power.

She glanced along the pew to see how the bereaved parents were coping. Peter had his head bowed. She couldn't see if he was crying, but Valerie was staring straight ahead. She wasn't looking at the coffin, but at the stained glass window above the altar, which showed Christ on his cross surrounded by Mary and the disciples.

The meaningless service eventually drew to a close. Few had joined in the hymns or repeated the 'amens' — were they all feeling as let down by religion as Barbara was? This time one of the undertakers picked up the coffin, and she was relieved Peter didn't do this a second time. They shuffled miserably to the churchyard, where more mumbo-jumbo was spoken before Judith was lowered into her grave.

Now came the strange custom of throwing

a handful of dirt onto the coffin. One by one, members of the family tossed soil into the hole. Barbara didn't want to do this, but Alex walked forward and she went with him. She couldn't bear to look into the dark interior, to see how small the box was, to imagine how cold and lonely the baby was going to be on her own. Tears blinded her, and only Alex's restraining arm prevented her from toppling in.

They stepped away to allow others to do the same. 'I've had enough of this, darling. I need to get away. I came in the funeral car; can I come back with you?'

'Of course you can — but don't you have to go back with your family for some sort of get-together?'

'No, my sister and Peter refused to have a wake. Did you know they're going to close the farmhouse and move in with his parents?'

'I did. It must be hard for your mother. She'll want your brothers home now, I expect.'

'Not straight away, Dad's going to be running both farms. He and Mum are going to stay there for a couple of days until everything's sorted and the Land Girls know exactly what to do.'

They wandered back to where Grandpa's ancient Austin was parked. He was already there and obviously waiting for them. 'I take it you're coming back with us, young man? Do you have to be on duty tonight?'

'Compassionate leave. Don't have to be back until tomorrow morning.'

The return journey was even bleaker, if that were possible. Nobody spoke; there was nothing to say that would make things better. Barbara huddled in Alex's embrace, incoherent with grief.

Grandma pulled herself together. 'You've got a couple of hours before the boys come home. Why don't you take your son for a long walk? The track around our grounds is passable even with a pram.'

'Actually, you've given me an idea. Alex, why don't we take the cart and go for a drive instead? The dogs can come with us. Charlie loves watching them running about.'

For a moment she thought he was too dispirited to answer, then he cleared his throat. 'Okay. I've got some mufti in your cupboard; we can change first.' He was wearing his best blues, she a black coat and hat borrowed from her grandmother.

The atmosphere in the car lightened a little. 'Excellent idea, Barbara,' said Grandma. 'Nothing like a bit of fresh air and sunshine to raise the spirits.'

'Why don't we all go?' Barbara suggested.

'Silver's quite capable of pulling four adults and a baby.'

'Are you sure, my dear?' asked Grandpa. 'You don't know how many more hours you and Alex have.'

'Grandpa, we need to be together today. Do you think it's too cold to take a picnic?'

Her grandmother swivelled on the front seat. 'Not at all. We can wrap up warm and take a thermos of tea. I'll ask Mrs Brown to sort something out whilst we change, and Joe can harness your mare. I can't remember the last time I went on a picnic.'

'It will be Charlie's first picnic as well.' Barbara was warming to the idea. 'He can crawl around in the cart whilst we eat; he'll be perfectly safe there.' For a few moments she'd actually forgotten they'd just been to a funeral. She slumped against the seat, her enthusiasm for the outing evaporated. She was about to tell the others she didn't want to go, when Alex took her hand and whispered in her ear.

'It's all right, darling. Life goes on. Valerie and Peter are grieving for Judith, but they don't expect us to do the same.' His words made sense, but seemed harsh in the circumstances. But then he faced the death of his friends on an almost daily basis and couldn't afford to dwell on things.

She rested her head on his shoulder and he put his spare arm around her waist. Her grandparents continued to discuss the picnic, and she was glad she hadn't cancelled the outing.

★ ★ ★

Silver whickered a greeting as Barbara came out carrying the large bag of paraphernalia needed for the baby. 'Hello, lovely girl. I hope you're feeling energetic, as you've got a lot of weight to pull today.'

'She's raring to go, Mrs Everton. Not been out since yesterday morning. I reckon a load of logs is a lot heavier than you four,' Joe replied.

When had he got so tall? He was a man now and not a boy. 'How old are you, Joe?'

His grin slipped. 'I know what you're thinking. I'll not be old enough to be called up until the end of next year. Mind you, I'd like to do my bit straight away — '

'Forget that, Joe. We need young men like you helping to replace the food the U-boats destroy,' said Alex as he appeared with their son, who crowed with delight when he saw the horse.

'Absolutely right, Alex,' said Grandpa. 'Plenty of time for Joe to fight for his country when he's old enough. Doing a sterling job right here at the moment.' He pushed the picnic hamper onto the cart and turned to take the pile of rugs and cushions from Grandma. 'Let me take those, Elspeth. I'll arrange them so we'll be more comfortable.'

'Thank you, Edward. I can't tell you how much I'm looking forward to this excursion.'

'I've never seen you in slacks before, Grandma, but they look very smart,' said Barbara.

'I'm not sure they are quite suitable for someone my age, my dear, but Edward persuaded me they would be more practical for scrambling in and out of a cart.'

Alex had taken Charlie to pet Silver and was talking seriously to Joe, and Barbara didn't like to interrupt them. 'I think Grandpa and I should sit on the box; and you, Alex and the baby can sit in the cart on the cushions. Is that okay?'

'As you're the only one who can drive, my dear, you must sit at the front. However, I'm perfectly happy to go in the back so Alex can sit next to you.'

Barbara didn't think leaving her grandparents to hang on to a lively baby whilst they bounced along the narrow track was a good idea. Alex came to her rescue.

'Right, I'm sitting up front with this little

rascal. Does anyone need any help to get in the back?'

Barbara had wanted her grandfather sitting beside her because there was more support for his back and somewhere to put his legs, but he seemed perfectly happy with the arrangement.

Joe had put an upturned orange box at the rear of the cart, which made an ideal step. 'Give me your hand, Mrs Sinclair, and I'll help you in.'

It took a further ten minutes before everyone was settled to Barbara's satisfaction. 'If you're ready, we'll get started.' She glanced over her shoulder. 'Exactly where are we going, Grandpa?'

'Follow your usual route, my dear, but turn left instead of right where the track forks. The lane is well-used, as it leads directly to the woods where Joe gets our logs from.'

Her mare hardly needed her hands on the reins, as Silver headed in the right direction of her own accord. The hawthorns and sloe bushes were hazed with white blossom, but there was little sign of spring anywhere else.

'We must be mad going for a picnic so early in the year,' said Barbara. 'We won't be able to sit on the ground; it'll be far too wet after all the rain we've had this month.'

Her grandmother answered from behind

her, 'That's why I put in two rubber sheets, Barbara, and plenty of blankets and cushions as well.'

'I was going to put in a couple of deckchairs, but Elspeth thought that was a bit much.' Grandpa chuckled. It was good to hear him laughing again.

The lane was a bit sticky, but not heavy enough to cause the tough little mare any problems. Charlie was waving and babbling with excitement and for once was content to remain in one place. The birds were singing in the naked branches, and Barbara saw several squirrels scampering up and down the trees. The lane entered the woods and she shivered. Even though there were very few leaves on the trees, the temperature definitely dropped.

'Another half a mile, my dear, and we'll reach a clearing,' said Grandpa. 'Plenty of room to turn the cart, and an ideal place for our alfresco lunch.'

Alex answered, 'Good show, Edward. Bit chilly in here to picnic.' He settled the baby more firmly on his lap. 'I think he's nodding off, Babs. Is that okay?'

'Yes, it's perfect. If he takes a nap we can eat our lunch in peace. It's a bit gloomy in here. I'll be glad to get out in the sunshine again.'

'Look, just ahead. I can see the clearing. There's even a patch of grass for Silver to graze on.'

'Joe put a hay net in for her, but I expect she'd prefer fresh grass.'

Charlie was fast asleep in Alex's arms. The baby looked so right where he was that it didn't matter who his natural father was; Alex was his daddy.

Barbara expertly turned the cart so they were facing the right way for the return journey. She jumped down and helped set up the picnic site. 'Those logs would be ideal to sit on and to use as tables.' She pointed to the pile of freshly cut wood. 'What do you think, Grandma?'

'Perfect, Barbara my dear, and with a cushion on top we'll be quite comfortable. Edward, will you bring the picnic basket over here please?'

Whilst the three of them organised the lunch, Alex made a nest from blankets and gently placed the sleeping baby in it. He carefully refastened the tailgate of the cart, ensuring that if Charlie woke he wouldn't come to any harm.

The tea was hot and, although a trifle stewed, was exactly right for a chilly afternoon. They munched their way through spam sandwiches, followed by jam sandwiches, and finished with a slice of treacle tart.

'Did you know, my dear, that it's illegal to feed the birds?' Grandpa called as she was scattering crumbs and crusts on the ground.

'Nobody's going to see me do it out here, unless you intend to report me?'

Charlie had missed his first outdoor meal, but he would have been a nightmare crawling around the wood and stuffing everything into his mouth. A sudden gust of wind blew two of the cushions across the clearing, and by the time they had been recovered the sun had gone in.

'We'd better get back pronto, Babs, or we're going to get soaked,' Alex said as he bundled up the rugs and blankets and prepared to throw them in the back of the cart.

'I'll sort Silver out whilst you get everybody on board. We should be ready to go in a few minutes. Try not to wake Charlie.'

When they were settled she released the brake and clicked her tongue. The mare leaned into the traces willingly and the cart rolled forward. They were still driving through the wood when the heavens opened.

'Put a rubber sheet over your heads and another one on your legs,' Alex shouted above the rain. 'Charlie should stay dry as well if you do that.'

The cart suddenly lurched sideways, and Barbara shot off the wet seat and tumbled over the side.

7

Barbara landed in the mud. She was terrified Silver would keep walking and she'd be run over by the wheels. As she gasped for breath, Alex's head appeared above her.

'Bloody hell, Babs, that was a spectacular exit. Are you okay down there?'

'Absolutely spiffing! Don't sit there grinning, Flight Commander Everton, get down here and help me up.'

Grandpa peered over the side of the cart. 'Do you require the attentions of a medical man, my dear?' He was trying not to laugh.

She wasn't going to get any sympathy, so she might as well get off the ground and back onto the box. She tried to sit up but for some reason was unable to do so. Her stomach turned, then she realised the back of her coat was trapped underneath the wheel.

She was tempted to pretend she was injured but decided against it. 'Is Charlie all right? And Grandma?'

'Both absolutely fine, my dear. Your son thinks it's all a bit of a lark,' Grandpa replied.

Alex jumped down and knelt beside her. 'Your coat is stuck.'

'Thank you for pointing that out. I wouldn't have noticed otherwise.' She was now soaked to the skin and no longer found the episode the slightest bit funny.

'Hang on, I'll move the cart forward a yard and then you'll be free.'

He scrambled up and went to Silver, encouraging the mare to move. Immediately he did so the pressure on Barbara's back vanished, and she rolled sideways and on to her knees. She was too cold and cross to do more than climb back onto the box and pick up the reins. She waited in silence for Alex to join her and then clicked her tongue. The mare tried to walk on.

'We're stuck. Babs, I'll get down and give us a push.' Alex vanished before she could comment. 'Stay where you are, Edward, no need for all of us to get wet.'

The only way they would get out of the rut was by lightening the load. Barbara climbed down and ran to Silver's head. 'Come along, sweetheart, you can do it.' She grasped the wooden shaft and threw her weight against it. The mare lowered her head and heaved. The combined effort was successful; the rear wheel jolted out of the mud and the cart rolled forward.

From Alex's foul language she guessed he'd fallen face-first in the dirt. Serve him right.

'I'm going to lead Silver. I think she'll go better if I do, and I'll be a lot warmer walking than sitting on the box.'

'I'll walk with you, Babs. Make it easier for your mare with us on foot.' Alex wasn't as muddy as she was, but he was almost as wet. 'What a palaver, as my mum would say. Good thing I'm not wearing my uniform. I think the Wing Co would take a dim view if I was.'

'I'm freezing, Alex. If you go the other side and hold onto the shaft, we'll get Silver to trot. The sooner we get inside and in dry clothes, the happier I'll be.'

By the time they arrived at the stable yard her teeth were chattering and even her knickers were soaked. She wanted a lovely hot bath, but first she must take care of Charlie and make sure her grandparents were okay.

'Alex, will you unload the cart whilst Joe looks after Silver?'

'Righto, I'll be in as soon as I can.' He already had the back of the cart open, and Grandpa handed him a somewhat damp baby. 'Come along, Charlie Bear. I'll take you inside so your mummy can get you nice and dry.'

Barbara didn't argue with the change of plan, but paused to check her grandparents could get out unaided. They waved her away and she ran indoors to stand dripping in the corridor. She could hear Mrs Brown clucking and tutting in the kitchen, so Alex must be in there. Quickly she stripped off her sodden coat and hung it on a peg, and then her mud-plastered shoes thumped into the shoe rack.

Mrs Brown appeared with Charlie in her arms. 'You and Mr Everton run along and get yourselves clean and dry. I'll change this little man and give him some toast to be going on with. And don't worry about bringing anything in; my Joe will do all that.'

'Thank you,' said Barbara. 'You're an angel. There are plenty of clean nappies and things in the box.'

Her grandparents were in the passageway removing their coats. They looked remarkably dry considering they'd been sitting in torrential rain for half an hour.

'Those rubber sheets worked wonderfully, my dear,' said Grandma. 'I don't think either of us need to change. You and Alex run along; I'll help Mrs Brown with Charlie, and your grandfather can make us all a hot drink.'

Upstairs wasn't as warm as the kitchen, but after the unpleasant conditions outside Barbara hardly noticed. 'We can share the bath, Alex, then we can put a bit more water in.'

'Why don't we use the one in the spare

room? It's a lot smaller and we won't need so much water.'

'Good idea. I'll go first as you're dirtier than me. I'll run the water, if you'll fetch our clean things.' They didn't need to take fresh towels, as the bathroom was always left ready for use. She didn't hear his reply but assumed he'd agreed, as he'd vanished into their bedroom.

There was no temperamental geyser in this bathroom, thank goodness, so Barbara dropped in the plug and turned the tap on fully, hoping the boiler had been working efficiently and there would be enough hot water for a decent soak. Whilst the water was thundering into the bath she stripped, tossed her clothes into the corner and wrapped herself in a large towel. She might as well get the worst of the mud off before she got into the bath.

The room was now pleasantly full of steam and she turned on the cold tap, ignoring the fact that there was already the regulation five inches in the tub. She reached in and tested the temperature. Still too hot, but there was nothing she could do about it now. The door opened and Alex came in wearing his dressing gown.

'I had a quick wash first, darling. Why don't you do the same?'

147

'Already done it. I should really wash my hair as well, but I'll just dry it with a towel and hope for the best.'

Before she realised his intention, he stepped in and flicked off her towel. His eyes were dark — he had more than washing on his mind. He shrugged his dressing gown off. 'We've never made love in the bath. Shall we give it a try?'

Her pulse raced and she nodded. 'We'd have been better in our bathroom; there's more room.'

He gripped her elbows and stepped over the side of the bath with her in his arms. 'Too much. We'd probably drown.'

The water was deliciously warm, and so were his lips and his everything else too. There was no time to worry about flooding the floor, or think about his reasons for wanting to start another baby. She was swept along by passion.

Afterwards she peered over the edge of the bath and giggled. 'Not too bad. The bath mat has taken the worst of the water.'

'I'll mop it up whilst you do your hair. You might as well wash it; it's already wet.' He gently eased her away and pushed himself upright, sending a second tidal wave of water over the edge. 'Practically afloat down there now. I'm going to need more than the bath mat.'

'Dry yourself first, darling, then use the towel — but make sure you don't use mine.'

Barbara relaxed against the back of the bath, watching him. She frowned. There were several new bruises on his back, and he was definitely thinner. 'Alex, how did you hurt yourself?'

'Nothing spectacular, sweetheart. Just a rotten landing a couple of nights ago.' He glanced at his bare feet. 'Not much point in drying these; I'm paddling at the moment.'

He'd sounded so blasé about his crash. He could have been killed, and she wouldn't have known about it. She smothered her sob with a flannel.

'Don't cry please, Babs. It was nothing. Couldn't even class it as a prang. My landing gear . . . ' He was crouched beside her, trying to prise the cloth from her face.

She sat up, glared at him, then gave him a push. 'I don't care about your bloody landing gear; that's not the point. You could be killed or injured and I'd be the last to know about it.' She stood up and shoved him aside. 'I don't want to have another baby until the war's over and there's no danger of me becoming a widow.'

He was sitting, naked, in a pool of water and didn't look too pleased about it. Then he grinned. 'Probably a bit late to tell me that, my love, but I do understand. Can I get up now, or are you going to attack me again?'

Reluctantly she smiled. 'Don't be ridiculous, Alex. Please let me out. We've been up here for too long already.' She snatched the remaining towel and, without stopping to dry herself, ran to the bedroom. She didn't trust him when he had that particular look on his face. She was safely in her underwear and pulling on a fresh pair of slacks when he strolled in.

'Bathroom's pristine. I've dumped the wet stuff in the bath for now.' He reached out and lifted a wet lock of hair. 'Are you going to dry this?'

'No time. I'll put it up so it doesn't drip down my neck. Are *you* going to stand there with no clothes on, or get dressed?'

'Don't put ideas into my head, sweetheart. Your grandparents already think we're sex-mad.'

Her cheeks burned. 'Don't say that. I won't know where to look when I go down.'

'I won't be long. I expect we'll need to put the kettle on again, as the first pot of tea will probably be cold.'

She scrambled into a blouse, added a cardigan and scrunched her hair up into a wet lump on top of her head. 'I'm going down. Aren't you putting on your uniform?'

He shook his head. 'No need. I'm not going out, and I don't have to be on duty until first thing tomorrow.' His smile was sad. 'I know I'm supposed to wear my uniform, but being in civilian clothes for a bit helps me forget this bloody war.'

Ignoring his state of undress, Barbara threw her arms around him and stood for a few moments giving him her love and support. She shouldn't complain; her life was so much easier than his. She didn't have to put herself in mortal danger every day. 'I'm so sorry, darling. I don't know why you still love me after what I did. I don't deserve — '

He put one finger on her mouth. 'You've got nothing to be sorry about. None of this is your fault. What happened between you and John was unfortunate, but if you hadn't slept with him we wouldn't have Charlie. Think about that — would you turn back the clock and not have him?'

'Of course not. He's everything to me.' She stretched up and kissed him. 'I love you so much, and I promise I'll be the best wife you've ever had. In future I'll do whatever you want without argument.'

'I might hold you to that. But as you're the *only* wife I've had, or intend to have, no problems there either, sweetheart.' His mouth curved and she saw the danger signs and wriggled free.

She laughed as she ran downstairs, then stopped, horrified she was laughing on such a sad day. Why was life so unfair to some people and good to others? Her marriage should be over, she should be in disgrace, but Alex had forgiven her and accepted Charlie as his own. If she conceived over the next few days, then so be it. She wasn't going to argue about having another baby if that was what he wanted.

★　★　★

The Everton boys were delighted to be going home, and Barbara was so busy sorting out their things the next morning that she hardly had time to miss Alex when he returned to the base.

'I'm going to ask Joe to drive the cases over, Grandma. Then they can go straight home from the bus this afternoon. I'm just going to collect their ration books from Mrs Brown. Is there anything else?'

'I don't think so, Barbara. You have already collected their clean laundry, haven't you?'

'Yes, and I've put their schoolbooks and so on in that box. I'm going to miss them, and I know Tom and David will too.' She checked that they were on their own in the study. 'Grandma, is Grandpa all right? He's definitely lost weight, and seems tired.'

Immediately her grandmother lost her bright smile. 'Oh my dear, I'm so glad you've mentioned it. I've been so worried, but I didn't like to bother you with my concerns. He's overdoing it. He should be enjoying his retirement and not working so hard at the hospital.'

'We need to speak to him together. Perhaps he'll listen then. I don't suppose we'll be able to persuade him to give up completely, but if he only went in two days a week instead of five, that would be a lot better.'

'If you've finished collecting the boys' things, there's no time like the present. He went in at dawn today and I just heard his car arrive in the yard.' Her grandmother smiled conspiratorially. 'He'll be exhausted, so with luck he won't have the energy to argue with us. I'll bring him in here, if you'll fetch the coffee.' She pursed her mouth. 'Not that that awful Camp deserves to be called coffee. I believe there might be some of the tasty carrot cake left if there are no biscuits.'

'I'm pretty sure Mrs Brown managed to get a tin of cocoa in Brentwood yesterday. Shall we have that instead of coffee? Charlie has only just gone to sleep. I'll put his pram outside the door so I'll hear him when he wakes.'

'Yes, let's do that. Please don't use the dried milk. Today we should have real milk, and if there are any biscuits bring those as well. Edward will be more receptive if you offer him cocoa and biscuits.'

When Barbara carried in the tray, her grandfather was stretched out on the Chesterfield being fussed over. She put down the drinks. 'Grandpa, we're in luck today — cocoa made with all milk and plenty of sugar, and some cake.' He opened his eyes and his lips twitched as he winked. 'Grandma, it's no use. He knows we're up to something.'

'Edward, you're impossible! Sit up and listen. Barbara and I have something to tell you.'

'I know what you want to say, and I agree.' He held out a hand for his mug and picked up a wedge of cake in the other.

'How can you possibly know what we're going to say? Are you a clairvoyant as well as a doctor?' Grandma said tersely. She didn't like being teased.

'No, Elspeth, my love, I'm not. However, when my two favourite girls bombard me with love and attention, I'd have to be

154

remarkably stupid not to realise what they want.'

Barbara collected her own drink and cake and curled up in a battered armchair opposite. 'Just in case we're talking about different things, Grandpa, we want you to cut back on your hours at the hospital. We understand you want to do your bit for the war effort, but we need you too. You're the centre of this family and we couldn't manage without you, especially as Alex is going overseas very soon.' There, she'd finally told him how she felt.

He sipped his cocoa and munched his cake and Barbara thought he hadn't heard her. Then he nodded and smiled. Despite the lines of fatigue and the hollowness of his cheeks, he suddenly looked years younger. 'You're absolutely right, my dear girl, and believe it or not I had already decided the time had come to step back. We've had a couple of younger chaps join us, army medics with injuries that stop them working on the front line.'

'Edward, that's wonderful news. Have you given in your notice already?'

He chuckled and his eyes sparkled. 'Better than that, I've been given my marching orders. Today was my last shift. I'm now emergency rota only.'

Barbara jumped up and rushed over to hug him. Initially he recoiled, but then he slowly put his arms around her and returned the embrace. 'I can't tell you how pleased I am! We've been so worried about you.'

'I know you have, my dear girl.' He patted the seat next to him and Grandma shifted along so they were either side of him. 'Elspeth and I have also been worried about you. Was it your secret about Charlie that was making you ill?'

'Yes, it was. Finally I can plan ahead without fear.' He held her and she sighed and rested her head on his shoulder. They relaxed together to the sound of the logs burning in the grate. Too soon, she had to sit up.

'I think I can hear Charlie muttering. I'd better finish my drink before he wakes up properly. He's getting too big to sleep in his pram and I'm worried he's going to tip it over any day.'

'Finish your cocoa, Barbara,' said Grandpa. 'It's too good to waste.'

'Okay, I will, but I'll just check before I do.' She peered around the door and immediately saw the baby had settled again. 'He's asleep, but I don't think it'll be long before he's crying for his lunch.'

She resumed her seat opposite her grandparents and drank the remains of her cocoa. Grandpa smiled and then sat up straight and looked directly at her.

'I've been thinking about filling my days now I'm retired. Would you like me to tutor you in medicine, my dear? You have an aptitude for it, and you already have your first-aid certificate.'

'Now I really do think you're clairvoyant, Grandpa. Alex and I talked about this the other week. We thought I'd have to wait until the end of the war to apply. In fact, we weren't even sure a married woman was allowed to study medicine.'

'There are certainly medics who are married women, but I should think they qualified when they were single. However, the more you can learn before you apply the more likely they are to take you, married or not.'

Grandma wasn't happy with his suggestion. 'I hope you don't expect me to take over your duties as a mother, Barbara, whilst you do this?'

This sharp remark shocked Barbara, and her excitement at the prospect of spending extra time with her beloved grandfather fizzled out. 'No, of course I don't, Grandma. Charlie comes first and I can study when he's asleep.'

She collected the mugs and picked up the

tray. The atmosphere in the room was tense, the way it had been when she'd first arrived and her grandparents were estranged. The last thing she wanted was to cause friction. 'On second thoughts, Grandpa, I'm not sure I'm sufficiently dedicated to be a doctor — all those long hours and so on. But thank you very much for your offer.'

She tiptoed past the pram and into the kitchen. 'Thank you, Mrs Brown. That was delicious. Did you ask Joe to collect the cases and boxes from upstairs?'

'He's already on his way to Home Farm; left half an hour ago. Don't look so fed up, miss. I reckon those lads will still be over here every five minutes.'

'It's going to seem very quiet with only Tom and David. My grandfather has just told us he's retired, so at least we'll have him here.'

The housekeeper nodded. 'About time, too; if you don't mind me saying so, he's been looking a bit peaky these last few weeks. A man of his age should be sitting back with his feet up and his slippers on.'

Charlie was crying. This was unusual, as he normally woke up from his afternoon nap smiling and happy. Barbara dashed into the corridor and unclipped him. As she picked him up, murmuring nonsense, the study door flew open and her grandmother stalked out, ignoring both of them.

'Come along, baby. I'll get you changed, and then you can have a nice drink, and we can go and meet your uncles from the bus.'

'I'm sorry, my dear,' said Grandpa. 'I think Elspeth and I upset the little man. He's not used to raised voices in this house.' He patted her shoulder and strode off to the billiard room.

She wanted to follow him and ask what the row had been about, but she had a horrible feeling it had something to do with her. Her name should have been Cassandra, as disaster seemed to follow her around. The past two weeks had been absolutely beastly, and now inadvertently she'd caused a rift between her grandparents.

The baby wriggled and screeched, wanting to be put down so he could crawl. 'All right, Charlie Bear, I'm going to change you and then we're going for a walk.'

* * *

'Babs, nothing is going to happen to Charlie, is it?' David asked as they walked back to the house from the bus stop.

'No, he's absolutely fine. Don't worry about it, sweetheart. Everyone's fit and well.'

Tom frowned. 'At the moment. But what about Alex? He could be shot down at any time.'

This wasn't a good start to the evening. 'Please don't remind me. I try not to think about it. But it's different; he's fighting for us, and . . . ' She didn't know what to say to them that would make the thought of losing Alex acceptable. Then Charlie came to her rescue by trying to throw himself over the side of the pram. By the time she'd sorted things out, the boys had forgotten.

'I've got some good news for you,' she said. 'Grandpa has retired. He won't have to go to the hospital unless there's an emergency. Isn't that splendid?'

'He promised to teach us to play billiards properly when he had time,' David said, skipping around and tickling the baby as he went past.

'And he said he would teach us how to play poker,' Tom added gleefully.

They raced up the drive, leaving Barbara to push the pram alone. The sound of a Spitfire overhead made her look up, and her heart plummeted. Was this the last of the new planes the squadron was waiting for?

The boys were trailing around disconsolately when she eventually pushed the pram into the hallway. 'We can't find him anywhere, Babs, and Grandma has gone to bed with a headache,' Tom told her.

'Never mind, boys. You don't have to start doing everything tonight, do you? You break up tomorrow and there'll be plenty of time in the holidays. Have you got homework tonight?'

'No, we've got a holiday task, but don't have to start that until next week. Come on, David, let's get changed and take the dogs for a walk.'

Barbara decided to eat with the boys when she discovered her grandfather had gone out in his car and told Mrs Brown he wouldn't be in for supper. The house seemed rather sad and quiet without the Everton boys, but her brothers didn't seem bothered.

'Babs, are you going to put the spare beds away or leave them?'

'They can stay where they are for the moment, Tom. I expect Ned and Jim will be over at some time during the holidays. Are you going to move back in with David, or stay in the playroom?'

'He's coming in with me, aren't you, Tom? I don't want to sleep on my own,' David said.

'Course I am, silly. Anyway, we like the extra beds because we can — ' He stopped and looked shifty.

'I do hope you weren't going to suggest

that you could jump on those beds.' Barbara tried to look cross and failed. 'You mustn't bounce on them or you'll go through the floor.'

'We won't. We only did it a couple of times. If we move them to the edge, we can use them to sit on when we play cards and things.'

'Good idea, Tom. Now off you go, it's almost bedtime.'

Barbara wasn't sure if she should check on Grandma, but didn't want to make matters worse if somehow she was to blame. After she'd put Charlie to bed she wandered into her bedroom and put the wireless on. The news was grim: another devastating raid on London had struck the East End in the docks, and over a thousand people had been killed or injured. Had more civilians been killed than servicemen or women?

She didn't want to hear any more news, so turned the set off and picked up her novel, a murder mystery by Agatha Christie entitled *A Man in a Brown Suit*. Tonight she wanted something exciting that she could immerse herself in and forget everything else. At nine thirty she heard the phone ringing and dashed downstairs to snatch it up.

'Babs, darling, sorry to ring so late.' She clutched the receiver, knowing what was coming next. 'The last Spit arrived today — we're leaving when the replacement squadron gets here. That means we get a forty-eight-hour pass before we go.'

'That's good news, darling.'

'You don't sound very pleased. I thought you'd be glad we could spend two whole days together.'

'Sorry. Of course I'm thrilled about that, and that you will be somewhere safer for a few months. But you'll be going away, and I'm going to miss you dreadfully.' She couldn't prevent the wobble in her voice.

'I know, sweetheart, but it's not forever. We should be back in the autumn. I could be in the army and stuck in Africa for the duration.'

'But you're not, so that's no comfort to me. Are you on duty tonight?'

'No, on reserve. We can stay on the base unless there's a big flap. We go to the forward camp at dawn. Is Charlie okay?'

'He's fast asleep and so are the boys. When will you know about your leave?'

'As soon as the other bods arrive and get settled, we get our passes. This gives the ground crew time to check our kites before we fly to the Isle of Man.'

Barbara was tempted to tell him about the row but didn't want to worry him when he would be flying in a few hours. 'I've not heard any German bombers. Hopefully it's going to be a quiet night.'

'Last night was bloody awful. Lost two kites in the drink.' He was quiet for a moment, then continued. 'Both flyers bailed out, so they'll have been picked up by now.'

'Does that mean you will leave two planes short?'

'Not likely! They weren't in my squadron — our new Spits are much faster and keep us out of trouble.'

'Fighting the bombers is more dangerous than patrolling the North Sea, so why aren't the other flights getting the newest planes?' Why were they discussing this when they had so little time left to talk about personal matters?

'Good question, Babs, and one I asked when all this was mooted. The others are getting new planes as soon as they arrive — but the girls can't fly the new kites out to the Isle of Man, so we get them first. Makes sense really.' There was the sound of voices in the background. 'Sorry, darling, I've got to go. There's a big queue for the phone.'

'Goodnight, darling, and take care. See you soon. Thanks for calling.'

'Night, sweetheart. Kiss my boy for me.'

The line went dead and she replaced the receiver on the cradle. She went to the bottom of the stairs and listened. Silence. Good, she had time to make herself a drink before going to bed. She switched off the lights and checked the back and side doors were secure. Grandpa had forgotten to lock the door when he came in so she did so now.

Two hours later she was woken by what sounded like stones being thrown against glass. She grabbed her torch and ran across the room, threw up the window and peered out.

'Thank God! Barbara, my dear girl, can you let me in? Not a good idea to wake Elspeth so late.'

'Good grief, Grandpa, I'm so sorry. I locked up because I thought you were in. Hang on, I'll be down in a minute.'

She closed the window and made sure the blackouts were drawn, then switched on a light, dragged on her dressing gown, and shoved her feet into her slippers. Her heart was thumping and her hands were clammy. Where on earth had Grandpa been until after midnight? Had there been a medical emergency? She pulled back the bolts and turned the key. The door swung open and her grandfather stumbled in and sprawled at her feet.

8

Barbara stared at him in bemusement. For a horrible moment she thought he'd had a heart attack, then he rolled over and smiled up at her. 'Give me a hand up, my dear girl. I'm afraid I'm a trifle inebriated. I'm not sure where I parked the car.' He chuckled and his breath almost flattened her. 'Don't know how I got her home. Never mind.' His voice echoed down the corridor.

She reached down and took his hands. It took several attempts before she got him upright because his legs kept folding under him, much to his amusement. 'For heaven's sake, Grandpa, it's the middle of the night, and we're going to wake everybody up in a minute if you don't keep quiet.'

Once she had him on his feet she wasn't sure what to do next. She'd never get him up the narrow, twisting stairs on her own and she didn't think it would be wise to rouse her grandmother. 'I'm going to take you to the library, Grandpa. You can sleep on the couch.'

'Excellent, just the ticket. Off we jolly well go. Shall I sing you a song?'

'No, please don't.' She wobbled him along

the corridor and into the library. She couldn't release her hold to switch on the lights, so guided him to his temporary bed by the light of her torch. She turned him and gently pushed. He collapsed with a sigh and was instantly snoring loudly. All she had to do was lift his legs up and find him a blanket. His head was already on a cushion. The back door was wide open, so she closed and locked it then ran upstairs to fetch a couple of blankets from the linen cupboard. He could be sick, so she'd better take him a basin as well.

She carefully rolled him into the recovery position, tucked him in and put the basin on the floor where he could reach it. What else? Maybe a towel under the basin would be a good idea just in case, and a large glass of water for the morning. Finally satisfied she'd done everything she could, she left him and returned to her room.

The clock in the study struck three — Charlie would be awake in a few hours, so she'd better get into bed. Although tired, she couldn't sleep, as her mind constantly reviewed the events of the night. Grandpa liked a drink or two but she'd never seen him the way he was tonight. Where had he been until midnight? Who had he been drinking with?

Then she remembered his remark about the car. She tumbled out of bed and got dressed. She must find it before someone else did. Grandma would be so embarrassed if her friends found out the respectable Dr Sinclair had been wandering about the village in a drunken state.

This was something Barbara couldn't do on her own. She might be out for some time, and there would be no one to hear Charlie if he woke up. Joe slept upstairs on the nursery floor, but she didn't think her grandparents would want him to be involved.

There was nothing else for it; she would have to wake the boys. 'Tom, David, wake up. I need your help.' She shook first one and then the other. David, surprisingly, was awake first.

'Babs, what's wrong? Are we having an adventure?'

'We are, David. I need you to put on your dressing gown and slippers, and I need Tom to get dressed. I'll explain everything when you come to my room.' She stopped at the door. 'Be very quiet; I don't want you to wake Joe or Grandma.'

By this time Tom was sitting up. 'We'll be down in a jiffy. Hurry up, David — Babs needs us.'

Whilst Barbara was waiting she checked

the baby was sleeping, and then returned to her room and put on the standard lamp by the fireplace. There were embers glowing in the grate, and she rammed in the poker and dropped a couple of logs on top. Hopefully they would catch and her youngest brother would have a fire.

David was going to be her babysitter, and Tom could come with her to find the car. She had a vague idea of how to drive but wasn't going to risk it. If she pushed and Tom steered, she hoped they could bring the car back safely — that was, if it wasn't in a ditch or something.

In less than five minutes her co-conspirators arrived, still pink-cheeked and tousle-haired from sleep. 'Right, boys, Grandpa needs our help. We must be very quiet and keep tonight's adventure a big secret. Do you think you can do that?'

They nodded, their eyes gleaming with excitement. 'What do we have to do, Babs? Do we have to rescue him from Germans?' Tom asked hopefully.

'Nothing like that, but he went out and had rather too much to drink and can't remember where he left his car. Tom and I have to find it for him and bring it back. David, I want you to look after Charlie if he wakes up.'

The little boy nodded. 'I can. If he cries, I'll

169

go into his room and talk to him until you get back. I promise I won't go to sleep. I've brought my book with me, so I'll read.' He grinned. 'It's a *Just William* book and it's really super.'

'Good, I'm sure you'll do an excellent job. Of course, if you're worried, you must wake Grandma.'

Tom sniggered. 'Don't do that unless you have to. We don't want her to know about Grandpa.'

'Okay, we'd better get a move on. Did you remember to bring your torch, Tom?'

He waved it in the air. 'Never go anywhere without my trusty torch, Babs. Will I get to drive the car?'

'Of course not, but you might have to steer whilst I push.'

Fortunately there were no clouds and the moonlight was sufficient to guide them, so they could save the precious batteries. The car wasn't in the yard, but Barbara hadn't expected it to be, although she should have had the sense to check first. 'I don't actually know where Grandpa went, so it might be hard to find his car,' she said.

'If I climb that tree, Babs, I can take a squizz into the lane and I might be able to see it.'

'Be careful, Tom. You don't need a broken

leg to add to our problems tonight.' He was an expert tree-climber and was at the top in no time. She moved beneath it so he wouldn't have to shout.

'I think I can see it. There's something just outside the gate. I reckon Grandpa didn't make the turn and went into the hedge.' He slid down, arriving at her side in a rush.

'Well done. Let's run the rest of the way. The sooner we get this over with the better.'

She was quite breathless when they skidded around the gatepost at the end of the long drive; she really must take more exercise and get fit again. Sure enough, the little black car was nose-first in the hedge, with the driver's door hanging open.

Tom was there first. 'It doesn't look too bad, Babs. We should be able to get it out okay.' He scrambled inside and then poked his head out. 'I've found the starter handle. I can get it going, and then you can drive it out of the hedge.'

'I wish I could, but I don't know how to put it into reverse. We're going to have to do it the hard way, one of us pushing and the other steering.'

'I reckon I could do it. I've driven the tractor loads of times at Home Farm.'

'Have you really? I hope Mr Everton knows about it.'

His teeth flashed white in the darkness. 'Of course he does. He's the one who showed me. If we go either side of the car and push, we should be able to get it out far enough for me to get the starter handle in.'

After a frantic few minutes of shoving and heaving, the car rolled backwards onto the road.

'Jump in, Babs. There's no point in you walking when you can ride. It won't take me a moment to get this started.'

His confidence was infectious and she jumped in the passenger seat. Not only was he almost as tall as she, but he had learnt to do something she couldn't do herself. 'Driving a car isn't the same as the tractor, Tom. I hope you know what you're doing. Are you sure it wouldn't be safer to push?'

'Ask me that again in a minute, Babs,' he said with a grin. He was definitely growing up. He grabbed the handle and vanished to the front of the car. There was a rattling and the engine coughed into life.

Her brother landed on the driver's seat and fiddled about with the knobs and levers. 'Hold on, Babs; we should be moving in a minute.' He jiggled his feet and moved the gearstick, and with a hideous grating sound the car shot backwards, narrowly missing the brick gatepost. Barbara almost swallowed her tongue. Tom thought the whole thing a lark.

'Just got to get it into first gear and we can go home.'

'Do we need the lights on, or can you manage to see as we are?'

'I'm not quite sure which switch turns them on. Can you shine your torch on the dashboard?'

She did as he asked, and he studied the array for a few seconds before reaching out and pushing a switch. To her horror a shaft of golden light shot down the drive. The black paint on one of the headlights had obviously scraped off in the accident, so they had the full beam instead of the pinprick which was all that was legal in the blackout.

Unfortunately, both she and Tom leant forward simultaneously and cracked heads. For a moment she couldn't see, as the pain blinded her; but when she recovered the light had gone. 'Are you all right, Tom? That was a frightful bang.'

'I'm fine. Hurts a bit, and I reckon we'll both have lumps on our foreheads tomorrow. We'd better get a move on; someone might have seen the beam in the village and come to investigate.'

The car was still chugging away. Tom waggled his feet again and the car lurched forward, and then stopped. His knuckles were white on the steering wheel and he was staring intently through the windscreen. He couldn't see well enough to drive safely.

'I'm going to get out and walk in front with my torch,' said Barbara. 'Make sure you don't run me over.' He didn't argue. She was forced to brace herself against the car bonnet, hoping she hadn't got concussion. She shook her head and regretted it; she was being silly. If Tom was okay, then she couldn't have done herself any serious damage.

However, when she stepped away from the car her eyes blurred and she almost passed out. She dug her nails into her palms and the sharp pain steadied her. Somehow she forced her feet to obey, and began the long trudge up the drive with the car spluttering and complaining a few yards behind her. She kept her eyes firmly fixed on the building. Looking down was impossible, as it made her head swim and her legs go wobbly.

Eventually they reached the cobbled yard at the side of the house, and Barbara staggered the last few yards. Gratefully, she propped herself against the wall and watched her brother park the car and turn off the engine.

'I say, Babs, you don't look very well. You need to go and lie down.'

Tom's voice seemed strangely distant, but

she understood. 'I'm sorry; I do feel a bit peculiar. I think that bang on the head has given me a bit of concussion. Are you sure you don't feel ill?'

'It was the top of my head that hit your forehead, Babs. You got the worst of it. Hang on to me, and I'll get you upstairs. I'm going to wake up Grandma. She'll know what to do.'

He was almost pushing her up the stairs in the end. Her head was spinning and she felt really sick. Definitely concussed — this was one of the things she'd learnt from her first aid course. Someone, she wasn't sure if it was Tom or David, guided her to her bed, and she collapsed on it. The last thing she remembered was asking for a basin.

* * *

David stared down at his big sister. 'She doesn't look well, Tom. I don't like it. Why doesn't she wake up and talk to us?'

'She said she had concussion. I'm going to wake Grandma; you fetch the bowl in case she's sick.' He looked at his brother. 'She's going to be fine. A bit of concussion is nothing, really.' David didn't look like he believed him. He'd better try again to reassure him. 'Honestly, Grandpa told me loads about it. It's not serious. Babs will just have a bad headache and feel sick for a few days, and then she'll be right as rain.'

'Why doesn't Grandpa wake up and look after her? I don't want her to be concussed, I want her to be awake.'

'You stay here while I nip downstairs and see if he's up. Is Charlie okay?'

David sniffed and wiped his nose on his dressing-gown sleeve. 'Fast asleep. I've been in to look at him loads of times.'

'Jolly good. Don't look so worried, she's going to be all right. You find a basin, and I'll go and see how Grandpa is.'

Tom forgot to be quiet and his heavy outdoor shoes clattered on the thin carpet of the stairs. If Grandma didn't wake up it would be a blooming miracle. He hesitated at the library door. He wasn't sure how to go about waking Grandpa up; he could be a bit tricky sometimes. Mind you, he was a good old stick, and so was Grandma — even if she was a bit of a stickler.

The door creaked open and he peered round. He couldn't hear anything, so he shone his torch in the general direction of the sofa.

'Turn that bloody light off! I've got a shocking headache.'

Tom dropped his torch and it went out. He

fell to his knees to scrabble about trying to locate it. 'It's me, Tom, Grandpa. Barbara's banged her head and she's passed out.' He found the torch and switched it on.

'Put the light on, there's a good boy.'

Tom wasn't sure where the switch was, so he shone the beam across the wall until he found it. Just as he was about to push it down there was an almighty crash, and Grandpa used words he wasn't supposed to.

'Are you all right, Grandpa?' The room was flooded with light, and he spun round to see his adopted grandparent sitting on the floor amongst the broken remains of a china bowl.

'Bloody stupid place to put a basin if you ask me. Give me a hand, my boy. I'm not quite myself as yet.'

Tom was trying not to laugh. He bit his lips and hurried over to grab hold of Grandpa's arm. 'Up you come. Mind you don't fall over the broken bits.' He couldn't stop the snigger escaping and waited for the explosion. It didn't come.

'I'm a silly old bugger. I expect you know I went out and had too much to drink. I've not done that since . . . well, for many years.' He was now upright and remarkably steady. 'Now, tell me how your sister came to be injured whilst I fetch my bag.'

Grandpa didn't say anything about the car

when he heard what had happened, but stopped and carefully examined the top of Tom's head. 'You've got a nasty bump, my boy, but the top of the skull is remarkably tough. The forehead is more vulnerable.'

'She was a bit groggy but managed to walk up the drive okay, then she sort of went really quiet and I had a bit of a job getting her up the stairs and into bed. David's been looking after her whilst I fetched you.'

He led the way into the bedroom and stopped so suddenly his grandfather cannoned into his back, sending him staggering into the room. Grandma was up, still in her nightie and dressing gown, with a strange sort of net thing on her head. She didn't look too pleased to see them.

'Good, you're here at last, Edward. David and Thomas, back to bed at once. Your grandfather and I will take care of things now.'

Tom grabbed his brother's arm and pulled him out of the room. Grandpa caught his eye, winked, and then closed the door firmly behind him.

'We've got to go downstairs and tidy up before we go to bed, David,' said Tom. 'I don't want Grandma to find things in a mess when she gets up tomorrow.'

'Are they going to have another row? She

was ever so cross, and wanted to know what was going on.'

'They'll sort it out. They're all lovey-dovey most of the time, aren't they?' He switched on the stairs light and this time made sure he was quiet. 'You go and get a dustpan and brush from the scullery, and make sure you don't wake up Mrs Brown when you go past her rooms.'

'What do we need that for?'

'Grandpa stepped in the basin and broke it. He said some very rude words. Good thing nobody else heard.'

It didn't take long to pick up the big pieces of china and put them in the wastepaper bin. 'Can you sweep up the little bits, David? I'm just going to lock the back door.' He'd already put the cushions tidily on the sofa and folded up the blankets, and the room looked the same as usual.

'Shall I put the bits in the wastepaper bin?' asked David. 'Or are you going to hide them somewhere?'

'I'll put them in a bucket under the sink in the scullery. I'm certain Grandma will never look in that.'

Between them they'd managed everything really quickly. 'Give me the blankets,' said Tom. 'We're going to need them.' He'd decided he and David should sleep in the nursery with Charlie so they could look after him when he woke up, because Babs wouldn't be well enough. As he led his brother into the passageway he could hear raised voices coming from her room.

Tom pointed to the nursery, and they'd just got inside when the door opposite opened and Grandma was ejected. 'Go to bed, Elspeth. Neither Barbara nor I require your presence here.' Grandpa pulled the door shut, leaving her outside. Her shoulders drooped and she looked really fed up. For a moment Tom was tempted to go out and speak to her, but then thought that might be a bad idea.

Would she think to check on the baby before she vanished? Too late to hide if she did, but she walked away and he heard the distant snap of her bedroom door closing.

'Come on, David. We've got to fetch our eiderdowns and pillows, then we can sleep with Charlie and make sure he's okay. No one else is going to.' He couldn't put on the light in the nursery, but they managed to make a respectable bed beside the cot by the light of their torches. 'Jump in. I'm going to close the door now.'

It wasn't too uncomfortable lying on the eiderdowns, and they were lovely and warm under the two blankets. Tom yawned. Thank goodness there was no school tomorrow. He was just drifting off to sleep when David poked him and whispered in his ear.

'What happened tonight? Where did you and Babs go and how did she hurt her head?'

Tom gave him a short version of the events and they were both giggling by the end of his story. Charlie stirred and Tom held his breath. 'Shush, we're waking the baby. I'll tell you the rest tomorrow.'

* * *

Barbara opened her eyes and blinked. What was Grandpa doing reading the paper in a chair at the end of her bed? She had a shocking headache and was desperate for a pee.

'Good morning, my dear girl. You gave us a nasty shock last night.' He folded his newspaper and put it tidily on his chair and then walked up to her. 'Let me give you a hand. I expect you need the bathroom, and you will probably be a bit wobbly.'

She sat up and waited for the dizziness to subside before swinging her legs onto the carpet. He expertly put his arm around her waist and gripped her elbows, and she was on her feet. 'I think I'm okay. I won't be a minute.'

Whilst she was in the bathroom she

thought she would clean her teeth and give her face a wash. Good grief! Now she remembered. She'd banged heads with Tom last night, which was why she had the most enormous lump on her forehead. As she was carefully drying her face, she realised the sun was up and the blackouts were drawn back. She'd been unconscious for hours. She hadn't heard Charlie screaming, so Grandma must have taken care of him.

Thoughtfully, she replaced the towel. She had a vague recollection of someone shouting last night; her grandmother had been in the room. Grandpa looked remarkably well for a man who had been incapable a few hours ago.

He was staring out of the window when she returned. 'Apart from a nasty headache, I feel absolutely fine this morning — or should I say this afternoon?'

He turned and smiled, then strolled over to join her. 'You aren't concussed, my dear, although I slept on your daybed just in case.'

'So I haven't been unconscious for hours?'

'No, just catching up on missed sleep. I think your body was taking advantage of that bang on the head. You've had a very stressful time these past couple of weeks.'

'I'm surprised you haven't got a headache as well, Grandpa,' she said with a smile.

'I certainly deserve to have one, my dear. I drank far too much last night. I do most humbly apologise for passing out at your feet. I gather from the boys you had a bit of an adventure on my behalf.'

'We did. Did you know Tom can drive? I've been so engrossed with the baby and Alex that I've rather lost touch with both of them. From now on I'm going to be a better big sister.'

He pointed to the bed and obediently she hopped in. 'They've got four other adults to talk to; they haven't missed out. Although I know you feel well enough to get up, I insist you remain in bed today. You had a very nasty knock on your head last night and you're going to feel a bit groggy, even if you're not concussed.'

'I don't like to leave Grandma and Mrs Brown to look after the baby for so long. I'll stay in bed for another couple of hours, but then I'm definitely getting up.'

'Your brothers slept in the nursery last night and got your son up, changed his nappy and dressed him. By the time Elspeth arrived they were ready to take him down for his breakfast. He missed his morning milk, but I don't think he's any the worse for that.'

'Is there any chance of some breakfast? I'm absolutely starving.'

He nodded. 'There used to be a strap you could pull that rang a bell in the servants' hall. I had them taken out, but I rather wish I hadn't today. No, my dear, stay right where you are; I'll go down and rustle up something. It will be more brunch than breakfast, but I'm sure Mrs Brown will find you something light and make you a pot of tea.'

She propped herself up on a couple of extra pillows and closed her eyes. He was right; she didn't really want to get up just yet.

Grandpa didn't come back, but sent her brothers with a tray. 'Come in, boys,' she said. 'Thank you for looking after Charlie.'

'He was just sopping wet, Babs. I don't think we could have coped with anything else,' Tom said with a grin as he plonked the laden tray across her knees. 'Grandpa said only to bring up toast and tea, but we've put on a boiled egg as well.'

'Wonderful. Is Charlie with your grandma now?'

'He's actually next door having a nap. We'll bring him in to you when he wakes up.'

David sat on the end of the bed, making sure he didn't spill her tea. 'They're not speaking, Grandpa and Grandma. It's horrible downstairs.'

'As soon as I've had my breakfast I'll go

down and speak to them. I'm sure it's nothing serious. I'd be very cross with Alex if he came home drunk, but I'd soon forgive him. Don't look so worried, David; it'll soon blow over.'

She shared the toast with the boys, ate the egg and drank two cups of tea. Tom went to check on Charlie without being asked and came back to say he was asleep.

'Good. Now I'm going to get up. Would you mind staying here whilst I go down and try and get to the bottom of this row? When Charlie wakes up we can go for a walk if you like. I'm sure the dogs need the exercise.'

'Can we ring Ned and Jim? Perhaps we could go over there later?' David asked.

'I don't think it's a good idea to go there at the moment. Mrs Everton promised to call as soon as things were straight.' Her little brother looked so disappointed that she quickly added a proviso. 'But there's no harm in asking. They could always cycle over here.' She looked at both of them. Tom was almost an adult, and David shouldn't really be called a little boy anymore. 'What about suggesting you go for a bike ride together? You've got some pocket money. If you promise to be careful, you could ride to Brentwood and buy some pop.'

'Really? That would be smashing — another

adventure,' Tom said eagerly. 'Don't be long, Babs. We want to find out if they can come. Can we go on our own if they can't? We've got some coupons left; maybe we can find a sweet shop selling something.'

Now that he mentioned it, her brothers might well be safer with just the two of them. 'Why don't you go without the Everton boys the first time? Give the family a bit longer to get over the tragedy.'

David was jumping up and down. 'That's the best thing ever, Babs. We'll be ever so careful and be back long before dark, won't we, Tom?'

'It might be best not to bother our grandparents with this,' said Barbara. 'I know I can trust you to be sensible, and we don't want to worry them, do we?'

They shook their heads solemnly, happy to bypass a possible veto as long as they didn't get the blame.

Charlie would be awake and demanding his lunch in half an hour, so Barbara knew she'd better get a move on if she was going to talk to her grandparents. Grandpa would be hiding in the library or the billiard room, and Grandma would either be in the kitchen or the study. Who should she tackle first? Although she was really close to her grandmother now, she remembered the frosty

186

reception she'd received when she'd first arrived.

Sure enough, Grandpa was reading his paper in the billiard room. He looked up with a friendly smile and put his newspaper aside. 'I thought I told you to stay in bed, my dear, but I suppose no one is going to take any notice of an old fogey like me.'

'I've taken a couple of aspirin and feel perfectly well, as long as I don't move my head about too much. Grandpa, may I talk to you?' She didn't wait for his agreement but sat down next to him. 'The boys and I are really worried about you and Grandma. Is there anything I can do to help put matters right?'

'I thought the bad feelings between us were long gone. We've been so happy since you got here. But I didn't like the way she reacted when I suggested I work with you to improve your medical knowledge.' He rubbed his eyes and his shoulders sagged. 'I know both of you wanted me to stop working, but I was enjoying it. Even someone as old as me wants to feel they are doing their bit for the war effort. I thought by teaching you, a medic of the future, I'd still be making myself useful.'

'You've done your bit, Grandpa. No one expects you to do any more.' What she wanted to say next was going to be a bit tricky. 'Do you think that Grandma was looking forward to having you to herself? You've always been so busy that you rarely do things together. Maybe suggesting you spend your spare time teaching me was the last straw?'

His eyes widened and she could almost see the penny drop. 'My word, why didn't I think of that? I was disheartened to see the unpleasant woman that Elspeth used to be reappear, so I went out and got drunk. We're a pair of silly old fools. I promise, my dear, we'll spend a few hours every week together.' He jumped to his feet like a much younger man and headed for the door.

'The boys are going for a bike ride on their own. They've been rather upset by all this and I think it will be good for them — '

'You don't have to explain to me, my dear girl. We might be their legal guardians, but we will always support your decisions.'

Well, that was easier than she'd expected. She would pop along and talk to Mrs Brown and see if there was any possibility of making the boys a packed lunch, then they could get off straight away and have longer to enjoy their excursion.

9

The days drifted by without any word from Alex, and everyone did their best to appear jolly. Barbara's grandparents were now speaking to each other, but there still seemed to be a distance between them that hadn't been there before. The boys, now that they had their independence, were rarely in the house. Sometimes they came back at lunchtime, but more often stayed out all day and only returned when they were hungry. Barbara wasn't sure they should be allowed so much freedom when there was a war on.

She was in the kitchen giving Charlie his lunch when the house shook. 'Look at that — there must be a whole squadron of Spitfires going over,' Mrs Brown said as she peered out of the window.

'That means Squadron Fifty-four will be leaving for the Isle of Man in a day or two. Alex should get a forty-eight-hour pass before he leaves. At least, I hope he does.'

'You'll miss your young man, but better to have him away than fighting them blooming Germans every night.'

'I know you're right, Mrs Brown, but I'm going to miss him dreadfully and so will the boys. Charlie will have forgotten him by the time he gets back.'

'Some children in the village haven't seen their fathers since the start of the war, Mrs Everton, and some won't see them ever again.'

There was no answer to that so she changed the subject. 'Tom told me they'd been meeting up with local boys and messing about on the river. It's a good thing they can both swim.'

'They'll come to no harm with those local lads. It will do them good to rake about with other boys. I reckon they've been a bit cosseted since they came here, if you don't mind me saying so. My Joe was never indoors until dark. They learn to look after themselves, and that can't be bad.'

Barbara's grandparents had gone out to lunch, so she made herself a sandwich and ate this whilst Charlie banged his spoon on the tray of his high chair. 'I'm going to take him out in the pram; he can have his afternoon nap in that. I'm going to walk down to Home Farm. If Alex rings, could you tell him he can catch me there?'

'I will if I'm here, but it's my afternoon and evening off. There's potato and cabbage to make bubble and squeak, and a few eggs to go with it.'

'I'm sorry, I'd forgotten it's my turn to make supper. I'll see you tomorrow morning.'

It had been almost three weeks since she'd seen her mother-in-law. Tom and David had cycled over to see their friends, but the boys had been staying with a relative. Why had Ned and Jim been sent away when they could have remained at the Grove and been able to see their parents every day? She wanted to find out, and the best way was face to face.

As she was pushing the pram down the lane that led to the farm, she heard the unmistakable drone of an approaching bomber. What on earth was it doing here in the middle of the afternoon, and on its own? It must be following the railway line that ran from Clacton-on-Sea to Liverpool Street — Alex had told her this was their favourite route into the East End.

There was nowhere for her to shelter and she was still half a mile from the farm. She bumped Charlie over the grass verge and into the shelter of an overhanging thorn tree. There should be enough foliage on this to conceal her. She wasn't sure why she was hiding; even a German wouldn't waste his precious bombs on a girl with a pram. Surely someone at Hornchurch would spot the enemy plane and send up a couple of Spitfires to shoot it down?

No sooner had she had the thought when the unmistakable throaty roar of approaching fighters filled the sky. The baby screamed in protest, but his wails were drowned out by the racket overhead. The German plane, realising the danger, started to climb, but not before he released his evil cargo. Barbara held her breath as three black shapes hurtled towards the ground. Two fell harmlessly into a field, but the third hit the railway line and exploded with a massive bang. The shock-wave almost pushed her off her feet, and the pram tipped sideways into the bushes.

By the time she'd pulled it out and picked up her terrified son the dogfight had moved away, but she could smell the smoke and hear the flames even at this distance. Charlie was inconsolable, and she walked about talking to him and rubbing his back for several minutes until he calmed down.

'There, there, little man. The nasty planes have gone and you can go back in your pram. Mummy is going to take you to Nanny's and she'll give you a nice drink of milk.' She was still fiddling about with the harness when she heard someone shout her name. She looked up to see four boys on bicycles pedalling furiously.

Tom arrived first, his face pale. 'Babs, did you see that? Those rotten Germans have smashed the railway line and Jim says there's a train due in ten minutes.'

'Can you stop it? Is there time to get to the line and wave something?'

'We're going to try. David and Ned are going to the farm to ring the station, but Jim and I are heading for the railway line. Can we take Charlie's blanket?' She threw it to him as he and his friend continued their frantic dash to avert a disaster.

'Be careful, don't go anywhere near the bomb crater,' she said.

The other two shot past standing on their pedals, heads down, determined to reach the telephone in time. She grabbed the pram handle and followed, but was still quite a way from the railway line when the train whistled.

Were the boys there? Were they going to be in time? Then she spotted them at the bottom of the tall embankment, scrambling across the grass, the blue blanket easy to see even at that distance. She was frozen to the spot, unable to take her eyes off the drama taking place. They were too late. The engine thundered past without seeing them or the blanket her brother was waving wildly above his head.

As if the world had slowed, she watched the

engine driver finally see the danger and apply his brakes, but far too late. The engine toppled into the crater and the first carriage reared up behind before beginning to tumble after the engine. Would the remaining carriages crash sideways and crush the boys? The hideous sound of splintering wood and twisting metal battered the countryside. Charlie screamed and tried to bury himself in her clothes.

She was holding her breath, staring round-eyed at the wrecked train, unable to move. Then her breath hissed through her teeth as Tom and Jim began to scramble up the embankment towards the twisted carriages. Thank God! She wanted to race towards the wreck, to offer what assistance she could, to make sure her brother and his friend kept out of danger; but her baby's needs came first. He clung to her and she couldn't prise him off and put him back in the pram. 'All right, darling, I'll carry you.' He was shivering and she'd given his blanket to the boys. She unbuttoned her coat and snuggled him inside. Immediately he stopped whimpering and his tiny body relaxed.

There was a tractor and trailer bumping wildly across the field; Mr Everton and some of his Land Girls were on the way.

Barbara's arms were aching when she

arrived at the farm. Mrs Everton was rushing around in the yard with the younger boys, putting out wooden boxes and dilapidated chairs. 'My goodness, what a dreadful thing to happen. I've rung the authorities and there's ambulances and fire engines on their way. We're the nearest house to the accident so I reckon they'll send any passengers who can walk to us.'

'Charlie was so terrified by all the noise I can't put him down, but I can put the kettle on and find all the cups and mugs if you like.'

'Poor little mite, why don't you let me have him? I've not seen him for ages.'

'I'm not sure he'll go to you — and I warn you, he's really smelly.' Barbara opened her coat and to her surprise, a tear-streaked but smiling little face appeared. 'Hello, Charlie Bear, are you going to Nanny so Mummy can help with the chairs?'

His head turned, and he beamed and held his arms out to his grandmother. 'Come along, my little love, let's get you clean and tidy and Nanny will find you a nice drink of milk and a biscuit.'

'Hang on a minute, you need his bag — '

'It's all right, Babs, I've got everything we need indoors.'

As soon as she'd gone, David and Ned crowded up to Barbara. 'We didn't tell her what Jim and Tom were going to do. Are they all right?'

'Absolutely fine, Ned. They didn't get there in time, but were still in the field when the train crashed. Your dad will be there by now and be helping with the rescue. Now, what else do I have to do?'

The sound of clanging bells in the lane that led to the railway bridge reminded her that shocked and possibly injured train passengers would be arriving soon, and they needed blankets and the first-aid box.

'I think we've got enough seats. Boys, come with me and we'll fetch what else we need.'

She expected to hear her son crying, but instead he was babbling and chuckling as if nothing untoward had happened. 'Mrs Everton, do you have any spare rugs and blankets we can take out? I expect whoever comes here will be cold, especially if they've got to sit in the yard.'

Her mother-in-law's face changed. 'They can't come in the house, I don't have the room . . . '

'I didn't mean to suggest that they should be indoors; of course they have to be outside. Blankets?'

'Here, you take young Charlie for a minute and I'll show the boys what they can take. I've got both kettles and all the pans on the range, so we'll have plenty of hot water. I've found my party teapot and two others, but I've not got all the mugs and cups out yet.'

'I'll start putting them on the table, Mrs Everton. I think Charlie could go in the high chair now, don't you?'

★　★　★

When the tractor chugged into the yard with a trailer full of bedraggled-looking people, everything was ready for them. Mrs Everton remained inside pouring tea, the four boys acted as waiters whilst the Land Girls dished out blankets and things, leaving Barbara to take care of the walking wounded.

'Thank you, miss. Just what the doctor ordered,' an elderly lady said as she handed Barbara an empty mug. 'I thought me time had come, honest to God, and I'm right glad to be sitting here drinking tea and not on the way to hospital like some of the other poor buggers.'

'Would you like another cup? There's plenty to go round.' The old lady nodded and Barbara beckoned to Tom. 'Could you fetch another cup please?' He took the mug and sped off. 'Thankfully, the train was fairly empty. I don't think many people were seriously injured.'

'The driver bought it, and the fireman, but no passengers, thank the Lord.'

Barbara smiled and continued to move around amongst the twenty or so sitting on the makeshift chairs, drinking tea whilst wrapped in a miscellany of blankets and rugs. Her first-aid training had come in handy and she bandaged and strapped several minor injuries, leaving the tea and sympathy to the Land Girls.

Eventually everybody was collected by a relative or taken in an ambulance. Barbara was helping clear the yard when her grandfather appeared in his Austin Seven. Her brothers reached him first. She hung back, allowing them to tell him their part in the adventure. She wasn't surprised to see him; after all he was the closest to the scene and probably the best doctor in the district, even if he was over seventy. He looked remarkably sprightly; he'd obviously enjoyed being called on to use his medical skills again.

'Is there a cup of tea available, do you think, Barbara my dear?' He walked towards her with his arm round each of her brothers. 'I gather you've been doing an excellent job.'

'Boys, can you go and find your grandpa a cup of tea? I haven't had time for one either, and I don't suppose you've had a drink. Why don't we sit down and catch our breath before we go home?'

They dashed off, leaving her alone with her grandfather. 'How many fatalities?' This was something she couldn't ask when the boys were there.

'Only the poor chaps in the engine died. There were a couple of broken legs, a few more serious cuts and bruises, but we were remarkably lucky this time. No idea what that bomber was doing here in daylight. I heard they shot it down over the channel, so he won't be back.'

The Land Girls had returned to their duties, leaving Barbara to finish putting things away. Fortunately there were still four chairs and a couple of orange boxes in the shelter of an open barn. 'It's getting a bit chilly, Grandpa, but we'll be warm enough in here. Mrs Everton insisted on looking after Charlie, and he seemed happy about it, so I left them to it. I feel guilty that I didn't come over sooner, but I thought seeing him might bring everything back.'

He sat down with a sigh. 'It's more than three weeks since the baby died. Life goes back to normal, my dear. It will take far longer for Valerie and her husband to get over it, but Mrs Everton is a strong woman; she's got her boys to look after and is obviously ready to see Charlie again.' He stared at her intently before continuing. 'You must forget about his conception. He is Alex's son and therefore their grandson. You have no need to feel guilty, my dear.'

'I know you're right, but — '

'No buts, Barbara. Things are as they are. I don't want to hear about it again. Now, it looks like the tea is coming out, and Mrs Everton is bringing your son to join us.'

'He's been right as nine pence, Babs,' she said. 'It did me good to have him here. Shall I put him in his pram for you?'

'Yes please. I'm just going to drink this, then I'll be going. I'll bring him over again soon.'

'Mrs Everton, how is your daughter? Has she returned home?' Grandpa asked the question Barbara hadn't wanted to.

Her mother-in-law didn't answer until she'd safely secured Charlie in his pram. 'She's a lot better, thank you, Doctor Sinclair. Peter's at the base now, but he's allowed to live at home so she moved back a couple of days ago. I'm hoping there will be another little one next year.' She wiped her eyes with a scrunched handkerchief. 'Another baby will never replace our Judith, but they can't grieve forever.'

'Absolutely right. Thank you for the tea, Mrs Everton — just what the doctor ordered.'

He stood up and handed Jim his empty mug. His attempt at humour had passed unnoticed by everyone apart from Barbara. 'I'll see you at home, Barbara and boys. It's beginning to get dark so don't hang about.' He turned to her. 'Why don't you come in the car? You can collect the pram tomorrow.'

'I might as well walk, thanks. The boys will keep me company. Come along and find your bikes; we don't want to be out in the dark.'

Barbara was glad they stayed with her and didn't cycle away; she enjoyed their company and they kept Charlie amused. When they turned into the drive she told them to go, and they vanished into the gloom. She could hear them greet somebody and then their voices faded. There was no moon tonight and she'd forgotten her torch; she hadn't expected to be out so late.

The wheels of the pram crunched noisily through the gravel and the baby clapped and kept peering over the side, although he could see nothing in the darkness. Barbara's heart almost jumped from her chest when someone spoke from the darkness.

'Hang on a minute, darling, I'll push. You must be knackered.'

'Alex! I just aged ten years. I wish you'd warned me you were coming. Why haven't you got your torch?'

'It's in the car. I heard you and didn't stop to get it.' He leaned into the pram to kiss his son, and then he picked Barbara up and swung her around like a child. 'I've got two whole days and nights to spend with my family. No more sorties for a while. I can't tell you how happy I am.'

His lips were cold and hard on hers and she pressed herself closer, then reluctantly stepped away. 'We have to get the baby to bed and he's not had his milk.'

'I'm sure it's easier pushing on the grass. You go ahead and make his bottle up; I'm right behind you.'

★　★　★

The next morning came too soon for Barbara. Despite their passionate lovemaking, she'd been unable to forget they only had one more night before he left.

'Stay where you are, sweetheart. I'll get Charlie and give him his bottle.'

'Are you sure? You need your sleep more than I do.' She didn't really want to get up, but had to offer. He shook his head and with a sweet smile went into the nursery, where she could hear him talking to Charlie. As she was settling under the blankets, she changed her mind and scrambled out of bed. From now until he left tomorrow night she would spend every second with him, not waste a moment doing things by herself.

His delighted smile when she walked in told her she'd made the right decision. 'I'll change him if you want whilst you go down and make his bottle and get us a cup of tea.'

'Don't get him dressed, darling. It's still really early. I've a feeling he might go back to sleep again if we bring him in with us.' Today she wasn't going to bother about the mussed sheets, just concentrate on what mattered.

The range was hot, so Joe must already be out taking care of Silver and the chickens. She touched the side of the teapot; this too was red-hot. She lifted the lid and saw there was more than enough for two mugs of tea.

The milk heated up quickly and she mixed it with a bit of boiled water and poured it into the bottle. She hoped Joe wouldn't mind her using the rest of his tea.

Alex and Charlie were already in bed. She handed Alex the bottle with a smile. 'You might as well do it; he looks so comfortable there.' She carefully put his tea out of the baby's reach and climbed into bed; it wouldn't be fair to drink her tea whilst Alex was busy, so she put it to one side as well.

She wanted to take a photograph of the two of them — something to remember when

Alex was gone. The camera had a few shots left on the film, and there should be enough light in the room to take a good picture.

Alex was so engrossed he didn't notice Barbara adjusting the focus on the camera, but he looked up as she framed the shot. She pressed the shutter and he smiled his heart-melting smile. She clicked again, and this time Charlie pulled the rubber teat from his mouth and beamed at her. She wound the film on and took two more pictures.

'Don't use up all the film, sweetheart. Let me get one of you two. When you get the roll developed you can send me a couple of snaps.'

She climbed in next to him and he handed the sleepy baby over. Charlie was still swallowing strongly, the milk almost gone. His eyes were half-closed.

Alex picked up the camera and hopped out of the bed. Barbara smiled at him and he used up the rest of the film. 'Will it be difficult to get these developed?' he asked.

'No, there's a man in the village who's got his own darkroom and he does them for us. Charlie's fast asleep; if you move your pillows to the edge I'll put him down in the middle. He won't roll out with us on either side.' The baby didn't stir when she gently placed him on the sheet.

'I can't remember the last time I had tea in bed, Babs. I'll treasure these memories whilst I'm away.'

'Please, can we not talk about it? I just want to enjoy the time we have and not think about the future. What shall we do today? I thought we could walk over to see your parents. Your mother was so thrilled to spend time with her grandson yesterday.'

'I was going to suggest we did that. I'd like to see my brothers as well. I didn't tell you last night that I called in to see my sister on the way over. Mum probably told you she's back home and already talking about trying for another baby.'

'I think it's too soon, but if it makes Valerie feel better then I'm sure it's the right thing for them. I'm waiting for your mother to tell me when it's okay for me to visit again.'

They chatted quietly whilst their son slept between them. Seeing Alex this morning had finally convinced her he really did think of the baby as his own flesh and blood. 'I won't know if I'm pregnant for another week or so. I'm still not sure how I feel about it, but I'll be pleased either way.'

He yawned and his jaw cracked loudly. 'Same here. I'll be happier if you're not — the thought of missing Charlie growing up is bad enough — but not seeing our next baby at all would be hard.' He slid down into the bed. 'Do you mind if I catch a bit more kip? Wake me up when young sir is dressed and ready to go.'

He was asleep as soon as his eyes closed. Barbara envied this ability but supposed all flyers had to sleep when they could. She was wide awake but didn't want to get up, so she might as well doze.

Tom and David had already cycled over to Home Farm by the time she, Alex and the baby were ready to go. The phone rang just as Barbara was doing the buckles up on Charlie's harness. Grandpa shouted down the corridor that the call was for Alex. Her heart plummeted; surely he wasn't being called back to base?

Alex was dressed in cord trousers and a battered tweed jacket. He wasn't supposed to be out of uniform even when on leave, but he said today was different. He wanted to forget he was a pilot for a few hours. 'Don't look so worried, Babs darling. It wasn't the base, it was Mum. She doesn't want us to come as Valerie's there for the day.'

'You go on your own, Alex. You must spend some time with your family.'

'If you don't mind, I'll do that. I'll borrow your cycle. I promise I'll be back by lunchtime.' He kissed her briefly, ruffled the baby's hair and was gone.

Barbara decided she might as well go out anyway. Perhaps she'd walk into the village and buy some stamps. She had to get used to doing things on her own now her brothers didn't want to be with her all the time. Feeling sorry for herself wasn't going to improve things; thousands of young women were living without their husbands, and not in such luxurious circumstances either.

'Just a minute, my dear,' said Grandpa. 'Elspeth and I would like to join you on your walk, if that's agreeable?'

'That would be lovely. Alex has gone to see his parents, so I was going to walk into the village, but I don't care where we go.'

The day was overcast and chilly, not at all spring-like. Grandma was looking elegant as usual in a smart blue tweed suit, fox fur, and matching pillbox hat. Grandpa was wearing what he always did: dark wool trousers and a double-breasted jacket.

'I'm not sure I should be walking with you two. I look like a poor relation.'

Grandpa chuckled and took the pram from her. 'I don't think I've ever pushed one of these contraptions before, but I'm retired now and can do what I want.'

'What a good idea, Edward. Then I can walk with Barbara. It's been far too long since we had a good chat, my dear.'

The excursion was cut short when Fred Fisher, the ARP warden, waved them down. 'You can't go into the village, Doctor Sinclair. Unexploded bomb discovered in a back garden. The family have been away with relatives, and their neighbours don't go out back anymore.'

'How long has it been there?' Grandpa asked.

'No idea, but I reckon it came down with that last raid on London a couple of weeks ago. We're waiting for the bomb squad. I've evacuated the village until it's dealt with.'

They turned back, disappointed that they couldn't continue their walk. 'Shall we walk up to the Farleys' old house, Edward? I've heard it's being turned into a convalescent home for RAF personnel.'

'I'm game. What about you, Barbara? I've not been there for years.'

She'd only visited Mountney Hall on one occasion, when Simon Farley had insisted on taking her for tea. She shuddered — thinking about the man who had almost murdered her gave her goosebumps. 'I think it's a good idea, Grandpa. I still have nightmares about what happened, and maybe seeing the house being used for something worthwhile might lay the ghosts to rest.'

'I think it's going to rain,' said Grandpa. 'We don't want to get soaked for a second time this month.'

Grandma clicked her tongue. 'In which case, Edward, we should be turning back.'

The gates were wide open, and Grandpa marched down the drive pushing the pram in front of him like a cavalry charge, quite unabashed by the strange looks he got from several workmen.

Charlie was squealing with joy; he loved to be bounced up and down in the pram. Grandma and Barbara were almost running in order to keep up with Grandpa. 'Perhaps he needs the lavatory, Grandma. I can't see any other reason why he's in such a rush.'

An officer in RAF uniform had greeted him and they were deep in conversation by the time Barbara and her grandmother arrived. Grandpa looked decidedly shifty — what was he up to? Then Barbara understood his hurry; he was offering his services to the convalescent home. How long would it take Grandma to work this out? The officer shook hands with Grandpa and wandered back inside.

'There you are, my dears. I've just been talking to the chap who is going to be running this place. I volunteered my services, and he was delighted to have me on board.'

Barbara waited for the explosion, but it didn't come. 'What a good idea, Edward. It will give you something useful to do whilst I'm at my WVS and WI meetings. Although I'm not sure why we had to come all the way down the drive with you; we could have waited at the gate and not got so hot and sticky.'

He grinned and his faded blue eyes sparkled, giving them a glimpse of what he must have looked like when he was a young man — as Barbara's father would have looked if he hadn't died so young.

'Absolutely right, Elspeth. I'd no idea you were still with me. I spotted the officer and wanted to catch him before he vanished.'

A few spots of rain began to fall. 'Do you have the pram cover, my dear?' asked Grandma.

'It's in the bag in the space behind Charlie. Hang on a minute; I'll put it on. At least you won't get wet, little man, even if your mummy and grandparents do.'

With the hood up and the cover on, Charlie was warm and cosy but still able to peer out and see what was going on. Barbara decided to push the pram herself and made a point of walking briskly so the others could talk to each other without interruption.

Fortunately the rain remained drizzly and

they arrived home just a little damp. 'I'll give Charlie his lunch,' said Barbara. 'Thank you for coming with me. I really enjoyed it.'

'My absolute pleasure, my dear girl,' said Grandpa. 'Now, I'm going to have some of that disgusting coffee essence. Will either of you ladies join me?'

Alex turned up mid-afternoon with Barbara's brothers in tow. They were all subdued; something was wrong. Tom and David disappeared upstairs without stopping to speak to her. 'Alex, what's going on?' she asked.

He shook his head and nodded towards her grandparents. 'Later; not now, darling.'

10

Barbara had no opportunity to ask Alex what had happened at the farm. Her brothers had opted for supper on a tray, so she hadn't been able to speak to them either. Her grandparents didn't seem to notice how quiet her husband was; they talked enthusiastically about the imminent arrival of the RAF convalescents and Grandpa's future role in their care.

'I rather thought, Edward, that the WVS might wish to become involved in the care of these brave men,' said Grandma. 'We're dreadfully underused at the moment. There are no more evacuees to send off, and hardly any bombs have dropped in the neighbourhood.'

'Don't sound so disappointed, Elspeth. We are fortunate to have escaped the horrors of the Blitz so far. Apart from the bombs dropped on the area around the base and on Hornchurch, we've been remarkably lucky.'

Grandma pursed her lips. 'You are being deliberately obtuse, Edward. We all want to be involved, to do our bit for the war; and organising parcels to be sent to prisoners of war isn't really what we had in mind.'

'Don't forget knitting gloves and balaclavas for the sailors, Grandma. I must have knitted a couple of dozen hats, but the gloves defeated me,' Barbara said with a smile.

'What about you, Alex my boy?' asked Grandpa. 'You're a bit quiet tonight. I expect your departure to the Isle of Man must be preying on your mind.'

He didn't answer for a moment. Then he looked up, his expression bleak. 'I don't know how to tell you all this, but Mum and Dad have decided to transfer to Hornchurch. Peter's farm's bigger than ours and it makes more sense for them to be living there. That means Jim and Ned won't be able to come here very often and Charlie won't see his grandparents much.' He shook his head. 'Valerie's made it quite clear she wants no contact with any of you — she can't cope with the thought of anyone else being happy at the moment. I think Peter being called up was the last straw.' He rubbed his eyes and looked impossibly tired and old for a man barely twenty-four.

'No wonder the boys were so upset,' said Barbara. 'The four of them are like brothers. David will be particularly unhappy. He and Ned are very close.' She stretched out and took his hand. 'It's not your fault, darling, and we all understand how difficult things are for your family. I'm sure by the time you come back things will be back to normal.'

'I don't see how, not with my mum and dad living in Hornchurch. Mum said she's happy for my brothers to come here for the occasional weekend, but Tom and David won't be able to go there. I did my best to talk Valerie round, but she's irrational at the moment.'

'There's nothing we can do about it, so we'll just have to get on with our lives and be grateful we've got each other,' said Grandma. 'I expect you and Alex will want to spend your last evening upstairs. We shall remain down here tonight, Barbara.'

'Thank you, Grandma, but this bad news has made me lose my appetite. I don't want dessert; if you'll excuse me, I'm going to check on Charlie.'

'I won't be long, sweetheart, but I'm not going to miss out on Mrs Brown's apple dumplings,' said Alex.

The baby was fine, so Barbara decided to go up and speak to the boys. To her surprise the light was off and the room quiet; they'd gone to bed very early. They didn't go back to school until next week, so there was plenty of time to talk about the Evertons' move before the end of the holiday.

She wasn't sure why the move was necessary. After all, Peter hadn't been posted away from home and could still be involved with the running of the farm — or had that changed as well? She was in her pyjamas and dressing gown when Alex arrived.

'I'll just have a quick shave, darling, and then join you. Don't bother to put the wireless on; we need to talk.'

Shaving at night when he was home was done for her benefit, after she'd complained about his bristles giving her a rash. Despite her sadness, she felt a pulse of excitement — he wouldn't be shaving if he didn't intend to spend the night making love to her.

He strolled out of the bathroom in his birthday suit and collected his pyjama bottoms and dressing gown from the end of the bed. 'I didn't tell the old folk everything. Things are far worse than I said. Peter's been told he can't sleep at home after all; that the dispensation was only for compassionate reasons, and it's expired. He's only going to get the occasional pass, like everyone else. He tried explaining to the adjutant that growing food was as important as mending aeroplanes, but they took no notice.'

'He must be devastated, and Valerie's plan to have another baby will be ruined as well. I really hope I'm not pregnant. That would be too cruel in the circumstances.'

He didn't join her on the sofa but stretched out on the bed. 'You're not kidding. It would be a disaster. You can imagine how upset my mum is about not seeing you and Charlie. She'll be able to come over sometimes when Dad comes to Home Farm, as long as Valerie doesn't find out. I wish I was going to be here to sort this mess out, but you'll just have to go along with it.'

'Thank goodness our boys have made some friends in the village this past week. It will make losing your brothers a bit easier to cope with.'

'I told Jim that although it's too far to cycle all the way over here in the evenings at the moment, as the nights get lighter it should be possible for them to meet halfway. Mum's okay with them coming here on a Saturday, as long as they don't tell Valerie.'

'It doesn't seem fair that the children have been involved. I know your sister's very unhappy, but I don't think allowing her to dictate how everyone else behaves is going to help her in the long run.'

'I know. You're right of course, but there's sod all I can do about it. Come to bed, darling. I don't want to think about it anymore.'

★ ★ ★

When Barbara, Alex and the baby eventually came down for breakfast the next morning the boys had already gone out. 'Your brothers said to tell you, Mrs Everton, they're going to spend the day with their friends,' said Mrs Brown. 'It's a right shame Jim and Ned are moving away. We'll miss them here, I can tell you.'

'Thank you. Did they take a picnic with them?'

'I made them up a couple of sandwiches; I hope that's all right.'

'Of course it is. I'd rather they had something with them than went hungry.' She turned to Alex, who was strapping their son into his high chair. 'That means we have the day free — what do you want to do?'

He had to report to the base that evening and his squadron would be flying away at dawn the following day. 'Not much. We can mooch about here. I hope Tom and David get back before I leave.'

'They always come back for tea, and you're not leaving before then, are you?' Every time she mentioned his departure he flinched, but they couldn't pretend he wasn't going. They needed to talk about it, make plans and decisions for the future, just in case he didn't come back.

Her eyes filled. She'd been trying not to

think about this ever since he'd told her. She couldn't look at him; didn't want him to see how upset she was. He was having enough trouble keeping his own emotions in check.

Neither of them wanted much breakfast, and it didn't take long to feed Charlie. There'd been no sign of Barbara's grandparents. Were they just being tactful, or had they actually gone out for the day? She was too miserable to ask the housekeeper.

'We'll make our own lunch, Mrs Brown, and I'll eat tea with the boys tonight.' Alex would have gone by then.

He carried the baby into the passageway. 'Shall we take the dogs for a walk? A bit of fresh air will do us good.'

The walk was abandoned after twenty minutes as it started to rain. Alex ran with the pram and Barbara ran alongside. The baby was laughing so much she couldn't help joining in. They erupted into the house and almost sent Barbara's grandparents flying.

'I take it, it's raining,' Grandpa said. 'Why don't you join us in the study for a hot drink?'

'Good idea, Edward,' said Alex. 'It's rotten weather today. I hope the boys don't spend all day outside and get soaked.'

When had Alex turned into a concerned parent? He sounded just like Barbara,

218

worrying about the welfare of his family. She was going to miss him so much. Even when she didn't see him or hear from him, knowing he was only a few miles away made his absence less painful. How was she going to cope with him being so far away? The fact that thousands of other wives, mothers and girlfriends were in the same position didn't make it any easier.

She hid her distress by spending several minutes removing her coat and boots. Today he was in uniform, his civilian clothes back in the closet for heaven knew how long.

'We'll join you in a bit, Edward. We just need to change this smelly baby,' Alex said with forced jollity. He was equally upset. His arm slid around Barbara's waist and he pulled her back so she was resting against his chest, their son on his right hip. 'I know, it's bloody horrible, but we've got to put on a brave face. Giving in will just make it so much worse and upset Charlie and your grandparents.' He kissed the top of her head and his warmth and solidity steadied her.

'I don't want to be upset, but I just can't help it.' She was finding it difficult to speak. 'It's not the fact that you're going away; I can deal with that. It's the thought that I might never see you again. That today might be the last day we spend together.'

His arm tightened and the baby protested. 'All right, baby, I'm going to take you in to your grandparents. I need to talk to your mummy. Go upstairs, sweetheart; I'll join you in a minute.'

She stumbled to their bedroom and sat rigid on the edge of the bed, her arms gripped tightly around her waist as if somehow she could keep the misery inside. This had been the worst few weeks of her life and she wasn't sure she could cope with his departure as well. She'd left the door open and saw him come in. His expression was wretched; she was making things so much worse for him.

'Babs, darling, you've got to be strong. You hold this family together. However hard it's going to be, you'll get through it. Charlie, your grandparents, and your brothers are relying on you.' He picked her up, placed her on his lap and rocked her like a small child.

She shivered and gulped but managed to hold back her tears. If she gave in she wouldn't be able to stop. 'I'm sorry; I'm making this so much harder for you. I'm being selfish, I know that. But I love you so much, and I need you.'

'Don't say that. You're the least selfish person I know; you always put everyone else first. We've got to talk; we've put it off too long. It's very unlikely I'll be stationed in Hornchurch again. I could be sent to Malta, Kent, or somewhere in Lincolnshire or Norfolk. Unless I get a long pass, we won't be able to meet.'

'I realise that. Pretending we could be together again in six months has made these past few weeks easier. We can write, and maybe you'll be able to ring me when you're back in Britain. The war can't go on forever. Please keep safe until it's over and you can come back to us.' She shifted onto the bed so she could see his face. His cheeks were wet; he was having as much difficulty as she with keeping things together.

They kissed — not passionately, but with a gentle sweetness. She was cradled in his arms when they heard the telephone ringing. 'We'd better go down,' she said. 'The call will be for you.'

They were halfway down the stairs when her Grandpa shouted up from the bottom. 'Alex, your CO on the line for you.'

'Go on, darling,' she said. 'I'll be with Charlie in the study. I promise I won't be silly about you going, even if you have to leave straight away.' She pressed herself against the wall, allowing him to squeeze past. He jumped the last few steps. Only then did she remember an old wives' saying that it was bad luck to pass someone on the stairs.

Grandpa was waiting for her and squeezed her shoulder sympathetically. 'Chin up, my dear. You will get through these next few days. Don't let his last memory of you be a sad one.'

She was too choked to answer, but nodded and rushed ahead of him, not wanting to hear the conversation in the library. Charlie was sitting on his blanket banging a wooden spoon on an old saucepan, but he dropped them and crawled towards her. She dropped to her knees and swept him up and kissed him. 'Hello, Charlie Bear. Have you been a good boy? Show me how you can bang your spoon.' She was about to put him on the carpet and patted his bottom. He definitely needed changing. 'Come along, smelly boy. Mummy's going to get you nice and clean.'

When she returned to the study, Alex was there and he was smiling. 'I don't have to report to base early, Babs. I was just given some really good news. I've been promoted to Squadron Leader. I'm taking the blokes to the Isle of Man. Richard is the new Commanding Officer at Hornchurch. Not sure where the old CO is going.'

'That's terrific news, darling, and no more than you deserve. Does it make any difference to the amount of sorties you fly?' She hugged him with her free arm and the baby crowed with delight.

''Fraid not. I go up when they go up. However, I'll be more involved in decision-making and should know what's going on a bit earlier.'

'Let's tell them the good news. Grandma will be thrilled I'm married to a squadron leader.'

The day sped past and Barbara couldn't stop herself glancing at the clock every few minutes, wishing the hands would stop turning; stop moving relentlessly towards the time when Alex's lift arrived.

The boys didn't appear in time to say goodbye and Alex was upset about that, although he didn't say so. He shook hands with Grandpa and kissed Grandma on the cheek, and then Barbara walked with Charlie in her arms to the side door.

She couldn't speak and neither could he. His kiss was hard and his eyes glittered. He kissed the baby and then without a word almost ran to the noisy motorbike and climbed on the back. He didn't wave, didn't turn round — just disappeared out of the yard, possibly forever.

★ ★ ★

'David, get a move on. We're going to be too late to say goodbye to Alex,' Tom shouted over his shoulder as he pedalled up the lane leading from the river. He gripped his brakes so fiercely he almost shot over the handle-bars. His brother wasn't behind him; in fact he wasn't there at all.

'David, where are you? Don't play silly buggers. We've got to get back.' His voice echoed down the lane but got no answer.

He really wanted to see Alex before he left. Babs was really cut up about his going. What with Judith and everything else, he didn't want to make things worse for her by not being there. Should he carry on, and then at least one of them would be there? Or should he go back and look for his little brother?

Tom heaved his bike round and pedalled furiously down the hill, yelling for his brother as he went. He couldn't leave him; it would be dark in an hour and neither of them had lights. His chest felt tight and his heart was pounding; he had a bad feeling about this. He'd no idea when David had disappeared. He should have been keeping a closer eye on him, not just carrying on without checking.

He skidded around the corner and smiled. His brother was sitting on the grassy bank, his bike beside him, obviously unhurt. 'What happened? Got a puncture?' David didn't answer. Tom increased his speed and arrived in a squirt of gravel and mud. The first thing he saw was that his brother's bike was okay, so that wasn't the reason for the delay.

'What's up? Did you fall off? Are you ill?' David didn't answer, but kept his head down and ignored him. Something really was up. Tom dropped his bike and squatted down beside him. David was crying. For a moment Tom hesitated; he didn't go in for all that cuddling stuff. Then he put his arms around David and held him close.

'What is it? Tell me. I can't help if you don't tell me.'

His brother continued to cry for a bit longer and then shuddered and sniffed and wiped his running nose on his sleeve. 'I don't want to say goodbye to Alex. Everything's rotten. Judith died, our best friends are moving away, and Alex won't be here anymore. He could die as well.'

'I know, but there's nothing we can do about it. It's going to be far worse for Babs; she needs us to be there. Alex will be really fed up we haven't bothered to go home in time to see him off.' David didn't move. Tom tried another tack. 'If you don't get off your bum and on your bike it will be too dark to see. We won't be allowed to go out on our own again if we're late.'

This seemed to do the trick, and his brother grabbed his bike and pedalled away, leaving him to catch up. They arrived at the entrance to the drive just as a motorbike was turning out. Alex was on the back. He tapped the driver's shoulder and when the bike coasted to a stop, he jumped off.

'Good show. I thought I wasn't going to get the chance to say goodbye. I'm going to miss you two. Are you too old for a hug?'

David threw himself into Alex's arms, but Tom held out his hand. There'd been a bit too much hugging going on lately. 'Sorry we're a bit late. We thought we might have missed you.'

'Not to worry, Tom. You're here now. Will you keep an eye on Babs for me? She's going to find it hard without me there.' Alex was rubbing David's back and offered him a clean handkerchief. He then dipped into his pocket and produced two crisp ten-bob notes. They were definitely ten shillings, because even in the fading light Tom could see the paper was mauve and not green. Alex pushed both of them into his hand.

'Thanks, Alex. And I'll definitely make sure Babs is okay.'

'David, old chap, I've got to go. I'll be in trouble if I'm late.' He had to peel David from him. 'Cheerio, boys. Make sure you write to me.' With a brief wave he hopped back on the bike and disappeared.

Tom turned to show his brother the money but David had already gone. He had a horrible suspicion his brother wasn't going to get over all the upsets of the past few weeks very easily.

Babs was okay about them almost missing Alex and was suitably impressed with the money they'd been given. She was so cut up about everything that Tom didn't want to tell her about David. When he'd offered him the money, he'd shrugged and refused to take it.

His brother was still sulking when they went to bed and he was fed up with trying to speak to him. When Babs came up to offer to read a story David ignored her too. She didn't seem too concerned; just kissed the top of his head (which was all that was poking out of the blankets) said good night and went back downstairs.

Tom's last thought before he dropped off was that he hoped his brother wouldn't start wetting the bed again like he had last year.

* * *

Surprisingly, Barbara slept well and woke the next morning knowing she was going to be able to cope. She was determined to stay positive, and think about the good things in her life and not the bad. Today she would sit down with the boys and talk things out; make sure they too would be able to adjust to the absence of Alex in their lives.

Charlie was still fast asleep. Mind you, it was only half past five; he didn't normally wake until around seven. Plenty of time for Barbara to wash, sort out the laundry, change the bed and make sure the boys didn't sneak off as they had done yesterday.

When her chores were finished she went upstairs to collect the boys' dirty washing from their bathroom. There was someone moving about in the playroom, so one of them was definitely up. She propped open the stairs door with the laundry hamper and went in to investigate.

'Good morning, David. You're up early. Are you coming down for breakfast, or waiting for Tom?'

He ignored her and continued to rummage through the box of Meccano. That wasn't like him; he was usually a happy and polite little boy. 'David, I'm talking to you. Please put that down and answer me.'

He sighed audibly and looked up with a surly expression. 'I don't want any breakfast with you; I'm staying up here on my own. Go away.'

'That's not very nice, sweetheart. I know you're upset about Alex and the Everton boys, but you don't have to be rude to me, do you?'

He scowled and resumed his search for a missing bit of metal, not bothering to answer. She couldn't understand why he was so angry with her — what had she done to upset him? Her stomach plummeted. Surely he hadn't found out about Charlie? She was tempted to leave him to it, but something prompted her to investigate further.

'I think we need to talk, David. I can't help you if you don't tell me what's wrong.'

He scrambled up and faced her, his face red with anger. 'I don't want to talk to you. I don't want to talk to anyone. Leave me alone!'

Tom appeared from the bedroom, his hair on end and his face concerned. 'Who's pulled your chain, David? It's not Babs's fault that things are horrible at the moment. There's a war on. Don't be such a wet blanket, and apologise to Babs right now.'

Barbara's youngest brother remained silent for a moment, and then his face crumpled and he threw himself into her arms and his body shook as he sobbed. He was mumbling incoherently as he clutched onto her. She couldn't catch what he was saying, but it sounded like he was saying he was sorry for being horrid. He was nine years old, a bit big to be carried, but she scooped him up and took him to the chair by the fireplace and sat down with him on her lap and rocked him until he was quiet.

Tom watched them anxiously. 'I'm sorry about that, Babs, and I should have warned you he was in a bit of a state. He was crying in his sleep and calling out for Mum. He's not done that before.'

She stroked David's head. He was breathing evenly now; he'd fallen asleep. 'I think I'll put him back to bed. Do you mind awfully staying up here with him until he wakes again? I'll bring you a tray.'

'That's fine. It's pouring with rain, so we can't go out on our bikes. I'll turn down his bed if you'll bring him in.'

Together they settled him and then she snatched up the hamper and ran downstairs, expecting to hear her son crying. The nursery was still blessedly silent. She peeked in and, sure enough, Charlie was curled up clutching his teddy and showing no signs of stirring. With luck she'd be able to make Tom some breakfast and take it up before she was needed.

Dammit! She'd forgotten the dirty clothes; she'd better nip up and get them first. Mrs

Brown was just getting the range roaring and looked round in surprise when she burst in. 'Morning, Mrs Everton. You're up with the lark, and no mistake. Here, you leave that laundry with me.'

'There's no need. You have more than enough to do already, taking care of this big house and doing all the cooking for us. I'll do it later. I've come to make a tray for the boys; David's not too well this morning, and Tom's going to stay with him.'

'You get your little one's bottle ready; I'll do the tray.'

In less than fifteen minutes Barbara was on her way back with an appetising array of items for the boys as well as milk for her son. She left this on top of his chest of drawers, and was about to take the tray when Tom arrived and took it from her.

Charlie sat up and beamed at her. Whilst she was feeding him she went over the scene with David. She hoped his unhappiness wasn't deep-rooted; that the events of the past few weeks hadn't triggered a delayed reaction to the loss of his mother and father. They had settled into life at the Grove, were delighted to have been legally adopted by their grandparents, and seemed content at school.

Maybe Grandpa would be able to explain

what was happening in David's mind. Psychological things were hard to understand. Could David's problem be linked to their mother's terrible depression, which had eventually driven her insane? Could the tendency to become depressed be inherited?

11

October 1941

Somehow the months drifted past and life at the Grove settled into an acceptable routine. Grandpa cycled to the convalescent home two or three times a week, and Grandma and her WVS cronies made regular visits as well. David recovered his normal sunny nature after a week of sullenness and seemed satisfied with seeing less of his best friend. Barbara's in-laws remained in Hornchurch; and Valerie, miraculously four months pregnant, was now happy for her mother to visit the Grove, although she still didn't want to see Barbara or Charlie.

Alex had returned from the Isle of Man and was based in Kent and flying reconnaissance missions over France. He'd not had the opportunity to come home for a visit, but had spoken on the phone a couple of times. Barbara was looking forward to seeing him when he got a forty-eight-hour pass at the end of the month.

On Saturday she was sitting with her brothers and Charlie in the sitting room. The baby was now toddling about and chattering constantly. He was adorable, and she wished Alex wasn't missing this stage of their son's life.

She tried to read the newspaper, but the children were making so much racket that reading was almost impossible. Charlie loved playing noisy games of hide-and-seek and hunt-the-thimble with his uncles.

Joe poked his head round the door. 'Excuse me, Mrs Everton. There's a telegram for you.' He held the envelope in his hand.

The room fell silent; even Charlie sensed something was wrong. Her head spun and she had difficulty getting to her feet. She didn't want to read it in front of the boys, even though they would know its significance.

'Look after the baby for me. I won't be long.' She snatched the telegram and ran upstairs to her bedroom. Her hands were shaking, her fingers clumsy, as she tore it open. Her eyes blurred as she read the dreaded words.

MRS A G EVERTON THE GROVE INGATESTONE ESSEX. WE REGRET TO INFORM YOU THAT YOUR HUSBAND. SQD. L. A G EVERTON MISSING ON OPERATIONS SAT 26TH. LETTER FOLLOWS.

Her world crumbled. Alex was gone

234

— dead. She'd never see him again. She couldn't cry. She was numb, unable to do more than stare at the words on the yellow paper. Vaguely she heard heavy footsteps approaching the room but didn't look up.

'My dear girl, let me see.' Grandpa gently removed the paper from her fingers while she sat unmoving on the bed. The bed dipped and he gripped her shoulders and turned her round to face him. 'Barbara, listen to me. This might not be as bad as you think. It doesn't say that Alex is dead; it says that he's missing. Until the letter arrives you mustn't give up hope.'

He had to repeat his words a second time before they registered. The blackness hovering around her head moved away. 'Missing? Not dead? I don't understand.'

'He has been shot down over the channel, but he might well be picked up. The water is relatively warm at this time of year, he will have his Mae West on, and he should be able to keep afloat long enough for a boat to find him.'

For a glorious moment she actually believed Alex could be alive after all. Then the hard, cold evidence told her otherwise. 'He was shot down yesterday. If he'd been picked up they would have said so. They only send a telegram when they think someone's dead.'

He shook her gently. 'Obviously they haven't found him, but a fishing boat could have done. If they were sure he was dead, they would have said so. Don't give up hope; your young man might still be alive.'

It was as if a physical weight had settled on her shoulders, making it almost impossible to stand up. 'I won't give up, not until I know for certain. But we have to face the truth, Grandpa — Alex could be dead.'

'I'll contact the Evertons for you.'

'I'm going to tell the boys; they saw the telegram and know what it means.' She closed her eyes and a trickle of fear moved down her spine. 'God knows how David will react. It took him ages to recover when Alex left and the Everton boys moved away.' Maybe if she talked about something else, kept busy, she could keep the grief from overwhelming her.

'Very well, my dear. You must do what you think is best for you and your brothers. David is vulnerable emotionally; he's going to need a lot of extra attention to cope with this. Poor little chap has had too much disruption and unhappiness in the past two years.'

This wasn't what she wanted to hear. She would need all her strength to get through the next few weeks whilst she waited to hear if Alex, by some miracle, had survived and been picked up by a passing fishing boat. If he was, then passed on to the Germans, he would be put in a prisoner of war camp — but he'd be safe, and his name would eventually appear on the list that was sent to the War Office.

'Until we hear otherwise, I'll believe that he's alive. You're right, there's a slim chance he's been rescued. I'm not going to tell the boys that he's dead, just that he's missing and we're waiting to hear who has picked him up.'

'Excellent, exactly the right thing to do. We need to see what's in the letter; that might give us a bit more information about what happened.'

As she approached the sitting room she could hear her brothers talking quietly and her baby chuckling and banging his spoon, but Grandma wasn't there. She hesitated. 'Grandpa, will you find Grandma and tell her the news?'

'After I've rung the Evertons, I'll try and find her. She's in the orchard picking apples. I'm surprised she didn't rope the boys in to help.'

'I'll send them out after I've spoken to them. In fact I think I'll go as well and take Charlie with me. We all need to keep busy. As long as I don't have time to dwell on things, I'll be able to cope.'

Tom was standing by the door, his face pale and his eyes huge. She took a deep breath and forced her mouth to smile. 'Alex isn't dead, thank God. He's just missing. I know that's a worry, but he went down in the channel and will have his life jacket on, and the water's not too cold. I'm sure he'll be picked up eventually.'

David was sitting cross-legged playing with the baby. He didn't look convinced, but made no comment. Tom grabbed her hand so hard it hurt. 'How long do we have to wait before we know for certain?'

'There's a letter coming which should explain what happened. If he was picked up by a German boat and taken to a POW camp it could be weeks before we know. We just have to hope, stay positive and get on with our lives as usual.'

She walked across and joined her baby and younger brother on the carpet. 'Waiting for news is going to be very hard, David, but Alex wouldn't want us to get in a state about things. We've got Christmas to look forward to; and although we won't have the Evertons here this year, I'm sure we will still have a lot of fun.' She was babbling. What had possessed her to talk about Christmas at a time like this?

Her brother hung his head and tears dropped onto his knees. She gathered him into her arms and cuddled him like she did

Charlie when he was upset. 'We'll get through this, darling. We've got each other, and Alex wouldn't want us to be miserable. We'll keep writing our weekly letters even if we can't post them to him at the moment.'

Tom arrived beside them and put his arms around David as well. 'We aren't the only ones with people missing. There's three in my class who don't know if their relatives are missing or dead. There's a war on; we've got to be brave.'

David stiffened and then threw himself backwards, sending both Barbara and Tom flying. By the time she was on her feet he was standing at the door, his face screwed up and almost unrecognisable. 'I don't care about the war, or anyone else. I want Alex to come home. It's not bloody fair!' He shouted the last words defiantly and then vanished. Charlie started to cry, upset by the shouting.

'Let him go, Tom. He won't listen to either of us when he's like this.' Barbara scooped the baby up and shushed him. 'There, there, it's all right, darling. They didn't mean to frighten you.'

'He misses having Ned around. I wish they'd move back to Home Farm,' Tom said as he scrambled to his feet. 'I'll just go and make sure he's okay. I won't try and talk to him.'

Barbara felt physically ill, as if she were coming down with influenza. She was trying to put a brave face on things, but in her heart she was already grieving. She wandered into the passageway and met her grandmother.

'Oh, Barbara, my dear, what dreadful news. I know exactly how you must be feeling. It is all very well for Edward to tell you there's still a chance he might be rescued from the sea, but we both know they don't send a telegram unless they think the person is dead.'

Hearing what she was thinking spoken out loud had a remarkable effect on Barbara. 'Grandma, I don't think he's dead. I did for a while, but now I'm certain he's alive somewhere. I'd know, I'm sure I would, if he was gone forever.' The band around her chest loosened and the world seemed bright again. 'It could be weeks or even months before we hear from him, but he will come back eventually. I'm not going to worry.'

'I'm so sorry. I didn't mean to upset you — '

'You haven't; you've done me a favour. If you'll excuse me, I must find the boys and tell them. David was very unhappy. He needs to know how I feel.' She briefly hugged her grandmother before running upstairs to the boys' room to pass on her good news.

She was a bit puffed by the time she got to the top floor; the baby was too heavy to lump about the place. 'I should have left you downstairs, Charlie Bear. You're a big boy now. I'll be glad when you can walk up on your own.'

Neither of her brothers were upstairs. Tom must have checked and returned down the main stairs, which were only used in the summer. There was enough light from the large glass rotunda in the grand entrance hall for her to look over the gallery and see her brothers weren't there either. The patter of rain made her look up. She hoped they hadn't gone outside.

On her way to the kitchen she met Tom. 'I can't find him anywhere, Babs. He must be out there. I'm going to get my coat on and have a look.'

There was a scrabble of claws on the wooden floor and the two dogs scampered towards her. 'He can't be outside, Tom. The dogs would have gone with him.' She bent down so the baby could touch the animals. 'This house is so huge, he could hide for a week and we'd not find him. I'll just check to see if his coat and boots are here, just to be certain he's not gone out.'

Tom got there first and yelled back down the corridor. 'They're here. He must be inside

241

somewhere. I bet he'll come out when he's hungry.'

'I really wanted to talk to both of you. I know it's a worry having Alex missing, but for some reason I'm certain he's okay, and I'm not going to walk about like a wet weekend and neither should you.'

'Well said, my dear girl. No point in making ourselves miserable when there's a chance Alex is perfectly well.' Grandpa had appeared from the sitting room. 'Elspeth has unearthed the dinner gong. Do you want to bang it for me, Tom? The racket can be heard all over the house and should make that young scamp come down to investigate.'

Sure enough, a quarter of an hour later a rather sheepish David joined them in the sitting room. Barbara was on her feet before anyone else. 'There you are. We're about to play Monopoly and Tom's insisting he's going to be the banker.'

He must have thought it strange to see all of them smiling and apparently unbothered by the devastating news in the telegram, but slowly his face relaxed and he grinned. 'It's my turn to be the banker — you promised, Tom.' He grabbed a cushion from the sofa and dropped it next to Barbara. 'I hope Charlie isn't going to

242

tip the board over like he did last time.'

'He's perfectly happy playing with me, David,' Grandma told him. 'And your dogs have been allowed in here this afternoon; I'm sure the novelty will keep him amused when he becomes bored with his bricks.'

'Good show. Pass the money to me, Tom. I'll finish dealing. You can put out the Community Chest and Chance cards.'

'Is there any chance of a cup of tea, do you think, Elspeth my dear? I'm going to need all my strength to cope with the game.'

Immediately Tom jumped to his feet. 'I'll go. You don't want to be carrying that fat lump about at your age, Grandma.' The door banged behind him and his words hung in the startled silence.

Barbara was relieved when her grandmother laughed. 'I'm not sure, Barbara, which of us should be most offended by that remark.' She reached out and tickled the baby under the chin and he giggled. 'Imagine calling this handsome young man 'that fat lump'. I'm not sure exactly what his reference to my age meant. *I'm* still in my prime, aren't I, Edward?'

'Are you suggesting that I am not? I might be over seventy, but I can still cycle up hills without stopping.'

'You would be better getting off and

pushing your bicycle, Edward, and not showing off.'

The teasing continued until Tom returned to tell them the tea was on its way. It hardly seemed possible they were able to joke and laugh together. Maybe they were being unrealistic, but there was no point getting het up until they had some definite information.

The boys helped Barbara put Charlie to bed, and she was able to reassure both of them and was pretty sure David was all right about things. The stress and anxiety had taken its toll and she decided to go to bed as well. Fortunately she was able to get downstairs before her grandparents transferred to her bedroom.

'I'm going to turn in now; I hope you don't mind. Grandpa, I don't want to see the letter when it comes. You open it and tell me anything you think I need to know.'

★ ★ ★

Edward sat back on the Chesterfield with a sigh. 'Mrs Everton was remarkably stoic about the news. She's taken the same attitude as Barbara — won't believe her son is dead until she hears definite proof.'

'What do you think, my dear? I'm afraid I don't hold out much hope of ever seeing Alex again, but in the circumstances I think it's wise to keep up the pretence for as long as possible.'

'Exactly, Elspeth. By the time she does hear, or it becomes obvious Alex is dead, she will have got used to the idea and it won't be such a blow. Let's get Christmas out of the way. If the poor chap is gone, it might well be the last happy one for some time.'

'I'm going to put Barbara on the rota for the comfort visits to Mountney Hall. She's still a member of the WVS, although she rarely comes to the meetings anymore. Those poor boys need all the support we can offer them. Although we've only got young men recovering from fractures and surgery, it's still heartbreaking.' She dabbed her eyes with a dainty lace handkerchief. 'One of the boys — and I use that word advisedly — is only eighteen years old. He's a pilot flying a Hurricane, and had to bail out and broke both his legs.'

'It doesn't seem possible we need such young men to fight the war. The life expectancy of an RAF pilot or air crew is frighteningly short. I should be very surprised if more than twenty per cent are still alive at the end of the war.' He stood up and brought them both a large whiskey. 'I'm afraid this is the last of the bottle, but I think we need it tonight. It's going to be a damned depressing Christmas this year — no toys for the boys and very little extra for us.'

They sat in companionable silence for a while, sipping their drinks. 'I don't suppose the inmates at the convalescent home will get much for Christmas either,' said Grandpa. 'Why don't we ask Tom, David and Barbara to forego their own presents and little luxuries and make up parcels for the RAF patients?'

For a moment he thought he'd upset his wife; she could be a bit tricky about things sometimes. Then she smiled at him and, despite his decrepitude, his pulse skipped a beat.

'I think that's a good idea, Edward. It will keep us all busy over the next few weeks, and that's exactly what we need.'

He swallowed the last warming drops of whiskey and decided to take a chance. 'Would you like an early night as well, Elspeth?' She flushed like a schoolgirl and nodded. 'You go up then, my love. I'll make sure everything is locked up and turned off down here.'

Intimate relations had only resumed a couple of years ago after a gap of eighteen years. They might be a pair of wrinkled old crumblies, but the thought of making love to his wife could still send a rush of blood

246

around Edward's body and make him feel young again.

* * *

The letter from the adjutant where Alex had been based duly arrived just over a week after the telegram. The boys were at school, Mrs Brown was watching the baby, and Elspeth had taken Barbara on her first visit to the convalescent home.

It was remarkably thick; surely it didn't take several pages to explain what had happened to Alex? It was too damn dark to read it in the passageway, so Edward took it into the library — this had become his own domain since his study had become the family sitting room.

He carefully opened the letter and saw at once there was only one sheet of paper plus a sealed envelope addressed to Barbara. He wasn't sure of the significance of this until he read the letter. He quickly scanned the contents and realised immediately the chances of Alex being alive were almost nil. He had been flying over France and on his way back had run into thick fog; his radio had failed and he'd not been heard of since. It had been impossible to send out search parties until the fog had cleared. When they went to look there was no sign of the missing plane, and nobody had reported picking him up.

The adjutant went on to say there was a remote possibility he'd been rescued by a fishing boat and might be with the French Resistance or in a German POW camp. They would continue to make enquiries and keep Barbara informed of any developments. There was the usual guff about being sorry, and what a splendid chap Alex had been.

The letter was the young man's final message to his wife, to be given to her in the event of his death. Edward sunk onto a chair and sighed heavily. This was a dreadful business. They couldn't declare Alex dead unless they had definite proof. Alex would be posted as missing for the next few months; and if he were declared dead, there could be no funeral to mark the loss of the man Barbara loved and married.

Thank God she had asked Edward to open the letter. They wouldn't have sent Alex's missive unless they were more or less sure he wasn't coming back. He wasn't going to tell anyone what he knew. Time enough after Christmas.

* * *

Barbara was relieved the information in the letter was no worse than she'd expected. As long as they were still making enquiries, she would remain optimistic. Her first visit to Mountney Hall was less traumatic than she'd expected; she made tea and took it round, wrote two letters for men with broken arms, and played a game of cribbage. She came away feeling she was finally making a contribution to the war effort. Keeping busy was helping her to deal with the lack of news. The longer it went on, the more worried she would be.

One morning three weeks later her grandfather threw down the paper in disgust. 'What next? From now on we have to take our own bags when we shop — the Ministry of Supply insists that only food can be wrapped. There won't be any Christmas cards, wrapping paper or similar things this year.'

'Then it's a good thing we're not having presents, isn't it, Grandpa?' said Barbara. 'The boys told me their school has to collect every little bit of scrap paper, bottles, tins, tops, and even bus tickets. It seems there's a competition to see which school collects the most.'

'Several of my friends have joined the circulating library at WH Smith, Edward,' said Grandma. 'Two pounds and three shillings for a year is quite reasonable, especially as for that amount you get preferential service and the very latest books.'

He snorted. 'Extortionate, Elspeth. There won't be any new books if there's a shortage of paper. And the gates are going tomorrow as well. I don't mind that so much; they've got to make the new planes from something.'

'All the railings in the village have gone. I suppose we're lucky to have kept our gates up to this point.' Grandma smiled at Barbara. 'How is the knitting coming along? I wasn't sure that unravelling old garments was a good idea, but needs must, and the finished articles look as good as new.'

'Mrs Brown has knitted jumpers for the boys and the baby — they all have stripes in various colours and are rather jolly. There won't be any fruit, chocolate or sweets to put in a stocking, but I wanted them to have something to open on Christmas morning. I've knitted four scarves so far.'

'It's a good thing I saved the wrapping paper from last year, Edward. At least we still have something to put around the gifts. I think if I iron the paper it will be quite satisfactory.'

'Are we still going to put up a tree?' he asked.

'I thought we could cut some branches from one of the yew trees and decorate that. I've asked Joe to start looking for evergreens and holly with berries as well.'

'It's a great shame we didn't keep back some of the tins and jars you got from Harrods a couple of years ago, my dear. A few of those luxuries would go down well this Christmas.' He carefully folded his newspaper and placed it on the side table. 'Right, I'm due at the Hall in half an hour. I'd better get a move on.'

Barbara followed him out. 'Matron said they are expecting a dozen more patients today. I'm glad we don't get the burns; they must be the hardest to deal with.'

'There's a good chap dealing with all that — Archibald McIndoe, a top man. There will be a lot of young men grateful to him.' He shrugged on his coat, tied his scarf and pushed a battered cap on his head. 'Not raining at the moment. It was bloody awful coming back last time. I'm not looking forward to the bad weather. I'm too old to be pedalling through ice and snow.'

'I'm coming tomorrow morning to see if I can help with any of the new arrivals. Mrs Brown is only too happy to take care of Charlie when she has time off. The extra money is coming in handy.' She frowned.

'She's getting worried Joe will be called up before the war ends. Do you think we'll still be fighting in 1943?'

'We are on our own at the moment. Unless the Yanks join us, I don't see how we *can* win. At least the Luftwaffe are being kept busy fighting on the Russian front, so the they don't come over here so much.'

'Be careful, Grandpa, and remember you promised to push your bike up the hill.'

'Don't have the energy to do anything else, my dear.' He chuckled. 'Coming back is great fun; takes half the time.'

She was smiling as she returned to the sitting room — she rather thought this was her first genuine smile since the day of the telegram.

★ ★ ★

The two-mile bike ride to Mountney Hall the next morning was unpleasant, the wind rain-filled and cold. Barbara hadn't seen her grandfather this morning; he and Grandma had gone out somewhere before breakfast. Charlie was perfectly content to stay with Mrs Brown. He loved being the centre of attention and, as long as he had his morning nap and a good night's sleep, was a happy little boy.

Despite the icy drizzle there were a few of the patients, with their blue-grey greatcoats draped over their shoulders, wandering around the gardens. The Farleys' old house didn't have enough land to warrant ploughing it up for the war effort. However, it now had a substantial vegetable garden growing enough for the patients and staff.

Barbara didn't have to wear a uniform of any sort for her visits, although Grandma wore her WVS outfit. As Barbara was no longer an active member, she hadn't been allocated one of the smart navy-blue uniforms. She waved at the men outside and pedalled around to the back, where she left her bicycle in the shelter of the open-fronted barn.

As usual she headed straight for Matron's office after hanging up her coat. 'Good morning, Matron. Is there anything in particular you want me to do this morning?'

'Good morning, Mrs Everton. We have a new batch of young men — I expect Doctor Sinclair told you about them. Three are non-ambulatory, three are recovering from surgery, and the other four are what you might call the walking wounded. Perhaps you would start with the men in Ward Three and see if they need any letters writing — then visit the surgical cases in Ward Two. The remainder of the new patients will be in the day room, I expect.'

'I don't have any more writing paper, Matron, but I do have some postcards, so I suppose they'll have to do. I've already stamped them, so I'll post them on my way home at lunchtime.'

She was busy until mid-morning on the wards and was late for her next duty; she always helped to serve the tea and biscuits. When she arrived in the kitchen she was immediately pointed towards a trolley. 'Can you take this into the day room, please, Mrs Everton? We're a bit low on sugar today, so tell the gentlemen only one spoonful each.'

'I will, Mrs Smith. I'm sorry I'm a bit late.' She grabbed the trolley and headed to the large, airy room that had once been used as a drawing room. Someone heard the rattle of her approach and the double doors were pulled wide open by two smiling patients. Immediately she began to pour tea from the huge enamelled teapot. She didn't need to walk around with cups and saucers; those who were able took them to their friends.

Most of the faces she recognised and could greet by name, but there was a group of four sitting at the far side of the room that she didn't know. They must be the men who'd arrived yesterday. The two patients facing her had both an arm and leg in plaster; she couldn't see what was wrong with the others.

She pushed the trolley across the wooden floor and stopped beside the group. 'Tea and biscuits, gentlemen? I'm afraid there's only one spoonful of sugar per cup today. However, we do have plenty of biscuits though they're all of the broken variety.' She picked up a cup and saucer and prepared to hand it to the man with his back to her.

At the sound of her voice he jerked forward, and his plastered leg sent the small coffee table crashing onto its side, scattering books and ashtrays in all directions. He turned his head. Barbara dropped the cup and saucer in his lap.

'Sod me! That's bloody hot, Babs,' John Thorogood said.

His friends were helpless with laughter and didn't offer their assistance. There was no way she was going to offer to mop up the tea. 'John, I'm so sorry. I didn't mean to drop your tea.'

He grinned ruefully. 'I should hope not. I'm a wounded hero and expect to be treated gently.'

A nurse arrived at a brisk walk to see what all the fuss was about. 'Good heavens, Mrs Everton! Don't just stand there — help me sort this out.'

'Yes, Sister. I'll pick everything up if you take care of Flight Lieutenant Thorogood.'

John interrupted, amused at her embarrassment. 'That's Flight *Commander* Thorogood to you, Mrs Everton.'

Her cheeks were burning and she dropped to her knees to right the table and collect the debris. She was grovelling at the feet of one of the airmen when he spoke to her. 'I take it you and Skip know each other, Mrs Everton. I'm surprised he never told us he was acquainted with a little cracker like you.'

Before she could answer John stepped in again. 'Stow it, Higgins — none of your bloody business. Show a bit of respect to Mrs Everton.'

Sister Edwards was helping him to his feet. 'Come along, Flight Commander. I'll take you back to the ward so you can change out of those wet pyjama bottoms.' Unfortunately she had a very loud voice and crystal-clear diction.

Every man in the day room looked over and laughed. John turned a spectacular shade of scarlet and snatched up one of his crutches, rammed it under his left arm, and hobbled away without another word or glance in her direction.

It took a further quarter of an hour to restore order and have the room in the pristine condition which Matron required. John didn't return, and Barbara was relieved she didn't have to speak to him again. How could he be convalescing in Ingatestone, of all places? Why hadn't he gone somewhere nearer his home in Hastings? He'd been as startled as she was, so he obviously hadn't come here deliberately.

Once the trolley had been returned and the cups and saucers washed up, dried and put back on the rack, her shift was finished and she was free to go. The watery sunshine was a slight improvement on the earlier drizzle, but a bitter November wind flapped her coat around her knees as she wheeled her bicycle onto the drive.

Having John so close was a disaster. He was bound to ask about her, and someone would tell him that she had a sixteen-month-old son. He could do the maths, and would want to know if Charlie was his child. If he saw him, John would know immediately. The baby looked more and more like his natural father every day.

12

Barbara arrived at the Grove without being aware of how she got there. She'd completed the journey in a daze, believing her life just couldn't get any worse. Tom and David would discover the truth; but even worse, her in-laws would basically lose a second grandchild. The fact that Alex had accepted Charlie as his own didn't mean his parents would be prepared to do the same.

Why hadn't Grandpa warned her John was there? If she'd known, she could have kept away from him, and given them the time to prepare for the inevitable meeting. The chaos she'd caused this morning would be a talking point at the convalescent home for weeks. John would be pestered with questions about how he came to know her and why they'd both been so shocked to meet.

There was no opportunity to speak privately to her grandfather until after the boys were in bed and her grandparents joined her in her bedroom to listen to the wireless. Barbara was reluctant to bring the subject up, but she wanted answers. Anyway, Grandma was going to see John for herself tomorrow and needed to be prepared so she didn't behave as stupidly as Barbara had done.

'Grandpa, why didn't you tell me John was one of the new patients?' They stared at her, obviously as shocked by the information as she'd been to meet him. 'You didn't know? Sorry, I thought you must have seen him on your rounds yesterday.'

He eventually recovered his voice. 'What a horrible coincidence! I spent my time on the wards and didn't meet the ambulatory patients. What happened?'

She told them and they were laughing at the end of her story. 'Now I come to think of it, John was as surprised as I was. Is it possible he didn't actually know he'd been sent to Ingatestone to recuperate?'

'I can't believe he'd have agreed to come if he'd known — ' Grandma paused and shook her head. 'I wonder if he had knowledge of Alex's disappearance and decided to come to see you.'

'No, that can't be true, otherwise he wouldn't have been so surprised when I offered him a cup of tea. What am I going to do? He's done nothing wrong. The boys love him and will want to see him. I don't see how he's not going to find out about Charlie.'

'Don't tell Tom or David,' Grandpa said firmly. 'You mustn't go there again — and I don't think you should either, Elspeth. I'll have a word with Thorogood tomorrow and see if I can get him transferred somewhere more suitable.'

'Won't he think that a bit strange? I've known John for years. His friendship was what kept me going.'

'Be sensible, Barbara. Imagine the hurt that will be caused if your secret becomes common knowledge. I liked him; I'll explain that with Alex missing, it would be wrong to see him. He'll understand. I'm sure he's already planning to move elsewhere.'

'What if the boys find out he was there? Remember, Grandpa, we're going to spend Christmas Day at the home. Mightn't somebody mention what happened?'

'We'll keep the boys busy so they don't have time to strike up a conversation of any length. Don't look so worried, my dear. We'll get through this together.' He glanced at his pocket watch. 'We'll discuss this later. It's almost nine o'clock.' He got up and turned on the wireless.

The news was so awful they didn't get to finish the conversation. Japan had attacked the US Pacific fleet at Pearl Harbor in Hawaii, and thousands of American sailors had been killed and most of their fleet destroyed.

'Good grief!' exclaimed Grandpa. 'What a dreadful thing — to lose so much in such a short time. One thing is certain: America will declare war on Japan and Germany now. We won't be fighting Hitler alone.'

It was hard to believe such an atrocity might prove to be a good thing for Britain. Barbara went to bed but was unable to sleep; every time she closed her eyes she imagined the devastation at Pearl Harbor. When she sat up to push away the nightmare her head was immediately filled with images of Alex, and her eyes filled. She missed him so much, and wanted to believe he was still alive, but was slowly giving up hope.

★ ★ ★

Edward hadn't told Elspeth about the letter Alex had sent for Barbara. He needed to sit and think about what to do for the best. He told her he had some paperwork to do for tomorrow and she was happy to go to bed.

He could do with a large whiskey, but he'd finished the last of the bottle the other day. Bloody nuisance, not being able to get the necessities of life. Since he'd retired from his general practice he no longer had petrol coupons, which was another inconvenience. He would have to make do with the dregs in

261

the sherry bottle. Better than nothing, he supposed.

The house was quiet. Mrs Brown and Joe were in their own sitting room. Although the lad slept upstairs on the same floor as the boys, he joined his mother to listen to the wireless in the evenings. Edward was damn tired, getting too old for all this cycling about the place in the freezing cold.

He stretched out on the Chesterfield and winced when he tasted the sweet sherry. He closed his eyes and let his thoughts drift. Sometimes things sorted themselves out in his subconscious, and then an answer presented itself.

Was young Thorogood's arrival in Ingatestone fortuitous, or an absolute disaster? Had he been sent by some higher power to be there for Barbara when she was forced to come to the inevitable conclusion that Alex was dead? Thorogood was his great-grandson's actual father — surely it was better for the boy to grow up with two parents, however strange the circumstances?

Before he spoke to the young man he would give Barbara the letter. Maybe there was something in it that would help them make the correct decision. He yawned, looked at the glass, and decided to leave the rest. Mrs Brown could make a trifle with it.

Getting off the sofa was more difficult nowadays. His joints ached, and things he'd done a couple of years ago without a second thought were now almost beyond him. The letter was locked in his desk in the library; he'd retrieve it and give it to Barbara tomorrow morning.

As he removed the envelope he had second thoughts. Even if John was sent away without speaking to Barbara again, there was no reason why he couldn't be contacted at a later date if necessary. He ground his teeth. Procrastination was not in his nature, so why couldn't he make a decision?

It was going to take Barbara time to recover from the loss of the man she loved, perhaps years. What if Thorogood met and married someone else before he knew about Charlie? His beloved granddaughter and great-grandson might have lost the chance to live in a happy family — and the blame would lie at his door. With hindsight, Edward wished he'd not agreed to her request to keep the letter from Alex's adjutant a secret. He wouldn't make a decision tonight, but sleep on it and see how the land lay in the morning.

★ ★ ★

The telephone was ringing when Barbara came down for breakfast, Charlie on her hip. She hurried into the library and snatched it up. 'The Grove, Barbara Everton speaking.'

'Thank God it was you who answered, Babs. It's me, John.'

'I recognised your voice. I was going to come and see you this morning. I'm dreadfully sorry about dropping a cup of tea in your lap.'

'Not surprised. I was pretty shocked myself. I wanted to tell you I'd no idea I was in Ingatestone. We were just piled into an ancient ambulance and driven here. There were no windows and it was fairly dark when we arrived.'

'Surely there was a convalescent home nearer your base?' She stopped. She'd no idea where he was stationed, so the question was silly. 'Where are you based, exactly?'

'Honington. It's in Suffolk. This might well be the nearest convalescent home. I don't want to cause any trouble — I'm going to see the chap in charge and arrange to be transferred somewhere else.'

'No, please don't do that. You need to stay with your friends.' The baby wriggled and she put him down to toddle around the room. 'Alex is missing. He disappeared on his way back from a reconnaissance mission a few weeks ago.'

'God, I'm so sorry. Don't give up on him; he might well have been picked up. It could be months before you hear anything. All the more reason for me to disappear. If you were my wife I wouldn't want you spending time with your ex-fiancé.'

'I can't talk to you now, John. I've got to get the boys off to school. Would you mind if I came to see you later on?'

'I'd be delighted. My parents were devastated when you cut them out of your life. They were upset that you broke it off, but understood when I told them you'd never really loved me the way I loved you. They were like your family when you were growing up and they would love to hear from you.'

A yowl of pain from the baby when he banged his head on the corner of the table interrupted the conversation. 'I've got to go. Expect me round about eleven o'clock.'

She flung the receiver back on the cradle and picked her son up and comforted him as she carried him into the kitchen, where her brothers were already eating porridge. Horrible, slippery stuff — she'd rather have nothing than eat that.

'Mrs Brown, could you possibly look after this young man again this morning? I'll ask my grandmother if she minds.'

'No need to, Mrs Everton. I'm going down to the village after breakfast. The fish van comes today and I'm hoping to get a nice bit of haddock to make a fish pie tonight. Having the pram for the shopping will be a great help. It won't matter if it's raining; he'll be nice and snug with the hood up.'

Barbara strapped the baby into his high chair and Mrs Brown handed him his spoon and pusher. 'I've got some lovely scrambled eggs for you, Charlie. Make sure you eat it all up, and don't spill it on the floor like you did last time.'

'Neggies, yum yum.' He clattered his cutlery on the high chair tray and bounced up and down in anticipation.

Barbara handed him two toast soldiers spread with Marmite to be going on with. 'Mummy's going to see Grandma — I won't be a minute. Be a good boy and eat your toast.'

She wasn't sure how her grandparents would take the news of John's phone call and her decision to see him. During the night she'd decided to tell him he was Charlie's natural father, but that Alex had accepted him as his own, so he could never tell their son the truth. John would have to be a loving uncle until Charlie was old enough to know.

Her grandparents were in the breakfast

room as usual at this time of the morning. Grandpa looked as if he hadn't slept — in fact he looked a bit nervous, which was most unlike him. 'John telephoned me and we're going to meet this morning. I'm going to tell him about Charlie.' She'd expected both of them to protest, to try and talk her out of it. Instead they looked relieved.

'I think that's the right decision, my dear. Elspeth and I have just been talking about it. Is there a risk he won't keep the news to himself? The boys shouldn't know; word will get back to the Evertons, and God knows what will happen then.'

'I've thought about that, Grandpa, and don't see how we can prevent them finding out. Remember we have already arranged to spend Christmas Day up there; they will meet John and could well see his resemblance to Charlie and ask awkward questions.'

'Also, Barbara, John will want to meet his son even if he can't acknowledge him,' said Grandma. 'That could also create problems.'

Grandpa shook his head. 'As long as this takes place when the boys are at school, I think the risk is minimal. However, he would have to come here, as it might raise a few eyebrows if we took the baby to him — and that's not an option at the moment, as I don't have my car on the road anymore.'

This was going to be more complicated than Barbara had anticipated. 'Perhaps it would be better to forget the whole thing and not tell him at all. He offered to try and get himself transferred. I wish now I'd not told him that wasn't necessary.'

'Isn't he walking about on crutches?' Grandma asked. 'Surely we could transport him in the cart?'

'Excellent idea!' said Grandpa. 'We'll wait until Mrs Brown and her son are out, and then you can get him with your little mare and her cart, Barbara.'

'Mrs Brown has offered to take Charlie shopping with her this morning whilst I visit. What time are you due at Mountney Hall, Grandpa?'

'Not until midday. Presumably you will have spoken to Thorogood by then, so there will be no awkwardness when I meet him.'

★   ★   ★

Barbara decided to push her bike up the hill. She didn't want to arrive red-faced and sweaty for her conversation with John. When she'd seen him, the image of her son, she'd known at once she still loved him — not the way she loved Alex, but as a brother. She'd treated him abominably and wanted to put things right. Her lips curved as she imagined his delight at hearing he had a son, and she hoped Auntie Irene and Uncle Bill, his parents, would be equally pleased at having a grandson.

Her hands clenched on the handlebars. What was she thinking of? He couldn't tell his parents. It would be too cruel for them to know about Charlie and never be able to see him, or tell anyone they were grandparents.

The closer she got the more the idea seemed wrong. She tried to put herself in John's place and imagine how it would feel to be told he had a son, but could never acknowledge him, or spend any father-and-son time together. Telling him, she realised, was more for her sake than his. If he knew her secret and also forgave her, then she would feel better — but at what cost to John and his parents?

Her bicycle crashed to the road. How could she have forgotten about Alex's feelings? For the first time since that dreadful day in the middle of October, she'd not thought about him. Was her decision to involve John in their lives because she was coming to accept that the love of her life had died?

She retrieved the bike and clambered onto the saddle. Her legs were leaden; she scarcely had the energy to turn the pedals. Telling John was not an option; she wasn't ready to believe Alex would never return to them. He would be devastated if anyone else knew he wasn't Charlie's father. He adored his son and wouldn't want to share him.

Barbara's eyes cleared and her energy returned. Alex wasn't dead. He would come back, and she wasn't going to do anything that might cause him unhappiness. She would tell John she had a baby — she could hardly keep that a secret — but there was no need for him to know Charlie's exact age. As long as he didn't see him, and her brothers didn't get the opportunity to talk about their nephew, there was no reason to worry.

Good grief! She was being dense. Why shouldn't David and Tom talk about Charlie? They had blond hair and blue eyes just like the baby. If she mentioned he had been born very prematurely, even his birthday wouldn't be a problem.

Today she left her bike propped against a tree and went in the front door. John was waiting in the entrance hall, balanced on his crutches. 'It's lovely to see you, Babs. Matron has given us permission to use her office — it's the only place we'll get any privacy.'

'I'd forgotten how tall you were, John. Even on crutches you're still huge.'

'Do you like the moustache? I'm rather proud of it myself. Thought I'd better grow it when I was promoted last year.'

'To be honest, I hadn't really noticed it until you said. Very dashing; makes you look older.'

The door to the office was open and he hopped in behind her. He propped his crutches against the wall and turned a chair so he could sit. She brought a second one around the desk so she was opposite.

'You look well, apart from a broken leg of course. How did it happen, if you don't mind me asking?'

'Are you sure you want to hear? It's a pretty grim story.'

'I do, but let's get a few things out of the way first. I should never have agreed to marry you, and certainly not slept with you — it was very wrong of me. I thought I was helping you, sending you away happy, but I just caused you unnecessary pain.' She risked a glance in his direction. He looked serious, but not angry. 'I do love you, John, but not in the right way. I fell in love with Alex the first time I met him; and once you'd gone to Canada to train, we met up again. I wrote to you immediately to break off the engagement, and then Alex and I decided to get married.'

'I could make some sarky comment about

you being on the rebound, but I always knew you didn't love me the way I wanted you to. I shouldn't have made love to you; it was a bloody awful thing to do in the circumstances. I'm just glad you and Alex got together. I'm so sorry he's missing, but don't give up hope. Miracles do happen.'

'I'm sure I'd know if he was dead — somehow I feel he's alive somewhere and will come back to us eventually. I don't want our son to grow up without a father. Are you sure Auntie Irene and Uncle Bill would like me to get in touch? I'd love to speak to them again. I'll give them a ring at Christmas.'

'They'd like that. Before I tell you how I got buggered up, you ought to know I'm not considered fit for service anymore. Perforated eardrum means I'm deaf and can't fly. I've been invalided out of the RAF and am going back to Hastings to help run the farm. Thought maybe I'd join the police force. Even with a gammy leg, I should be able to do that.'

'You've got a degree from Oxford, John. Surely you can do something more exciting than be a policeman?'

'Like what? I'm not interested in being an accountant or sitting behind a desk. I'm hoping to become a detective eventually.'

'I'm sure you'll make an excellent plain-clothes man. Now, tell me about your crash.'

'There are a few things I need to explain before I start. I'm part of Bomber Command. Fly a Wellington; have done since I returned from Canada. Useless planes — far too slow, and too small a bomb load to be very effective. Another reason they don't want me; they want chaps to fly the Lancaster now.' He stopped and grinned. 'God! Why am I droning on about stuff you're not interested in? I'll get on with my story.'

As soon as he started telling her what happened, his eyes became unfocused. Was he experiencing the event again?

★ ★ ★

As he started talking it was as if he were back on that ill-fated night at the beginning of October. He and his five crew were airborne with one hundred and forty other bombers, intending to drop their load somewhere in Germany, when the squadron was recalled.

★ ★ ★

His navigator, Bill Hawkins, replotted the course. 'Can't say I'm sorry to have aborted the mission, Skip. The flak is murderous tonight. Wonder why they don't want us.'

'No idea, but it'll be good to get a bit of shuteye in my own bed for once.' The intercom crackled and the rear gunner asked if he should jettison the bombs over the North Sea. 'We'll let you know, Sammy. Sit tight and keep your eyes peeled — don't want to be shot down on the way home.'

There was time for a quick cup of coffee from the flask as they droned over the North Sea. He told Sammy to dump their load. The plane rocked as the bombs released, and he automatically adjusted the controls to compensate. Not far now; they should be safe from German fighters over British soil.

'We'll have to join the queue to land. I reckon we'll have to circle a couple of times until it's our turn.' They were all relaxed. Germany was a distant memory — nothing to do with them tonight.

They were on their second circuit when Bill shouted, 'There it is, Skip. Down we jolly well go. Might even be time to nip down to the pub for a pint.'

John lined up with the runway lights and came in. Immediately the wheels touched down he knew something was wrong. The aircraft was juddering and bumping all over the place. Then out of nowhere he saw a massive gun emplacement. Somehow he'd missed the runway and landed on the grass strip that ran beside the concrete. He couldn't stop in time — there was going to be a crash.

'Hang on. For God's sake, brace yourselves.'

He managed to turn the plane to the left, but it wasn't enough. The careering Wellington hit the concrete, and the sound of tearing metal drowned out everything else. His world went black for a second, and then his instincts kicked in. The smell of burning filled the cockpit. He had to get out and make sure his crew did also. Bill had vanished — he couldn't see him in the swirling, acrid smoke.

He pulled the lever above his head to release the escape hatch and stood on his seat. He scrambled out and jumped onto the port wing, shocked to see his plane had split into three pieces and burst into flames. There was nothing he could do for his men. If they weren't already out, they'd bought it. The ammunition would go off in a minute — he'd better get a move on.

His foot slipped as he jumped, and he landed heavily on his back, knocking the air from his lungs. He could hear the fire tenders approaching as he staggered to his feet, prepared to run for his life. He was a few *yards away when the Wellington blew up. Something smashed into his leg and he screamed.*

He woke up in hospital, his leg in plaster and deaf as a post. Eventually the nurse was able to tell him that Bill had gone for a Burton, and his rear gunner was horribly burned and fighting for his life — but the rest of them had suffered nothing worse than cuts, bruises and broken bones.

★　★　★

His eyes refocused and he looked up to see Babs staring at him, her eyes wide. 'Bloody stupid thing to do, but not entirely my fault. I discovered afterwards the runway lights went on the blink just as I was on my final circuit.'

'You sound so matter-of-fact, John. I can hardly take it in. Hearing you tell your story makes me realise just what the RAF is going through. I'm really glad you can't fly anymore. At least you'll be safe now.'

'I should feel guilty, be desperate to find a desk job, or become a trainer for the new blokes. But to tell you the truth, I feel as if I've done my bit. You're only supposed to fly three hundred hours before you get grounded — most of the blokes don't live that long. My crew, what's left of them, are out of combat duties from now on. We've clocked up more than the required hours, so we can let someone else take over with a clear conscience.'

All the time he'd been flying, risking his neck bombing Germany, he'd carried a photograph of Barbara in his pocket. He didn't blame her for giving him the boot; he'd pushed her into something she hadn't wanted. But he'd always love her, and doubted he'd ever find anyone to take her place.

She was the most beautiful girl he'd ever seen. Like him, she looked older than her years, and was a bit thinner than she had been, but was still an absolute knockout. Just being friends with her, being able to talk to her sometimes on the telephone, have her back in his life, would have to be enough.

Maybe another chap would try his luck, make a move on her whilst she was vulnerable and her husband was missing, but he wouldn't do that. He'd never tell her he still loved her and would take her and the baby on in a heartbeat; she needed his friendship, not more grief.

'When will you have the plaster off? Are you still in the RAF, or have you been demobbed?'

'My leg was broken in three places. I was in

traction for weeks; don't expect to be chucked out of here until spring sometime. My papers should have arrived by then, and I'll go straight to Hastings.'

A nurse burst into the room and stopped in confusion. 'I'm sorry, I'm looking for Matron.' She vanished with a flurry of starched apron.

Babs was already on her feet. 'I'd better go, John. I promised I wouldn't be more than a couple of hours. I'll see you on Friday when I have another shift.'

She smiled and left him to push himself upright and hobble back to the day room. He was halfway there when he changed his mind. He couldn't face being ribbed by his mates about meeting Babs. He hoped for her sake Everton turned up alive and well; but if there were no sign of her husband by the end of the war, well . . . he might be in with a chance.

★   ★   ★

Barbara had to intercept her grandfather before he began his rounds. He had to know she'd changed her mind and hadn't told John the truth. She checked with a passing nurse that he wasn't already on the premises, and then hurried out to rescue her bicycle from the hedge.

She saw him pedalling slowly towards her up the drive. She waved and met him halfway. 'Grandpa, I've decided it's better not to tell John anything. I still believe Alex will come home. Until I know otherwise, it wouldn't be fair on him for this secret to come out.'

'Good decision, my dear girl. How is Thorogood? Will he be able to fly again?'

When she'd explained John's story he nodded. 'He's a lucky beggar and so are his crew. I'm surprised they're happy to release him and haven't insisted he become a desk wallah. Probably because he's going to be farming, and we need all the food we can get.'

'I'm going to tell the boys John's here. They are very fond of him, and at one time thought he was going to be part of the family. Fortunately they don't break up until two days before Christmas, so won't have an opportunity to visit until Christmas Day. Between us we can make sure they don't spend too much time with him. If they mention when Charlie was born — '

'You mustn't worry about that, my dear. Why on earth should the boys want to talk about your baby when they can hear first-hand about Thorogood's daring exploits?'

'Thank you. I don't know how I could manage without your good advice. I'll see you later. I'd better get a move on; Mrs Brown will be back from the village by now.'

As she rocketed down the hill, the clouds parted and she was bathed in golden light. The ice around her heart melted, and for the first time since she'd received that dreadful telegram she truly believed Alex was alive and would one day walk through the door.

13

The boys came home on the last day of term rather subdued. Barbara was concerned they were regretting having agreed to do without Christmas presents so their points could be used to buy token gifts for the patients at Mountney Hall. She followed them upstairs, but as Charlie was scrambling up in front of her she arrived several minutes after them. They were already out of their uniforms and into corduroy trousers and thick woolly jumpers.

The baby ignored his uncles and toddled towards the rocking horse. 'Me ride, me ride horsey.'

Tom reached him first and lifted him onto the horse. 'Hold on tight, Charlie Bear. The horsey's going to gallop.'

Whilst her son was occupied, Barbara went in to speak to David. 'You both seem a bit fed up. Did something happen at school?'

'No, Babs. It's just going to be horrible this year with no tree, no presents, no one here for Christmas, and Alex missing as well.'

'You and Tom have got more toys in your playroom than you need. I was going to suggest you sort out some things you don't play with and we could give them to the children in the village.'

Her brother scowled. 'No, we're keeping everything for Charlie. He'll want it soon.'

'That's all right; it was only a suggestion. Aren't you looking forward to seeing John? He's got loads of exciting stories to tell you. When I told him about your collection of war souvenirs, he said he had a few things he could give you.' This did the trick and immediately David was smiling again.

'Crikey! Ned and Jim have the best collection at the moment. Maybe ours will be better if we get some good stuff.' He rushed into the other room, and she could hear him excitedly telling Tom that going to Mountney Hall on Christmas Day wouldn't be so rotten after all.

She remained upstairs with the boys, watching them play together. Her brothers were so good with Charlie — far more patient than she was, if she were honest. 'We'd better go down to tea, boys. It's shepherd's pie and baked apples tonight.'

Life was much simpler now her grandparents ate in the kitchen in the evenings. She smiled when she remembered that not so long ago they'd all dressed for dinner. How times had changed. She must ask Grandma if she intended to return to the old ways when the war was over.

She would have been quite happy if Joe and his mother ate with them, but Mrs Brown was adamant that wouldn't do. At least there was less washing-up and dashing back and forth to the breakfast room, the way things were. Breakfast and lunch were still segregated, but Barbara always ate in the kitchen with her son, as he was too messy to do so anywhere else.

The dogs were curled up in a huge basket with the cat and too lazy to do more than wag their tails when she came in. The kitchen table was covered with a damask cloth — the one concession to formal dining; the cutlery wasn't the heavy silver or the crystal.

'Is there anything I can do, Mrs Brown? It smells delicious.'

'Nothing, thank you, Mrs Everton. Mrs Sinclair said to eat without them tonight. The doctor has been delayed — some sort of emergency up the road, and she's going to have hers on a tray with him when he gets back.'

The meal tasted as delicious as it smelled, and even Charlie managed to eat without covering himself and those sitting next to him with his food.

'Can we get down, please, Babs?' Tom asked politely.

'Finish your mouthful first, then you can go. I've left the wireless tuned in so you can listen to ITMA in my room if you want.' Jack Handley and his programme, *It's That Man Again*, was a huge favourite with all the family.

'You coming up to listen, Babs? I like it more when you're there,' David said plaintively.

'I wouldn't miss it for the world. I promise I'll be along as soon as I can. I just have to sort this little fellow out and get him in bed. He doesn't need a bath tonight, so I shouldn't be too long.'

Charlie fell asleep immediately and she was in time to catch the last half of the programme. They played a few games of cards, and then it was time for her brothers to go to bed. As she was tucking David in, he grabbed her hand.

'I want to see John immediately. It's too long until Christmas Day.'

'Good heavens, it's only three days, David. I'm sure you can contain your impatience until then.'

'We'd like to see him, Babs. He's like a big brother to us. We could cycle on our own — it would give us something to do tomorrow,' Tom added.

She wasn't sure she wanted the boys to see John without supervision, but they were so

284

keen she didn't have the heart to say no. 'I'll ring first thing and ask Matron if she minds you coming — but I'm not promising anything. If you do go, you can't stay long and must be very quiet.'

Tom raised his eyebrows and sighed loudly. 'We're not stupid, Babs. We'll be on our best behaviour, promise.'

'Do you think he'll have anything to give us tomorrow?' David asked.

'I shouldn't think so, but it won't do any harm to ask,' Tom replied. 'Can we still go if it's raining?'

'There's no point in worrying about it until we know you can actually go. Now, I'm going to turn the lights out — no reading tonight.'

There was the sound of footsteps in the passageway outside. Joe was on his way to his bedroom at the far end of the corridor. The boys shouted good night to him and he answered cheerfully.

'It's raining cats and dogs out there,' he said. 'Don't reckon we'll have a white Christmas this year. Good night, lads.'

'Gracious, I'd no idea it was ten thirty already,' said Barbara. 'Go to sleep. I'll see you in the morning, and we can decide what's going to happen then.'

★　★　★

285

Matron was delighted at the prospect of having the boys visit. 'Send them along, Mrs Everton. A couple of lads will cheer the patients up no end. If they come at coffee time they can help give out the drinks in the day room.'

Tom and David were hopping up and down beside her and she smiled and nodded. 'I've told them they mustn't stay for too long. They should be with you around ten o'clock.'

'Tell them to come round to the kitchen door; I'll need to check they have clean hands and no mud on their shoes before I let them in. I know what little boys are like — mud magnets, all of them.'

Barbara hung up. 'Right, Matron is happy for you to go as you'll cheer up the patients. However, she expects you to make yourself useful. You will be serving hot drinks in the day room.'

'Super, I'll like doing that,' said David. 'It's not raining at all — can we go now?'

'In half an hour. She wants you there by ten.' Barbara explained where they were to leave their bikes and warned them that there would be a hand and shoe inspection before they were allowed inside.

When they were ready to leave she checked they had on their smartest clothes and that their socks were pulled up to their knees.

'Wear your school macs, boys, and your caps — I want you to look your best.' She stepped back to check their appearance before letting them go. 'Okay, try and stay clean — don't ride through the puddles today.'

Charlie no longer wanted a nap during the day, although sometimes he fell asleep on the floor. This morning he did exactly that, and Barbara was able to carry him upstairs and put him in his cot. She was tempted to sit down with a book but decided to clean her bathroom instead.

She was cleaning the bath when her grandfather walked in. 'It might be easier if you got in, Barbara. Your arms aren't long enough to reach the far side of that monstrosity.'

'I know, but as I don't use it very much anymore, it doesn't need much of a clean. We use the one in the guest room as it's much smaller. I'll leave this for another time. Did you want to speak to me?' He looked so serious her heart plummeted.

'You'd better come and sit down, my dear. I'm afraid I've just received a letter from the War Office. It's not the news you were hoping for.'

She tossed the cleaning cloth into the bath and followed him. She didn't want to know what was in the letter.

He waited until she was sitting bolt upright on the sofa before joining her. 'It would appear, my dear, that a fishing boat picked up debris in the channel which proved to be from Alex's Spitfire. They have revised their opinion and now listed him as missing, presumed dead. I'm so sorry, my dear girl. I'd hoped your young man might have survived his crash.' He put his arm around her but she resisted. 'I was in two minds whether to tell you, and thought I might leave it until after Christmas, but decided I had no right to withhold information from you.'

'Where exactly was the debris found?' She didn't know why she'd asked this; she'd be none the wiser if she did know where it came from.

'I assume, my dear, that it must have been somewhere close to the shore. I doubt fishing boats would be far from the coast because of the risk of being torpedoed or bombed.'

'I see. Does that mean I am a widow? That we have to hold a memorial service?' Why was she asking these stupid questions? Alex couldn't possibly be dead — she would know if he was.

'I really don't know, my dear girl, but I have a feeling that in wartime the usual seven years doesn't apply. I think they will issue a death certificate fairly soon.'

A stranger seemed to have taken over her brain, and what she was saying bore no relation to what she was thinking. 'I don't want it to be made official. You mustn't tell the boys, or his parents. I don't want to ruin their Christmases as well.'

His face sagged and he looked old and tired. It wasn't his fault he'd had to tell her the RAF had given up on Alex and thought he was dead. She should have opened her own mail, and then he wouldn't have known anything about it.

'I'm sorry, Grandpa. That was unkind. From now on I want to open any letters myself — it's not fair asking you to do it. Although this is definitely a blow, I'm not giving up hope entirely. Until I receive an official notification saying he's dead, I won't accept it.' On impulse she stretched up and kissed his leathery cheek. 'If he's not a POW then he must be with the Resistance, and they don't send a list of names to anyone, do they? I don't know how long it would take for him to be smuggled through France to somewhere safe, but it could be months, couldn't it?'

His eyes glittered but he managed a watery smile. 'Best thing, my dear. I'll not say a word to anyone, even Elspeth. However, in the circumstances I think I really should give you this. It came with the original letter; I regretted not giving it to you at the time.'

He handed her an envelope. Her name was scrawled on it in handwriting she immediately recognised. Her throat closed and she felt as if someone had punched her in the chest. She didn't need to open it to know what it was. Alex had written this to be given to her if he died. She shook her head and wanted to thrust it back but her fingers remained clenched around it.

'I'll leave you in peace to read it, my dear. I'll be in the sitting room if you want to talk to me.' He walked out, his shoulders slumped, looking every one of his seventy-three years.

She didn't want to read it; wanted to tear it up, forget she'd ever seen it, but knew she couldn't. This might be the last communication she had from Alex, and she must treasure his words. She was about to tear it open when something stopped her. She scrambled to her feet and hurried into the nursery.

Charlie was sleeping soundly, bottom in the air with his face resting on his hands. She moved a small basketwork chair across and positioned it close to the cot. Reading this possibly posthumous letter was going to be the most difficult thing she'd ever done; being close to her baby would make it easier.

My darling Babs,
If you're reading this I will be dead and you will be broken-hearted. I don't want you to grieve for me — I will have died, like thousands of other young men, in defence of my country.

It wasn't what we planned. I imagined us growing old together with a house full of beautiful children. I couldn't love Charlie any more even if he was my own flesh and blood; I want you to know that I don't regret anything that happened. If you hadn't slept with John, we wouldn't have our beautiful baby.

Hitler is to blame for me being taken from you — hate him, but don't hate me for leaving you. I love you, sweetheart, and always will. From the moment I set eyes on you, when you came over on your bicycle to buy fodder and bedding for your horse, I knew we were destined to be together. We didn't have very long, but we shared a love few people are lucky enough to experience.

I don't want you and Charlie to be alone. I want you to tell John that Charlie is his son; he'll do the right thing and offer to marry you. Knowing the two people I love most in this world will be taken care of when I'm gone is a comfort to me.

No, don't shake your head, darling girl — I don't expect you to rush off right now. But when you've had time to think about it, you'll know that I'm right. Forgive me for being selfish. I don't want you to fall in love again and have another man replace me in your heart — by marrying John I know that won't happen. He will take care of you, give you more children and be a good father and husband.

Look after yourself and our son, and remember that I love you and will always be with you — not in person, but in your heart.

Yours in eternity,
Alex.

She was numb. She'd read his words but couldn't take them in. This was all wrong — she wasn't meant to see this until he was gone. A shiver started at the base of her spine, and then she was shaking uncontrollably. Reading the letter was like signing his death warrant. Somehow it made a possibility into a certainty.

If she gave in to her grief, it would rip her apart. She had to stay strong for the rest of the family. Until she held Alex's death certificate in her hand she wouldn't believe he was never coming back. She concentrated on the baby breathing serenely beside her, forcing her own breath to match his. Eventually she was calm and had the strength to carry on — at least until she had the proof in her hands. She carefully refolded the letter and returned it to the envelope, then pushed it into the very back of her underwear drawer.

She returned to her position on the floor and drifted off to sleep, only to be woken a short while later by a little hand tugging on her hair. 'Mummy, Mummy, my wake-up now. My done big poo.'

She gently untangled his fingers and stood up. 'Have you really, Charlie Bear? Then Mummy had better get you changed before we go down. I think I can hear your uncles coming up to see us.'

The door burst open and David tried to shove past his brother in order to get to her first. 'It was absolutely super, Babs! We've got loads of things for our collection.' He wrinkled his nose. 'Charlie, you smell rotten.'

The baby jumped up and down in his cot. 'My done big poo.'

The boys backed out, holding their noses. 'Are you coming down, Babs? We'll get everything ready to show you,' Tom said as he firmly closed the door.

'I can't wait to see them. We'll be down in a minute, won't we, smelly boy?'

Her grandfather looked at her anxiously as she came in, and she smiled and nodded to reassure him. 'Okay, show me what you got,' she said to her brothers.

Spread out on a newspaper on the kitchen table was a selection of what looked mostly like junk. Tom and David picked up each piece and explained its use and value to their collection. 'Nobody else has got as many different bullets as we have, nor have they got a bit of a Messerschmitt with the swastika on it,' Tom told her proudly.

'I hope those bullets are empty, young man,' said Grandpa. 'I'm not having live ammunition in this house.'

David picked a handful up and shook them vigorously. 'See, Grandpa? All empty.'

'Make sure the baby doesn't get hold of any of it, Tom,' said Barbara. 'When you've finished sorting it out, put it with the rest of your collection in the barn.' She didn't like the idea of any sort of bullets, even dead ones, being kept in the house.

'We're not stupid, Babs. Once this is done and we've written it in our notebooks, it's going outside.' He nudged his brother. 'I reckon we've got dozens of swapsies now,

David. We definitely have the best collection of war souvenirs in the whole of Essex — if not the world.'

Barbara left them eagerly discussing their treasure and herded Charlie down the passageway and into the sitting room. Fortunately Grandma was still at one of her meetings; Barbara needed to speak to her grandfather in private. He quietly closed the door behind them and collapsed with a heavy sigh onto the sofa while she pointed her son in the direction of his toy box.

'Play with your bricks, darling, whilst your mummy talks to Grandpa.' He beamed and began to throw toys in all directions, chattering to himself about houses and bricks. Satisfied he'd be occupied for a while, she joined her grandfather on the sofa.

'I don't want to talk about the letter, Grandpa, so please don't ask me. I'm going to pretend nothing has changed. We both know that's not true, but there's been enough upset this year already. Grandma doesn't know about the plane, does she?'

'No, my dear girl, she doesn't. I didn't have time to tell her, as the letter arrived after she'd gone to her meeting. If you can carry on as normal, then I shall do the same. I take it you're not going to speak to the Evertons either.'

'Absolutely not. Let them have as many months as possible to recover from Judith's death before they learn about Alex. I'm hoping the official notification won't arrive for several weeks. Obviously I shall have to . . . well . . . I'm not going to think about it at the moment.'

Watching Charlie playing was pure entertainment. He was a constant delight, and it was hard to be sad with him toddling about.

'Did the boys say anything about John, Barbara?'

'Actually, they didn't. I think they must have been so busy cadging souvenirs from everyone that there wasn't time to talk to him at length. I'll ask them tonight.'

'Excellent — let's hope it remains that way. It's going to be a very different Christmas Day tomorrow. I gather from Elspeth that everyone will still have a stocking in the morning. I'm glad Tom and David will have something to mark the occasion.'

'Remember our first Christmas here in 1939? We bought so much. I wish I'd put some of the toys away for this year.'

'Hindsight is a wonderful thing, my dear, but the boys are older and probably wouldn't appreciate the things we gave them two years ago if they were given today.'

'We're having a special supper tonight, so

Mrs Brown tells me. She wouldn't say what she was preparing, but the kitchen certainly smells delicious. At least we have a cockerel for lunch tomorrow and plenty of fresh eggs and vegetables.'

'Have you wrapped up the gifts for the patients? It might be a good idea to do that as a family. After all, we've all donated our points in order to buy them.'

'Grandma is in charge of the wrapping paper. She's been ironing the sheets she saved from last year. The boxes are in the library; I'll get the boys to bring them in after lunch.'

Keeping busy was the best way to stop unwanted thoughts from ruining their Christmas. By the time the dozens of presents had been wrapped, the sitting room looked like Father Christmas had emptied his magic sack all over the floor. Charlie had been happily occupied with the oddments of colourful paper and was now helping David put the presents back into the boxes.

'There are a few packets of Woodbines left over, Babs. What shall we do with them?' Tom asked as he waved them about.

'I bet they'd rather have lots of cigarettes than woolly socks,' David said. 'Why don't we wrap them together?'

'Is there anything else we could put with them, Grandma? Have we got any knitted items, sweets or biscuits?'

Grandma rummaged through the cardboard boxes. 'I've found two handkerchiefs, a bag of Paradise Fruits, and a pair of cufflinks.'

'Excellent — pass them over, Elspeth, and the boys and I'll do the final parcels. Good thing we had some brown paper and string in the cupboard. Is there anything sparkly we can add to these final gifts so they look a bit more cheerful?'

'We cut up all the old Christmas cards to use as tags, but I think I might have some raffia in my sewing box.' Grandma headed for the door but paused as she got there. 'It's almost time for supper. Put everything back and then go and wash your hands, boys.'

The celebration supper was leek and potato soup, and liver and bacon casserole, followed by a magnificent pink and white blancmange. 'That was delicious. Thank you, Mrs Brown, we all enjoyed it — especially the baby.' Grandpa nodded at Charlie, who was liberally coated with blancmange.

'I'm sorry about my son's table manners, everyone, but this is his first real Christmas and I want him to join in with everything — however messy.'

'Thank you, Mrs Brown, it was really lovely,' said Tom. 'Can we go upstairs and listen to your wireless, Babs?'

'Go ahead. I'm going to give this little man a bath tonight but I'll join you as soon as he's down.'

'I hope we don't have to share his water tonight, Babs. He's disgusting.' Tom grinned at the baby but didn't get within arm's reach.

'Make do with a good wash, you two. You had a bath a couple of days ago so can't be that dirty.'

Charlie, for once, didn't protest when Barbara lifted him out of the bath. 'Good boy. Let me get you dry, and then I'll wrap you up in a warm towel and take you into the nursery. It's Christmas Day tomorrow, and you will have a stocking of your very own. Father Christmas won't forget us even though there's a war on.'

He chuckled and stood up on her lap and threw his arms around her neck. 'Nice Mummy. Me lub you.'

'And I love you too, darling. Now, let's get you into your pyjamas.'

When Barbara went up to switch out her brothers' light, David whispered to her. 'Will there be anything at all tomorrow morning?'

'Wait and see. If you've been a good boy, Father Christmas might come.'

'That's what we thought — wouldn't be Christmas without a stocking.'

'Christmas is about more than presents,

David. It's time to celebrate the birth of Christ.'

Tom spoke from the darkness. 'Not much 'peace and goodwill to all men' around, is there?'

'Let's try and forget what's happening, just for one day, Tom.' Her eyes brimmed, but she forced the tears back and swallowed the lump in her throat. 'Good night, boys. Come down to the sitting room when you wake up.'

Her voice sounded normal; she didn't think they'd realised she was crying. She ran to her bathroom and splashed her face with cold water. She couldn't go downstairs until she was calm. It was going to be much harder than she thought pretending nothing was wrong.

Now Charlie was older and could call out if he wanted her, she thought it safe to leave him on his own upstairs for a short while. She listened at the bottom of the stairs every fifteen minutes or so — but he'd not woken even once in the past three months, and her grandparents preferred to sit downstairs.

She took a deep breath, put on a smudge of lipstick, and was ready. Filling up all the stockings was something she'd always enjoyed; somehow tonight it wasn't going to be the same. The gifts she'd managed to accumulate had been safely hidden in the back of her enormous walk-in closet. Each little item had been wrapped and labelled. Grandma had also been collecting things to put in the stockings, and now the boys were in bed they could start filling them. There was a sock filled for Alex, but she didn't take that down.

She was able to forget whilst they sorted out their gifts and put them in the correct place. Three old pillowcases were being used for the children, their names carefully embroidered on each.

'There. Don't they look splendid, Edward?' said Grandma. 'What a good idea to use a pillowcase for the boys, Barbara. We would never have got all their bits and bobs into a sock.'

'I can't hang them on the fireplace with the others, Elspeth. They're too heavy. Where shall I put them?'

'Put them on the sofa, my dear. We're going up so don't need to sit on it. All you have to do is take the stockings for Mrs Brown and Joe and hang them in the kitchen somewhere; then we can go to bed.'

'Good night, Grandpa, Grandma,' said Barbara. 'I'll see you in the morning. Do we let them have their sacks before we go to church, or make them wait until we get back from Mountney Hall?'

'What do you think, Edward? Anticipation is part of Christmas morning, so I think it might be a good idea to keep them waiting until after lunch. It will seem a bit flat if there's nothing to look forward to.'

'I agree, Grandma. By the time we've had breakfast it will be time to leave. I'm quite looking forward to arriving at the Hall by horse and cart. Very Dickensian.'

Barbara checked the baby and then prepared for bed. She was dreading the silence and darkness. It was going to be impossible to shut out the terrible idea that she'd lost Alex forever. However hard she tried to keep it alive, the flicker of hope was fading. She wouldn't give in; wouldn't accept the inevitable until she actually held a death certificate in her hands.

She wasn't sure she believed in God anymore — but just in case there were a supreme power listening to her, she prayed that Alex might be alive somewhere; that he was being sheltered by the French Resistance and would somehow make his way back to England. Putting it into words helped to steady her, and eventually she fell asleep still able to cling to the faint hope that things would work out in the end.

14

There was no time to be sad the next morning. Barbara was able to lose herself in the bustle of getting the children into their Sunday best. They were running late, and breakfast had to be eaten rapidly if they were to get to church.

When they emerged the sun was shining and the world seemed a better place. It took far too long to exchange greetings with the congregation, and they had to hurry home. The only one who enjoyed the experience was Charlie, who loved being bumped in his pram. He was able to walk now, but it took much longer that way.

'Look, Babs, Joe's got Silver ready,' said Tom. 'He's even put all the presents in the cart. And Mrs Brown's waiting for Charlie.'

'Good show,' said Grandpa. 'We can jump in and get away immediately. They have lunch at one o'clock sharp, and it's almost twelve now. We haven't got time to waste.' He led the charge to the pony cart and soon they were all safely inside. 'Is everybody warm enough? Do we have enough rugs?'

'We are absolutely splendid, my dear. Snug

as a bug in a rug,' Grandma replied.

Barbara unwound the reins and clicked her tongue, and her mare moved away smoothly. She couldn't remember the last time she'd ridden Silver, and she missed being out in the countryside on her own. Despite the fact that the cart was laden, her horse trotted up the hill eagerly, her ears pricked and her neck arched, obviously enjoying the experience. They arrived in record time and were welcomed by a group of airmen in pyjamas, boots and greatcoats.

She thought it strange they weren't allowed to dress if they were well enough to wander about the place. 'Merry Christmas, gentlemen,' she said. 'I do hope we haven't kept you waiting too long.' The cart rocked to a standstill and her brothers jumped out and began to pass the gaily filled boxes to the waiting men.

Whilst this was being done, Barbara pulled Silver's winter rug over the horse's back and gave her a nosebag of oats, carrots and chopped bran. 'We won't be long, sweetheart. Stand here like a good girl and enjoy your Christmas treat.'

David raced back to collect the last box. 'Hurry up, Babs! Everyone's waiting. They've got a massive tree and decorations and everything.'

'I'm coming. I had to make sure Silver was warm and comfortable. Do you think we've got enough parcels for everyone?'

'I reckon we have. John said quite a few of the patients have gone home for Christmas. There are only about twenty of them, and we've loads more things than that. Why can't John come back with us for lunch?'

Barbara almost stumbled up the steps. Her mind raced as she tried to think of a reasonable excuse. 'Remember, David, I was once engaged to him. I don't think it would be right to have him stay when Alex isn't there.'

'Fair enough, but it's a shame. He's like one of the family, really. Maybe he can come after Christmas, before he goes home.'

Somehow she managed to reply. 'Of course he can, and let's hope Alex is home before John goes back to Hastings.' She didn't want John anywhere near Charlie. He was bound to notice the familial resemblance and draw the correct conclusions. Whatever Alex wanted, she couldn't imagine herself married to John. He might be the baby's father, and everything else that Alex had said, but she would never agree to share a bed with someone she wasn't in love with, however much she wanted a bigger family and a father for her son.

Mountney Hall was almost unrecognisable from when the Farleys had lived there. Before, there had been an army of servants and the atmosphere had been chilly, and not just because of the lack of heating. The tree was indeed magnificent. She wondered where the decorations and twinkling lights had come from. The boys piled the presents around it and when she looked at the men smiling and happy at the thought of getting a gift, she was glad they'd made the effort.

John was propped against a radiator. He raised an arm in greeting but made no effort to join her. Someone had moved an upright piano into the vast entrance hall and struck up a lively rendition of 'We All Want Some Figgy Pudding'. When this was over, Matron stepped into the space and clapped her hands. Silence fell immediately. 'We would like to welcome Mrs Everton and the Sinclairs and thank them for their kindness,' she said. 'It is much appreciated by everyone, and we would like to give something to the children to express our gratitude.'

A young man in a wheelchair was pushed forward with two large, rather oddly shaped parcels on his lap. 'Here you are, Tom, David. We hope you like what we've given you.' He grinned at Grandpa. 'They're a bit heavy; we'll get a couple of our fitter bods to take them out for you when you go.'

Tom and David were suitably grateful, and then began the happy task of handing out gifts. Whilst they did this, Barbara and her grandmother helped distribute the tea and mince pies. 'Where did they get the mincemeat from, Grandma? Mrs Brown couldn't make any this year because there was no dried fruit to be had anywhere.'

'I expect servicemen, and especially wounded heroes like these, are exempt from a lot of the rationing. I do hope there will be one for each of us.'

One of the nurses overheard this remark. 'Don't you worry, Mrs Sinclair — we've packed up a nice box of goodies for you to take back. The least we could do. You and your family coming here with all these presents has made Christmas Day really special.'

'How kind of you,' said Barbara. 'It wasn't necessary at all, but will be much appreciated.'

There were so many parcels that all the airmen received at least two each, and they were happily swapping gifts so that nobody had more than one pair of knitted socks and no cigarettes or sweets. Someone touched Barbara's elbow and she glanced over her shoulder.

'John, Merry Christmas. You seem to be moving about a lot better than you did a couple of days ago.'

'I am. It took me a while to get the hang of these crutches. You look a bit pale — haven't you been sleeping well?'

'We were up late finishing wrapping the parcels and doing the boys' stockings. I'm missing Alex dreadfully; it's horrible not knowing where he is.'

'He wouldn't want you to worry; he'd want you to carry an as usual. Keep the home fires burning, and all that.'

'I'm doing my best. I've really enjoyed this morning. Are all these men pilots?'

He shook his head. 'No, but they are all aircrew of some sort or another. Have you written to my parents? I mentioned that I'd seen you and the boys and that you were going to contact them.'

She flushed, feeling guilty that she'd not yet found the time to do this. 'I'll ring them as soon as I get back, I promise. We have to go soon. I can't leave Silver standing for much longer; it's far too cold.'

'I hope the boys can visit again. The blokes love having a captive audience for their tales of derring-do.'

'Yes, I'm sure they will be back. I can't tell you how thrilled they were with the memorabilia they were given a couple of days ago.'

His smile reminded her how fond she was of him. 'That's a relief, because that's what their Christmas presents are. We had a good rummage around in our kitbags and came up with a load more bits and pieces that anyone else would call rubbish.'

'Absolutely perfect. They will definitely have the best collection of war souvenirs in the neighbourhood now. Take care of yourself, and I'll make a point of coming to speak to you when I'm here next. I don't want to lose touch again.'

As soon as they got back, Barbara and the boys laid the table in the breakfast room and sat down in good time. Even eating one of their own cockerels didn't detract from the tastiness of their lunch. Barbara had been worried David might be upset, but he tucked in with as much enthusiasm as everyone else.

'I expect you know what those parcels are, boys, so do you mind taking them outside to sort? Mrs Brown and Joe will be eating their own lunch in the kitchen right now, and Grandma certainly doesn't want the mess in the sitting room.'

'That's okay with us, Babs,' said Tom. 'Do you mind if we leave opening our other things until tea-time? It'll be too dark in the barn to see what we've got if we don't go out now.'

'I think that's a good idea, Tom. We will all wait until tea-time.' Grandpa waved his hand and Barbara's brothers threw down their napkins, mumbled thanks for the meal, and dashed out.

They listened to the King's speech at three o'clock, and then Barbara put Charlie down for a nap. If he was going to stay up after tea to open his presents, he needed a sleep or he would be disagreeable and grumpy. She didn't want to be on her own and have time to think, so she returned to join her grandparents in the sitting room. There was also that difficult phone call she'd promised to make.

She had no need to look up the number, as she knew it by heart. Auntie Irene never answered the telephone if Uncle Bill was there to do it for her. Whilst it was ringing she closed her eyes and imagined the house in which she'd spent so many happy days. Someone lifted the receiver.

'Merry Christmas, it's Barbara — '

'Babs! Well I never! We just got our John's letter telling us he was in a hospital near you. I can't tell you how pleased your Auntie Irene will be to hear from you again. Hang on a minute, I'll go and fetch her from the kitchen.'

A few minutes passed and then John's mother was on the line. 'How are you? And your brothers? We were ever so upset when you stopped writing to us, Babs. You've been like a daughter all these years. Never mind you didn't marry our John, we still think of you as part of the family.'

When she eventually put the phone down, Barbara wondered why she'd left it so long. She'd promised to go and see them as soon as travel was possible again, and to visit John as often as she could. They'd asked her to send photographs of herself, her brothers and her baby. That was the last thing she was going to do, as Charlie's resemblance to John was even more obvious in black and white than in the flesh. It seemed unfair that they were denied knowledge of their first grandchild, but telling them would destroy her in-laws, especially as they might have lost Alex as well.

As she was undressing for bed she decided that Christmas Day, considering the circumstances, had been remarkably enjoyable. The children had loved their gifts, although if she were honest, Charlie preferred the wrapping paper to the contents. She'd achieved her aim, so whatever happened next, it wouldn't forever cast a shadow over the festive season.

★　★　★

The weeks passed and still there was no confirmation from the War Office that Alex was dead. Barbara began to believe it had all been a dreadful mistake; that he was alive somewhere and trying to find his way back.

She continued to visit the Hall, as did her brothers, and looked forward to spending time with John. There had been complications with his leg and he'd been transferred to the hospital at Romford for further surgery for a while. His friends had left, but he seemed remarkably relaxed about being the inmate who had been there the longest. He never mentioned Alex, so neither did Barbara. They talked about the war, about his exploits as a pilot, and about the time they'd spent together in Hastings when she was growing up.

At the end of February Mrs Everton arrived for one of her regular visits and immediately asked if Barbara had heard from Alex. 'It's almost four months since he went missing. Surely we should have heard something by now?'

'His name hasn't appeared on a POW list, but that doesn't mean he's not in one somewhere. I think he's with the Resistance.' She hated lying to her mother-in-law, but this wasn't the time to worry her. Valerie's baby was due soon, and she wasn't going to spoil a happy family event.

'That's as may be, Babs, but it's hard for all of us not knowing.' She was helping Charlie arrange his farm animals, and the little boy was holding each one up for her to name. 'That's a pig — can you say 'pig'?'

'Piggy goes honk-honk, Nanny. Cow goes moo.'

'Who's a clever boy, then? He's very advanced for his age. I don't remember Alex or the other two being able to talk so early.' She smiled lovingly at the toddler. 'I expected him to have the Everton hair, but I think he looks more like Mrs Sinclair than he does you. Your mother was fair-haired, and so are your brothers, so it's not surprising this little man looks like them. Mind you, he's got your curly hair, hasn't he?'

'He has. Now it's longer you can really see the curls. I suppose I should cut them off; blond curls make him look a bit like a little girl.'

'No, no one could mistake him for anything but a boy. He's a joy, and it's such a shame our Alex is missing him growing up. By the way, once Valerie has had the baby we've decided to move back to Home Farm. My Bert has got everything organised in Romford and the house is bigger here, and Ned and Jim want to come home.'

313

'Will Valerie come with you? You won't leave her on her own?'

'She's decided to move in permanently with her in-laws. She doesn't want to live with this new baby in a house where little Judith died. It's for the best; it's nearer to the base, so Peter can nip home on his bicycle when he gets an hour off.'

'Has she said anything about seeing me? I really miss her. I don't have any other friends in the area.'

'She's sort of blanked you out, and she doesn't even talk about Alex. Maybe in a year or two she'll be ready to pick up where she left off. She's not the same; I don't think she ever will be the happy, optimistic girl she used to be.'

'Losing a child has to be the worst thing that can happen to a woman. I don't blame her, and just wish I could make things right between us, but in my heart I know we'll never be friends again. Charlie will be a constant reminder of what she lost.'

'I have to be careful not to mention him, or you, after I've been here. I know I shouldn't say so — after all, I am Valerie's mother — but I don't think her behaviour's normal. Good heavens, the country would grind to a halt if every mother who had lost a child in the last few years acted like her. Sometimes I want to give her a good shake and tell her to get on with her life and stop being silly.'

'It must be very hard for you. My grandfather says she's suffering from some sort of mental disturbance caused by grief. It's not really her fault, and she might well snap out of it when her life is happy again.'

'I've got no time for all that newfangled mental illness nonsense. In my day people just got on with things. People die, children die — it's part of life, and there's no point dwelling on it.' She reached down, kissed Charlie, and then stood up. 'I'd better make a move, Babs. I don't want to keep Bert waiting. Promise you'll let me know if you hear anything from the War Office?'

Barbara couldn't make that promise, so ignored the remark and handed Mrs Everton her coat and hat. 'Tom and David will be thrilled to know their best friends are moving back soon. Thank you for coming; I really look forward to your visits. Let me know when the baby's born, won't you?'

'Of course I will. You're a good girl; Alex was lucky to find you. Goodbye, my dear. Don't bother to show me out — it's far too cold.'

When Tom and David returned from school, Barbara gave them the good news and immediately they shot upstairs to change, then vanished into the barn to organise their collection. She'd had a cursory glance at the piles of twisted metal, bloodstained webbing, empty bullet cases and other miscellaneous junk, but had to take their word that they now had the best collection in Essex. How on earth they could know that, she'd no idea, but if it kept them happy at a difficult time then she wasn't going to argue. They spent more time out there nowadays than they did in the house, but her grandparents said boys should be outside and she mustn't worry about it.

At the beginning of March a phone call came telling her Valerie had had a girl, and mother and baby were doing well. Mrs Everton said they would be back at Home Farm by the middle of the month. It would be wonderful having her in-laws within walking distance again, and Ned and Jim would no doubt be able to spend far more time with her brothers than they had in the past few months. She gave the good news to her brothers when they returned from school that night.

'We've got a big surprise planned for when our friends come over,' David told her. 'We've been really busy and want all of you to come out on the big day and see what we've done.'

'I wondered what you were up to out there in the barn. Why don't you make a definite arrangement for all of them to come here for a birthday tea as soon as they're home?' She had turned twenty-one the previous week but had told the family to ignore it, as she'd had a big party last year. Both Tom and David had birthdays in the next two weeks and it would be nice for them to have a bit of a party.

'We can ask them at school tomorrow. Do you think it will rain when they come?'

'I've no idea, David. I'm not clairvoyant.'

'It'll be the Easter hols soon,' Tom said. 'The weather should be decent by then. Are we going to do painted eggs this year, Babs?'

'Mrs Brown has been blowing eggs and rinsing out the hollow shells for you. There should be plenty for you to decorate.'

'I can't wait — I'll be into double figures at last,' David said. 'Tom will be able to wear long trousers next year at school, like Ned.' He pointed to his brother's knees. 'You look silly in those now you're so tall.'

'Thanks a bunch, little brother. I really wanted to know that.'

Barbara left them amicably bickering and guided Charlie into the sitting room. This was empty, as both her grandparents were at the Hall today. As the weeks had trickled by she was beginning to flinch every time she heard the letterbox, expecting it to be the dreaded death certificate.

When the Evertons were safely installed at Home Farm, and her brothers were happy, she would contact the War Office and ask what was going on. After the birthday party would be a good time. She blinked away tears — no time would be a good time. The delay must be good news, surely? Perhaps they'd heard something; nothing concrete, nothing they could pass on to the family, but enough to postpone the confirmation of Alex's death.

★ ★ ★

The weather improved, the daffodils spread their golden glory along the garden borders, and the day for the family celebration arrived. Barbara's brothers spent so much time in the barn that she was becoming a bit worried about what they might be doing for their surprise. She tackled Joe about it the day before the party.

'Have you any idea what my brothers are planning, Joe?'

'No, Mrs Everton, they're a bit secretive. They keep the barn door shut and I've not been invited in to have a deco.'

'Never mind, I'll just have to contain myself until tomorrow afternoon. Don't forget that you're invited to the party, but there's no need to dress up. It's very casual.'

She bumped into her grandfather in the kitchen. 'I've got a bit of bad news for you, my dear. The boys have asked John to come tomorrow and I could hardly tell him he couldn't come. His plaster cast has been replaced with a brace, and he's borrowed a bicycle to get here.'

'Oh dear! I'll just have to ask Mrs Brown to keep Charlie out of the way. He can't toddle around outside anyway, so hopefully no one will think there's anything odd about him being absent from the party.'

'I think you're worrying unnecessarily, my dear. The resemblance between John and your baby is not as pronounced as you think. However, as your in-laws will be present at the boys' birthday party, it's probably better to err on the side of caution.'

'I've been enjoying talking to John — he'll always be a special friend to me — but I can't help feeling guilty. It doesn't seem fair on Alex.'

His expression changed. 'On that delicate subject, I take it you've heard nothing else since the letter you received just before Christmas?'

Was now the opportune moment to tell him what Alex had written? Her stomach contracted. Not today — she'd wait until the birthday party was out of the way and then do what she had to do.

'No, I've heard nothing. I don't want to think about it at the moment, if you don't mind. If I hear nothing on Monday I'll start making enquiries.'

★　★　★

'Are you quite sure, Barbara, that you want to hold the event in the kitchen?'

'Yes, if you don't mind, Grandma. Nobody's dressing up, and the main event is outside in the barn, so the kitchen is ideal. Also, I don't want Joe to feel uncomfortable, and he might if we were eating in the breakfast room. I'm going to put a pretty cloth on the table so it will look nice.' Charlie was sleeping upstairs and she thought she'd better go and check he hadn't woken up. 'I'm glad the baby's had his nap. I don't want him to be cross when everyone's here.'

There were jam tarts, fairy cakes, scones and sandwiches but no birthday cake; she didn't think her brothers would mind in the circumstances.

By the time Barbara returned with Charlie, the Evertons had arrived. She'd realised she couldn't really hide her son away, as his grandparents would want to spend time with him. Hopefully they would be too busy to make any unfortunate connections between John and Charlie.

'I'm so glad you could come today,' Barbara greeted them. 'Tom and David have been bursting with excitement ever since they knew their best friends were coming back to live nearby.'

'To be honest, Babs, our boys have never settled in Romford. There's no place like your own bed and bits and pieces around you, is there?' Mrs Everton held out her arms, and Charlie trotted over and allowed himself to be picked up. 'What a handsome chap you are in your new trousers. Have you got a kiss for your nanny?'

'My a good boy. My won't be bad, Nanny.' Charlie beamed and gave her a sloppy kiss. 'Down now, me down now.'

Mrs Everton released him and he toddled over to hug Grandpa's knees. Barbara couldn't hear what he was saying, but seeing them so happy in each other's company made her smile.

'Have you any idea what the big performance is, Babs?' Mrs Everton asked.

'I think my brothers are going to give us a show of some sort. It's definitely something to do with their collection of war souvenirs. They haven't allowed anyone into the barn to see, so it's a mystery for me as well.'

There were voices in the passageway outside the kitchen, and two men in RAF uniform came in. The first she recognised, but the second was a stranger. He was half a head shorter than John and had dark hair and grey eyes. He looked remarkably pleasant.

'Babs, I hope you don't mind, but I've come with my good friend Flight Lieutenant Simon Hodgkin — he turned up for a visit unexpectedly and was able to bring us in his car.' He grinned and pointed to his walking stick. 'To tell you the truth I wasn't looking forward to cycling with a gammy leg.'

'I'm delighted to meet you, Flight Lieutenant. Any friend of John's is a friend of ours. I'd like to introduce you to my in-laws, Mr and Mrs Everton.' He stepped forward and shook hands with them.

'If you'd like to hang your coats in the boot room, John knows where it is. However, I've got to warn you, we have to go outside shortly for some entertainment put on by my brothers.'

The young man had a firm handshake and a charming smile. 'Thank you for your gracious welcome, Mrs Everton. We've brought a contribution to the feast — hope you're not offended.' Like a magician he produced a shopping bag bulging with interesting shapes from beneath his greatcoat.

Whilst John showed him where to put his coat, she unpacked the goodies. 'Look at this, Mrs Everton. Where on earth did he find a tin of real coffee, a box of sugar lumps, and three bars of Rowntree's chocolate?'

'I expect servicemen get more points than we do. My word, Bert, see what else is in here.' Mrs Everton held up a giant tin of peaches, a tin of condensed milk, and a box of assorted biscuits. 'What a treat! Much better than buying presents for the boys.'

Barbara left the biscuits on the table to add to the party tea, but she put the rest of the things away in the pantry. Her grandparents could have the coffee and the boys could have the chocolate. The peaches and condensed milk would make a perfect dessert for lunch tomorrow.

Ned banged on the kitchen window. 'Tom says everyone must come out now and they're going to start the entertainment in a minute.'

'Righto, I'll collect everybody and bring them to the barn,' Barbara shouted back. Mr and Mrs Everton were already on their way, so all she had to do was find her grandparents and tell John and Simon to go straight out.

The sun was shining and the weather was remarkably mild for the end of March. Nobody really needed a coat on today. Whatever was going to happen was obviously an outdoor event, as Ned and Jim were directing everyone to the front of the house. Barbara picked Charlie up and followed her in-laws. Grandma joined them, but Grandpa strolled over and stood beside John and his friend.

At first Barbara didn't know why they'd gone round to the front. Then she saw a circle of tubes pushed into the circular bed full of daffodils, tulips, forget-me-nots and a variety of other spring flowers. She had a bad feeling about this. The tubes looked suspiciously like homemade fireworks. No one else seemed to have realised; the Evertons were engrossed in a conversation with Grandma, and Grandpa was talking to John and his friend. Joe had been roped in to help with the display and he didn't seem particularly perturbed, so maybe she was worrying unnecessarily.

Tom shouted for attention as David ran from one tube to another with a lighted spill. The fireworks fizzed and crackled and golden sparks shot into the air from a couple of them. Then a group of five in the centre of the bed toppled into each other. The air was split by a sheet of flame, and a deafening explosion followed. Charlie screamed and Grandpa fell backwards into the dirt.

15

Barbara couldn't go to his aid, as she had her hands full of hysterically screaming baby. As the smoke cleared she saw John and his friend crouching over the body doing some sort of first aid. She should be there; she knew what to do when someone had a heart attack. Her heart twisted. He looked so ill — his face was grey and his lips a horrid blue colour.

Grandma hadn't moved. She was standing rigid, her face white, staring at Grandpa stretched out in the dirt. Mr and Mrs Everton were comforting the boys. Had anyone thought to ring for an ambulance?

'Hush now, darling. That was a nasty noise, but it's gone.' Charlie continued to cry. He would be better inside. Maybe he was upset because his grandpa was on the ground. She shouted to John, 'I'm going to ring for an ambulance. I'll send Mrs Brown out with some blankets.'

John raised his hand but didn't look round. She met the housekeeper on the way out with an armful of rugs. 'My word, what a dreadful thing to happen. My Joe is ringing for the ambulance.'

'Thank you, Mrs Brown. I've got to take Charlie inside and try and calm him down. Could you look after Mrs Sinclair for me? She seems to be in shock.'

As soon as they were in the house, the baby's wails subsided and he fell into an exhausted sleep in her arms. She couldn't put him down as he'd entangled his hands in her coat, so she decided to wait outside until the ambulance arrived.

Joe met her in the passageway. 'The ambulance will be here in half an hour. I rang the Hall, Mrs Everton, and the doctor's on his way right now. He'll look after Doctor Sinclair until he gets to hospital.'

'Thank you,' said Barbara. 'I'm going to change the baby. Perhaps you could put the kettle on for us, Joe? A cup of hot, sweet tea will help with the shock.'

She tried to blot out the image of her beloved grandfather spreadeagled in the flower bed. If anything happened to him, the family would fall apart — he was the centre. With Alex possibly dead, they were going to need Grandpa more than ever.

She gently placed the sleeping baby on the floor, cleaned his face, and quickly changed his dirty nappy. She'd just completed the unpleasant task when Mrs Brown burst in. Her sudden arrival woke Charlie, who immediately started to grizzle again.

'He's come round. Your John and the other gentlemen are carrying him in. I'm going to make up a bed for him on this sofa.'

'I'll get out of your way,' said Barbara. 'Come along, sweetheart; Uncle John and his friend are bringing your grandpa here to have a lie down. I expect he needs a little nap after all the excitement.'

'Granpa poorly, me kiss him better.'

'When he's had his sleep, darling, I'm sure he'd love to have a cuddle with you.' She scooped him and his disgusting nappy from the floor just in time.

The makeshift bed was ready, and Mrs Brown stood by the door to make sure it stayed open as John, Simon, Mr Everton and Joe came in carrying Grandpa. He was conscious and smiled at Barbara.

'You're doing fine, sir,' said John. 'We'll get you comfortable on here whilst we wait for the ambulance.' He acknowledged Barbara's presence with a nod as he guided his three helpers towards the sofa. Goodness knew how he'd managed with his bad leg.

Where was Grandma? Why hadn't she come in? Surely she hadn't been taken ill as well? Barbara was about to rush out when her grandmother arrived.

'Mrs Brown is going to bring you

something to eat and some tea,' Grandma said. 'I've asked everyone else to return to the kitchen. We don't want to waste all that lovely food.' She smiled brightly, but her eyes glittered and her knuckles were white.

Barbara wasn't sure if food and drink were a good idea for the patient, but she didn't argue. Mrs Brown had gone, presumably to see to the rest of the guests. She wished she could be of more use, but her baby's needs must come first, and Grandpa had plenty of willing helpers. It didn't take long to get him settled, and she thought his colour was a bit better now he was propped upright and snugly wrapped in blankets.

'Grandpa, do you want a cup of tea? Or should we wait until you've been examined by a doctor?'

'I've got a dicky heart, my dear. Known about it for some time. One of the reasons I agreed to retire. I had a minor heart attack. I'll be perfectly well with a bit of rest when I've taken a couple of aspirin for my headache and a glass of brandy for the stress.' His voice was remarkably strong for a man who'd looked at death's door five minutes ago. 'Elspeth, my love, why don't you fetch the aspirins from the medicine cupboard whilst Barbara gets me something to eat and drink?'

'I'll do that. I won't be long.' She vanished,

followed by everyone apart from John.

Once Grandma had gone, Grandpa spoke to John. 'I don't need to go to hospital; there's nothing they can do. Get someone to cancel the ambulance, will you, Flight Commander?'

'I'll do it myself, sir. There's the medic from the Hall coming — I hope you'll let him give you a quick check?'

'If I must.' He beckoned to Barbara and she hurried over, not sure he was ready to be bounced on by the baby. 'Hello, little one, you going to give your old grandpa a kiss?'

Charlie struggled to be released and Barbara put him on the edge of the sofa. 'Grandpa needs to rest, darling, so don't jump on him. Just give him a little kiss and get down.'

'Don't stand about chatting, my dear. We're waiting for our party tea, aren't we, Charlie Bear?'

'I think you'd better wait until the doctor has examined you, Grandpa. I think I hear him coming now.'

An hour after the incident things were more or less back to normal — apart from the flower bed, which looked as if a bomb had gone off in it, which Barbara supposed it had done. She left her grandparents enjoying afternoon tea on a tray and went to join the crowd in the kitchen. Simon had returned with the doctor, but John was still there. She was rather glad that he was; his help had been invaluable and he deserved to share in the family party.

Relief that Grandpa was going to be all right appeared to have made everyone hungry. They were milling about the table tucking into the party food, and the atmosphere was remarkably jolly. Tom and David were in big trouble, but dealing with them could wait until tomorrow.

Charlie was content to sit in his high chair and gobble down anything that was given to him by his adoring audience. Barbara finally had time to speak to Tom and David and reassure them that no lasting harm had been done, despite their best efforts to blow everybody up.

She looked around the kitchen but couldn't see David. The other three were huddled in a corner looking a bit shifty, but still able to eat cake and sandwiches with gusto. 'Tom, where's your brother?'

He looked round. 'Don't know. Come to think of it, I've not seen him for ages.' He dropped his plate on the floor and jumped up. 'In fact, I don't think he's been around since the fireworks blew up.'

'Right, we'd better get searching.' John was

taking charge again. 'Babs, can you do the house with Ned? Tom, you go with Mr Everton and I'll take Jim.'

Nobody argued. The young man Barbara had known all her life had changed into a forceful and authoritative figure. Alex would never have suggested she marry John if he'd known how much his replacement had changed. If she weren't so desperately in love with her husband, she might find John an attractive proposition.

She wasn't going to bother the invalid with this further bit of bad news. David was hiding somewhere; he must have felt the debacle was entirely his fault, as he'd been the one to put the light to the fuses. If he'd run away before he knew his beloved grandfather was going to be fine, he might think the explosion had caused his death. No wonder he'd run off.

The search continued until dark but there was no sign of him. Grandpa had been escorted to bed with John on one side and Joe on the other. Somehow they kept the news of David's disappearance quiet. Barbara had learned on her first-aid course that shock and worry were bad for heart patients.

The Evertons had gone home, taking Ned and Jim with them. Barbara had made up the bed in the Green Room for John. No one had actually invited him to stay; it had just been assumed. Tom was distraught and blaming himself. 'I should have kept an eye on him. He begged me to let him light the fireworks and I couldn't refuse — after all, it's actually his birthday today, not mine. We searched everywhere. Are you going to contact the police, Babs?'

'Not yet. The weather's mild enough, so wherever he is he shouldn't come to any harm in one night.' Involving the authorities would make it impossible to keep the news from her grandparents, and they didn't need any more worry at the moment. Grandpa had resigned from his rounds at the Hall; from now on he had agreed to take it easy.

'I expect he'll come back when he's hungry,' John said. 'Don't worry about it, Tom — we'll find him tomorrow. Your sister's right, he'll be okay.'

After her brother had been persuaded to go to bed, John joined Barbara on the sofa in her bedroom. She was relieved the double bed was at the far side of the room and almost invisible with only the standard and table lamps switched on.

'We both told Tom that David's in no danger, but I'm desperately worried,' she said. 'He's a vulnerable little boy and takes everything to heart. When my sister-in-law's baby died last year he became very withdrawn. It took a lot of support and reassurance from all of us, especially from my grandfather, to bring him out of it.' She couldn't stop the tears trickling down her cheeks. She vividly remembered the last time someone living at the Grove had been missing overnight — the poor girl, a live-in housemaid, had been murdered. The murderer had almost done the same to Barbara. If John hadn't turned up she would be dead.

'Please don't cry, Babs. It's not the same as when Marigold went missing. I know that's what you're thinking, but back then there was three feet of snow and there's not a maniac on the loose in the neighbourhood. David's a sensible lad; he'll find somewhere to hole up for the night.'

He moved closer to her on the sofa and she didn't protest. Just for a moment she would allow herself the comfort of his arms around her. John was her friend, nothing else, and he wouldn't take advantage of the situation.

He stroked her hair and she sobbed on his shoulder, finally letting the worry and grief of the past few months surface. She sat back, wiping her eyes and blowing her nose noisily. 'I'm so sorry. I didn't mean to break down. It's just been such a strain keeping up a brave front when inside I'm falling apart.' She leaned away from him and he took the hint and returned to his position at the far end of the sofa. 'Grandpa's collapse and then David disappearing were the last straw. I promised my grandfather I would contact the War Office tomorrow and try and find out why we haven't had the final confirmation that Alex is dead.' There, she'd finally spoken the words out loud. She couldn't keep on pretending her husband was coming back.

'How long has it been since they sent the last letter?' She told him. 'That's odd, I've not heard of any family having to wait more than two months. You really should ask what the hell's going on — they must know something that you don't.' He smiled warmly, but his eyes were sad. 'The only reason I can think of is that they've heard he's still alive and are trying to confirm it. Don't give up hope just yet, Babs. As I told you before, miracles do happen. I shouldn't be alive — but I am.'

Without conscious thought she decided to tell him the truth. For some reason she was certain he wouldn't make a fuss, and neither would his parents when he told them. He loved her unconditionally and would never do anything to deliberately hurt her.

She stood up and held out her hand. 'Come with me, I want to show you something.' She led him into the nursery, letting the light from the corridor spill over the cot. Her son was spread out like a starfish. Even asleep and with his eyes shut, his resemblance to his father was obvious. 'Charlie is your son, John. Alex and my grandparents know, but nobody else. Please promise me you'll only tell your parents.'

He didn't answer, just walked softly to the cot and reached in and stroked the baby's hair. Why didn't he speak? Was he shocked? Would he make demands and ruin all their lives?

He backed away, put his arm around her shoulders and guided her back to her bedroom. 'Thank you for telling me, but I'd already worked it out for myself. Although he's got the same colouring as your brothers, I knew at once when I saw him this morning that I must be his father. I wasn't sure you knew, and I would never have said anything.' His expression was serious as he continued. 'What I did was unforgivable. If you hadn't married Alex your baby would have been born a bastard, your reputation ruined, and your grandparents put in an invidious position. You did the right thing — I shall be eternally grateful that Everton married you. I don't deserve to be part of your lives.'

She was stunned by his reaction. What a dear, kind man he was. 'I have to tell you that even if Alex is dead, I could never marry you.

I don't need the financial security, and Charlie will grow up surrounded by loving adults.'

He lent back and stretched out, flinching as the ankle flexed on his bad leg. She jumped up and fetched the stool and without a second thought placed his foot on it.

'Thank you. You're a wonderful girl, Babs, and I just wish we could have loved each other, but there's nothing we can do about it. Are you sure you don't mind if I tell my parents they have a grandson? I expect he'll be the only one they get.'

'No, of course not, but I'd prefer it if nobody else knew.' She joined him on the seat, her mind whirring with ideas. 'He can come and stay with you in the holidays when he's older. Perhaps you could tell people your wife died and that Charlie lives with his maternal grandparents?'

His eyes shone and his smile was happy for the first time. 'That would be fantastic. But we will have to tell Charlie the truth — anything else would be quite unacceptable.'

They were only talking about this because they both thought her husband was dead, despite their earlier comments. Alex would never agree to such an arrangement, and she had only revealed her secret because in her heart she believed she would never see him again.

She didn't want to talk to John any more. She wanted to be on her own to come to terms with the unbearable truth.

'I'm tired, John. Can you find your own way to bed? We need to be up at dawn and resume the search for David. I can't believe we've been talking about Charlie's parentage when we should have been thinking about my brother out there on his own in the dark.'

'I'll see you in the morning. And you mustn't worry — everything will turn out okay.'

★ ★ ★

Barbara scarcely slept, and was awake and dressed long before her baby was likely to surface. She crept through the darkened house and made her way to the kitchen. To her astonishment the light was on and the range burning brightly. Both Joe and Mrs Brown greeted her with worried smiles.

'We thought you'd be up early, Mrs Everton,' said Mrs Brown. 'I've made a nice pot of tea, and there'll be toast and marmalade in a jiffy. I thought you might like me to look after your little one whilst you're out searching for young David.'

'That would be wonderful, thank you so much. As soon as I've had my breakfast I'm going to cycle up to the Hall. I know we asked them to have a look and they didn't find him, but I still think he might be there. Could you come with me, Joe? You could use my grandfather's bicycle.'

'I'd be happy to, Mrs Everton. I've just got to give Silver her morning feed and let the chickens out, and I'll be ready.'

'Do you mind listening for Charlie, Mrs Brown? I'll put out his clothes and things, and you know what he has for breakfast. I should be back before my grandparents wake up, but John might well come down whilst I'm gone. I don't want him rushing about on his bad leg today.'

As she was creeping about in the nursery she remembered it was Sunday. There was no chance of anyone going to church today. She hoped both the vicar and the Almighty would understand that family came first. Grandpa had been told to stay in bed for a few days and take it easy, so he wouldn't be going anywhere.

She turned at a slight sound behind her and saw Tom peeping round the door. He too was fully dressed. She waved and pointed to the floor; he nodded and disappeared. He was waiting for her outside the kitchen.

'Is Grandpa all right, Babs? I listened outside the door but couldn't hear anything. If you're going out to look for David, I'm coming with you.'

'If he'd taken a turn for the worse we would know, Tom. Joe and I are going up to the Hall, and you can come. Grab a quick cup of tea and a piece of toast and we can get going.'

Outside it was barely light, but fine for cycling. As Barbara puffed up the hill she kept repeating the words, '*Let him be there, let him be there.*' If he wasn't, they would have to notify the police, and that would make matters so much worse for him when he did reappear. She refused to consider even the faintest possibility that anything untoward had happened to him.

She wheeled her bike around to the back of the building and the other two followed her. There were lights on in the kitchen, and she could see nurses and orderlies busy getting the early-morning teas ready.

She'd better let someone know they were going to search the grounds. She knocked — usually she walked straight in, but she didn't want to presume. When a nurse opened the door she quickly explained why they were there.

'We had a bit of a look round yesterday, Mrs Everton, but didn't find any sign of the little lad. You go ahead, and I hope you find him soon. We were sorry to hear about Doctor Sinclair. How is he this morning?'

'As far as I know he's much better. If you don't mind, we'll get on with the search, because if we don't find him here we'll have to notify the police.'

Joe went to search the various outbuildings whilst she and Tom headed for the summerhouse. This was the first opportunity she'd had to ask Tom how they'd made the disastrous fireworks.

'There were live bullets with the stuff we got at Christmas and I looked it up in a book in the school library. If they hadn't toppled over they would have been really good.'

She wasn't impressed with his explanation. 'What were you thinking of? Handling gunpowder is so dangerous. Apart from the fact that you gave Grandpa a heart attack, you could have blown yourselves up. There's also the matter of the flowerbed. I can promise you, Thomas, both you and David are in very serious trouble. Don't think that because your brother ran away it will make any difference.'

The summerhouse looked neglected: the glass in the windows was filthy, and the honeysuckle and climbing roses sadly over-grown.

'Look, Babs — the door's ajar. I think he might be in here.' He was there before her and wrenched the door open. 'David, you idiot, you only made matters worse by running away.'

She sent up a quick prayer of gratitude and followed him inside the dim interior. A bedraggled and sorry little boy was huddled in the corner of the building. 'Grandpa is fine,' she told him. 'We've been so worried about you. Promise me you'll never do anything so silly again.'

Although David was in disgrace, he needed a cuddle before he faced the music. He flung himself into her arms and sobbed uncontrol-lably. She rubbed his back and talked soothingly to him until he was done. He was filthy, cold and hungry but otherwise unharmed. She hadn't realised he'd run off yesterday without putting on his coat.

'Here, sweetheart, put my coat on. I got lovely and warm after I cycled up that hill.' He snuggled into it, releasing her hand just long enough to put his arms into the sleeves before clutching her again. 'Let's get you home. You need to have a nice hot bath and something to eat, and then pop into bed with a hot-water bottle.'

How were they going to transport him home? She hadn't really thought this through. Maybe Joe could take him? She kept her arm around his shoulders and Tom held his hand as they returned to the kitchen. Joe saw them coming and his homely face lit up.

'There you are, David. You've given us all a bit of a fright. Come on, I'll give you a piggyback, and then you can travel home in style on my crossbar.'

David shook his head and shrunk into Barbara's side. 'Never mind, darling,' she said. 'I'm sure we'll work something out.'

He was shivering, his nose was running, and she was pretty sure he wouldn't be able to walk the two miles in the state he was. Someone must have seen them from the windows of the Hall, as Simon emerged from the front door and ran towards them.

'Thank God you found the little boy. I'm so sorry we didn't search more thoroughly last night. The doc says to bring him in for a quick check-over before I run you back. You'll have to leave your bike here, Mrs Everton; I won't be able to fit it in my little jalopy.'

They trooped into the welcoming warmth and Matron ushered them into her office. 'There now, young David, you sit up here and let me have a look at you.'

He kept his head pressed into Barbara's

side, refusing to go anywhere near the chair. Barbara knelt beside him. 'David, we can't go home and see Grandpa until someone has checked that you've come to no harm. I'll sit on the chair and you can sit on my lap.'

He nodded. She sat and he scrambled on top of her. Matron gently peeled open the coat and put the stethoscope to his chest, then she took his temperature and checked his pulse. 'There, that wasn't too bad, now was it?'

Barbara kept her arms tight around his shaking body and raised an eyebrow in query. Matron nodded and smiled. Tom was standing right behind her but Joe hadn't come in. Simon was waiting in the doorway.

'Okay to go? Good show. I'll bring the car round to the front. Tom, Joe's outside with your bicycle. If you set off now you should be home the same time as us. I've already rung and told them you found your brother safe and well.'

'See you at the Grove, David,' Tom said. 'I'll get a bath on for you. You can have it really full — blow the regulations.'

'Come along, David, we're going home in style,' Barbara said. 'John will be so pleased to see you.' Again no response from her brother, but he didn't resist when she stood up with him in her arms. He clutched to her neck and his legs encircled her waist. He was a bit heavy, but she'd manage the short distance to the car.

'Thank you, Matron,' she said. 'I'm sorry about all the fuss. I'm afraid I won't be able to come here for a while, as I'll be needed at home.'

The car was waiting, and Simon helped her into the back seat with David still attached to her like a limpet. She was getting a bit worried about his silence; he'd not said a word since she'd found him. When they arrived John was standing in the yard. He threw open the car door and peeled David from her. She expected a protest, but he transferred his grip to John. Tom and Joe arrived as they were going inside.

'A nice hot bath, young man, then breakfast in bed for you. Mrs Brown has put a couple of hot-water bottles in, and she's making scrambled eggs, toast and Marmite.'

John continued to talk to David as he carried him upstairs. Barbara followed close behind, worried he might not be able to manage two flights of stairs. Twice he paused and leant against the wall for a moment. She was relieved when they reached the nursery floor.

The bathroom door was open and welcoming clouds of warm steam filled the room. 'I'll take over from here, thank you, John,' said Barbara. 'Have you seen my grandmother this morning?'

He gently lowered David onto the bath mat before answering. 'She came down for the breakfast tray a little while ago and said Doctor Sinclair was feeling well and insisting he could get up later.'

'Did you hear that, sweetheart? Grandpa is fine, and so will you be once you're warm and cosy and have had a lovely breakfast.' She stripped off his clothes and lifted him into the bath. He drew his knees under his chin and huddled miserably in the waist-high water. She snatched up a flannel, dipped it in the water and briskly washed him.

She continued to talk nonsense, hoping her soothing words would eventually get a response of some sort. 'There — lovely and clean. Out you come. I'll get you dry and into your pyjamas and then you can hop into bed.' He raised and lowered his arms and legs when instructed but kept his head down and didn't speak at all. At least she didn't have to carry him into his bedroom. He allowed himself to be guided there and flopped into bed when she pulled back the covers.

Tom arrived carrying the breakfast tray. It smelt appetising and was David's favourite food. However, he turned away and curled into a ball. No amount of coaxing from either of them persuaded him to sit up and eat. Eventually Barbara thought they were doing more harm than good.

'Never mind, darling, I'm sure Tom will eat your breakfast. You have a nice sleep and I'll be up to see you in an hour. Everything will be absolutely fine.'

Even as she said the words she had a horrible, sinking feeling that there was something desperately wrong with her brother. Although Grandpa had insisted her mother's insanity had been caused by childbirth, she couldn't help feeling David was showing the same mental vulnerability.

16

David refused to get up the next morning and remained huddled in bed with his face to the wall not responding, even to his brother. Barbara decided to leave him where he was for the moment.

'Tom, you'd better get dressed and have your breakfast or you'll miss the bus. I'll write a note to say David's unwell. Can you hand it in to his form master?'

'Can I stay off as well, Babs? I can sit up here and keep him company, then you don't have to keep running up and down.'

'Just for today, Tom. I'll ring the school. If I tell them about Grandpa, I'm sure they'll understand.'

'Do you hear that, David? I'm getting a day off school too. When you feel like it we can get the soldiers out, or maybe have a Meccano challenge?'

He was still holding a one-sided conversation when Barbara dashed back to the kitchen, where Mrs Brown was keeping an eye on Charlie whilst he ate his toast. Grandma must have collected her breakfast tray and taken it upstairs, as it wasn't on the

347

sideboard anymore.

'Thank you, Mrs Brown. I'm afraid neither of the boys will be going to school today. By the way, is John anywhere about?'

'He's gone up with Mrs Sinclair. He'll be back in a minute. It's a good thing he's staying here — what with Doctor Sinclair being in bed, we could do with a man about the house.'

Barbara was about to tell the housekeeper that John would be going back to the convalescent home today, when she reconsidered. When her grandparents were told about David's condition she was going to need all the help she could get. She couldn't look after Charlie and spend time with her brother. John might well jump at the chance of spending time with his son; but if he didn't want to, he could try and jolly David from his depression.

He limped in a few moments later. 'You'll be pleased to know your grandfather looks better than he did before the heart attack. A few days' rest in bed is just the ticket. How's the runaway? I take it neither of them is going to school this morning.'

'David's refusing to talk to anyone and he hasn't eaten anything since he got back. Tom asked if he could stay off with him, and I thought that was a good idea in the circumstances. I'm really worried about David. I keep thinking about what happened to my mother — '

'Babs, don't be ridiculous. The situations are completely different. Mrs Evans had been ill for years, and was certifiable. Your brother is just overwhelmed by all the upsets of the past few months.' He pulled out a chair and seemed relieved to sit down.

'I hope you're right. I don't want to tell the school why he's really staying at home. I thought I'd just say that his grandfather has had a heart attack. I'm sure the boys should be allowed at least one day's leave.'

'I'll sit with the baby if you want to make the phone call now.' He hesitated and the tips of his ears turned pink. 'Actually, Babs, I was wondering if you would like me to stay on for a bit and give you a hand until everything's back to normal. I was going to be discharged at the end of the week anyway; a few days earlier won't make any difference.'

'If you're sure, John, I'd be grateful for your help. I really want to spend some time with my brothers.'

His smile made him look like the boy she used to know. He was such a handsome man. Life would have been so much easier if she'd fallen in love with him and not Alex. Her stomach lurched as she remembered she'd promised her grandfather she would ring the War Office today. She shivered. It wouldn't hurt to leave that until the end of the week — the longer she remained in ignorance the better.

'Good show. I need to let the medic know I've discharged myself. I'm hoping Simon's still around and can bring my things down for me. I've not had time to talk to my parents; I don't want to put this in a letter . . . ' His voice trailed away and his smile faded.

Mrs Brown was busy at the range but they both realised she was listening. Had he revealed too much? 'I don't think they would mind hearing David's not well; it's not as though it's life-threatening,' said Barbara. 'But if you want to use the telephone to tell them you're staying here, then of course you can do so.'

He recovered quickly. 'It's just that they are very fond of your brothers, and they'll remember only too well what happened to your mother. Perhaps I won't mention anything about it, and just tell them about your grandfather and so on.'

'I must phone the school; I don't want the boys to get into trouble when they go back. Be a good boy, Charlie Bear, and Mummy will be back in a minute.'

Once outside the kitchen she leant against

350

the wall for a moment, recovering her equilibrium. She thought they'd got away with it, but they would have to be more careful. Mrs Brown wasn't famous for her discretion and if she got wind of the truth, it would be all over the village.

Barbara spoke to the school secretary and was given a sympathetic reception and passed on to their head of house. He suggested that as her brothers had not had any time off this academic year, it would be in order for them to stay at home for the remainder of the week. The Easter holidays began on Thursday, so they would only be having three extra days.

Before she returned to the kitchen, she would pop up and see her grandfather. She knocked on his bedroom door and was invited in.

'Good morning, my dear girl. I can't tell you how pleased I am to see you. How is the runaway this morning?'

'You weren't supposed to be worried about it, Grandpa, but I expect you wheedled the information out of someone. David's very withdrawn; I'm just going up to see how he's doing. I'll try and persuade him to come and see you, if that's all right. He might feel better when he sees how well you are.'

Her grandmother was sitting in a comfortable armchair knitting something boring by the light from the window. She smiled at Barbara. '*Mea culpa*, my dear. I can't keep anything from your grandfather, but I promise you we didn't know until David was home yesterday. Have you rung the school?'

Barbara explained what had been arranged and it met with their approval. However, when she told them that John was staying until he left for Hastings at the weekend, they were less enthusiastic.

'Are you sure that's a good idea, Barbara?' said Grandpa. 'The more time he spends with Charlie the more likely he is to guess the truth.'

'Actually, Grandpa, I told him last night. Charlie might be the only grandchild his parents ever have, and it just wouldn't be fair for them not to know.'

She waited for the exclamations of shock, but they didn't come. Her grandparents exchanged a knowing look and then both nodded approvingly. 'We think you've done the right thing, my dear,' said Grandma. 'John's an excellent chap, and it's not his fault he isn't married to you as he'd expected to be. Mind you, he shouldn't have slept with you in the first place — things could have been very different, and you would have joined the growing number of unmarried mothers.'

'That's what he said when he apologised, but there was no need. I can't imagine my life without my son, so I'm very glad we did behave badly.'

'Your grandfather insists that he's getting up tomorrow — that he's bored up here. Do you think John could bring the radio?'

'Does he play chess?' said Grandpa. 'I wouldn't mind a game or two. Keeps the old brain cells working.'

'He's an excellent player, far better than me,' said Barbara. 'I'm sure he'll be only too pleased to spend an hour or two with you. By the way, Grandpa, I've decided not to make that phone call until after he's gone. Another week won't make any difference either way. Also, if they confirm what we fear, I'll have to tell the boys, and that might push David over the edge.'

'Don't be so melodramatic, Barbara,' he said sharply. 'Your brother isn't falling into a mental decline. He's miserable and feeling guilty. He'll snap out of it in his own time. Get him painting eggs; that should cheer him up.

'Another thing — before you go, we can't let them get away with it just because David's fed up,' said Grandma. 'Have you had any thoughts about their punishment, Barbara?'

'I was thinking about stopping their pocket

money until they've sorted out the flowerbed and replaced the plants that were destroyed. Also, no unsupervised cycle rides until the summer. What do you think?'

They both nodded. 'Excellent!' said Grandpa. 'When I was a boy I would have been given a damn good hiding — but I don't approve of corporal punishment.'

'I don't want to stop Ned and Jim from visiting, as that would be punishing them as well. I'll go up and give our two the good news. Maybe knowing the worst will make it easier for David to sort himself out.'

She'd expected to hear Tom's monologue, but the nursery floor was silent. She went into the playroom, which was deserted. They must both be in the bedroom. She pushed open the door to see Tom sitting beside David, reading a book. His brother was in the same scrunched-up position he'd been in an hour ago. From the look of the breakfast tray only Tom had eaten anything.

'Right, boys, I've just been talking to our grandparents and I've come to tell you what your punishment is going to be.' Tom put his book down and tried to look nonchalant, but his shoulders were rigid. David remained as he was. She gave them the details and when she finished she waited for their reaction.

Tom spoke first. 'Blimey, we expected much worse than that. We're both really, really sorry for what happened.' He elbowed his brother in the back. 'So you can come out of your sulk, little brother. We're not going to be sent away to boarding school, or beaten with a big stick, or anything else you might have thought up.'

Barbara was almost sure David moved a bit. 'That's the bad news. The good news is the school has given you the rest of the week off — they think you are both exemplary pupils and can have compassionate leave because of Grandpa's illness.'

This definitely got a reaction. David rolled over and pushed himself up on his elbows. 'You didn't tell them what I did? Grandpa is going to be okay?'

She smiled and nodded. 'Yes, David, and John is going to stay here until he returns to Hastings on Saturday. So if you want to get him to tell you some gory war stories, you'd better get yourselves organised and come downstairs.'

David grinned. 'I'm busting for a wee. Get out of the way, Tom, unless you want me to — '

'That's quite enough of that, thank you, David. I'll take the tray back; I'm sure Mrs Brown can find you both something else.

David, when you're dressed . . . '

He didn't wait to hear the rest of her suggestion, but shot past, and the bathroom door banged seconds later. Tom threw his arms around her.

'I was so worried, Babs. He does get in such a state about things. Will he be okay now, do you think?'

'I'm sure he will, especially as you've got more than two weeks of holiday and your friends are back in the neighbourhood.'

'Do we really have to walk to the farm? It'll take us twice as long.'

'If I were you, Tom, I wouldn't argue about your punishment. I think you've both got off very lightly. I'm sure Ned and Jim will be happy to cycle over, so you won't have to walk every time you want to see your friends.'

David reappeared as she was leaving the room with the tray. 'I'm starving. I don't mind eating what's left on there.'

She smiled at him. 'I think we can give you something a bit more appetising than cold toast and congealed scrambled egg.'

On her way down to the kitchen she called in to her grandparents to give them the good news. 'David's snapped out of it — I think he was terrified we were going to send them away. They're going to call in on the way down, so prepare yourself for the invasion.'

'It's almost coffee time, my dear, and Elspeth tells me we have the real McCoy. Perhaps you could persuade young Thorogood to bring it up, and then we could have a quick game of chess before luncheon.'

Her grandmother snorted inelegantly. 'There's no such thing as a quick game of chess, Edward. However, if John is prepared to spend time with you, then I shall take the opportunity to make some phone calls and write a few letters.'

'I don't need a nurse. I'm perfectly capable.'

'You wouldn't stay in bed, Edward, which is why someone needs to be here at all times.'

Barbara left them amiably wrangling about this. They both seemed remarkably cheerful, considering her grandpa had had a heart attack. It might have been a mild one, but you couldn't be too careful.

The sound of her baby chattering and laughing echoed up the stairs. She arrived in the passageway to find John struggling to put on Charlie's harness. 'Here, let me do it. Sit still, you little rascal; we can't go out in your pram unless you're strapped in.'

'I thought we could take him for a walk around the village, Babs. I didn't want to spend too much time in front of Mrs Brown. She's already giving me peculiar looks.'

'I don't think that's a good idea either. Grandpa wants you to take him some coffee and have a game of chess. I'll take Charlie for a walk; I need a few things in the village.'

What she needed was time to think, and pushing the pram was an excellent way to do this. Having John stay was proving to be more of a worry than a help. They were going to have to be extremely careful nobody saw John with Charlie — especially Mrs Brown, who already had her antennae pointed in their direction.

Something else they hadn't thought about was how Barbara's in-laws would react to their daughter-in-law's ex-fiancé staying under the same roof whilst their son was missing in action. She still couldn't bring herself to consider his status as anything else.

When she returned, the atmosphere in the house was more cheerful. She'd noticed as she came in that the Everton boys' bicycles were propped against the brick wall in the courtyard. There was no sign of John, so he must be upstairs with Grandpa. Charlie was eager to get out and run around; an hour was the absolute maximum he wanted to be restricted in the pram.

★ ★ ★

The next few days flew past, and Grandpa declared himself well enough to get up and attend church on Good Friday. John was going to go, but Barbara and Charlie were remaining behind. She was worried Mrs Brown or the boys might think this rather odd, but nobody commented. Her son was not famous for his patience, and the solemn Good Friday service was definitely not the place for a noisy toddler.

The house was strangely quiet with everybody gone; even Mrs Brown and her son Joe were at church this morning. With the news on the eastern front being so bad, perhaps everybody wanted to pray for those who'd been captured and interred in Japanese concentration camps.

The service lasted about an hour and a half, and it would be a further half an hour before the family returned. What should she do with this unforeseen leisure time? The baby was having an unexpected mid-morning nap in his cot, so she was at a loose end.

When the churchgoers returned, Barbara had made a huge rhubarb crumble using up the last of the margarine, a large saucepan of soup, and had the vegetables cooked ready to make a giant Spanish omelette. The table was laid in the kitchen, Charlie was sitting at his high chair banging his spoon, and the dogs and the cat had been turned out to enjoy the spring sunshine.

David rushed in. 'What's for lunch, Babs? I'm absolutely famished, and the new vicar droned on for hours. I nearly fell asleep.'

'By the time you've changed out of your Sunday best, lunch will be on the table. Tell Tom to go up with you.'

Mrs Brown arrived, hastily tying on her wrap-around apron. 'My word, Mrs Everton, you didn't have to make the lunch for everyone. Joe and I will — '

'No you won't, Mrs Brown. We're all sitting down together today. We've got your lovely fresh bread to go with the soup, and I've made a delicious carrot salad to go with the omelette. The table is ready; all I have to do is put the eggs in the pan with the cooked vegetables.'

One by one her family arrived in the kitchen. Grandpa seemed in better health than he had been before his attack, and she thought the few days he'd had in bed had done him the world of good. John looked serious, and older than his twenty-three years — in fact he looked older than Alex had before he left last year. How could it have been last year? It was unthinkable he had left his family almost a year ago. He would scarcely recognise Charlie now.

The eggs were almost set in the enormous frying pan she'd discovered in the scullery, the soup was bubbling, and the crumble smelt delicious. 'Everybody, come and sit down. I'm going to serve the soup. John, would you cut the bread for me? I'm afraid there isn't any butter or margarine as it's been used, but the bread's so fresh you'll hardly notice.'

The bowls of steaming soup were handed to Mrs Brown and she placed them on the table. There was even a small amount, well-cooled, for the baby. Barbara joined them at the table, enjoying sitting with the people she loved the most. Only as she began to spoon soup into Charlie's ever-open mouth did she notice John was where Alex used to sit.

Her hand slipped and the liquid slopped onto the tray of the high chair, much to Charlie's delight. Her brothers laughed, and she was able to cover her momentary upset by jumping up to fetch a cloth to clean the baby and the high chair.

'That was absolutely splendid, my dear girl,' said Grandpa. 'I do hope there will be sufficient left for supper.' He dropped his spoon into the empty bowl with a satisfied smile.

'I'm glad you enjoyed it, and judging by the

361

empty dishes you weren't the only one. Tom, will you and David collect the bowls and take them through to the scullery please?'

The conversation around the long kitchen table had centred on the arrival of the Americans in East Anglia. 'Did you see the Flying Fortresses go over yesterday?' David asked Tom, who was sitting next to him.

'I did — they're absolutely enormous. No wonder they can't land at Hornchurch. They need runways twice as long as the ones used for the Spitfires and Blenheims.' He looked at John, his face alight with enthusiasm. 'Do you think the Yanks will win the war for us now they're over here?'

'I'm sure they will, Tom. They're better equipped and fitter than we are. However, it won't happen overnight. I can't see this being over any time soon.'

Grandma reached out and patted his hand. 'You and your crew have done your bit for the war. I'm just relieved you survived and can go home to your parents. There are far too many families who have lost loved ones.'

The words silenced the chatter. David spoke into the vacuum. 'When's Alex coming home, Babs? Shouldn't he be back by now? We haven't seen him for almost a year.'

Barbara ignored his question and continued to portion out the omelette onto the waiting plates. Grandpa eventually answered. 'I am pretty sure we'll hear something after Easter, David. Now, go and help your sister dish up the lunch.'

Conversation returned to less contentious subjects and, apart from Barbara, everybody enjoyed their food. Fortunately she'd only given herself a small portion. She didn't take any crumble and custard, and just wanted to get away from the jollity and talking. If she walked out now she would ruin everybody's lunch, and she couldn't do that.

Charlie solved the problem for her by filling his nappy in a dramatic and extremely noisy way. The stench was unbearable; even her brothers were holding their noses. She collected the baby and made a hasty retreat. The cheer of relief from those remaining at the table followed her up the stairs.

The unpleasant task completed, she took Charlie into her bedroom so he could wander about whilst she sat on the window seat. She vividly recalled the first time she'd sat here, her face battered from her mother's attack, scarcely able to believe she'd escaped a life of abuse and unhappiness.

★　★　★

Grandpa had welcomed her unconditionally, but it had taken her grandmother several weeks to come to terms with having an unknown grandchild living with them.

How much had happened in less than three years. She'd met and fallen in love with Alex and had almost been murdered by a psychopath. Then her son had been conceived, and the following week she'd met Alex again and slept with him. All that in the first few months she'd been living here. It hardly seemed possible, looking back at it now.

She wouldn't change a thing. If she hadn't run away from Hastings, she would never have found her grandparents, her brothers wouldn't have been adopted, and she wouldn't be married to Alex — wouldn't be his widow.

Charlie scrambled into her lap. 'Mummy sad? Don't cry, Mummy. Me loves you. Kiss it better.' He covered her face with wet kisses. She hugged him and rocked from side to side, trying to stop the misery from escaping. If she gave in she would fall apart, frighten her son, and ruin John's last few days here.

She gulped and swallowed, but the tears kept coming. There was a commotion downstairs, but she ignored it; she was in no state to investigate at the moment. Someone was thundering up the stairs. She had to pull herself together. There was something happening, and she couldn't hide in her bedroom when she was needed.

Her bedroom door flew open. Her eyes widened in shock. Even unshaven, painfully thin and dressed like a tramp, she knew who it was. Her world tilted and for a second she couldn't move.

Alex was beside her in one stride and his beloved arms were tight around her. She couldn't speak. The tears turned into sobs.

'Darling, sweetheart, don't cry. I'm back, and I'll never leave you again. I'm sorry you were told I was dead.'

Charlie screamed and started to kick and struggle. 'Bad man, go way, you bad man.'

He shot away as if scalded, but the baby continued to scream and cry until Alex had retreated to the door. Her son's violent reaction stopped her hysterics like a slap in the face. 'It's all right, Charlie Bear, it's your daddy come back from the war.' The baby continued to cry and attempted to bury himself in her arms. Alex leaned against the door looking defeated.

'He doesn't remember you. He'll be fine once he gets to know you again. You frightened him bursting in like that.'

Alex slowly pushed himself away from the door. 'I'm sorry, sorry about everything. I shouldn't have come back. I should have realised you'd moved on.' He brushed his hand across his eyes, shook his head and left.

She couldn't run after him, not whilst Charlie was so distressed. What was he talking about? Where was he going? Her head was spinning. He'd come back to her, but something was dreadfully wrong. She stroked the baby's head and talked to him quietly. 'Don't be a silly boy. Stop crying, and let's go down and find your daddy.' She had a brainwave and, with the child still clinging to her, she hurried to the dressing table and picked up the family photograph. 'Look, Charlie, see in this picture. This is Mummy, this is you when you were a baby and not a big boy, and this is your daddy — the man who just came in.'

He reached out and touched the image. 'My daddy?' He shook his head vigourously. 'Bad man not my daddy, no like nasty man.'

If Alex changed into his uniform, had a shave and got his hair cut, he would look more like his photograph. It must have been a dreadful shock for him to have been rejected like that, but he was an adult and should understand how difficult it was for his son.

She took Charlie into the bathroom and washed his snotty face. 'There, darling, all clean. Now, we must go downstairs and find your daddy. He will be wondering where we are.'

This was the wrong thing to say. 'Not down, stay here with my mummy.' His grip was so tight she could hardly breathe.

'All right, Charlie Bear, shall we go and play with your train in the nursery?' This suggestion stopped him crying, but he still didn't want to be put down. She desperately wanted to find Alex, hug him, kiss him, hear where he'd been all these months — but it would have to wait. Half an hour ago she'd thought Alex was dead, and now he was home. Their reunion would have to be postponed until the baby was in bed.

Ten minutes later Charlie was calm and happily pushing his little wooden train around the carpet, when there was a knock on the nursery door. Instead of asking the person to come in, Barbara scrambled to her feet and opened it herself. The last thing she wanted was another upsetting confrontation between the baby and his father.

It wasn't Alex, it was John. His face was white, and he looked as distraught as Alex had. She gripped the door frame as her knees threatened to buckle. She was so stupid. She'd forgotten John was sitting downstairs as if he belonged there.

He didn't need to tell her what had

happened; she had guessed already. 'He's gone again, hasn't he? He saw you all at the table, didn't he?'

He nodded. 'I'm so sorry. I shouldn't have come here. I'm going to try and find him — explain how things are, and that he got the wrong end of the stick.'

'No, that's the last thing you should do. He'll have gone to his parents' house. I'll go there myself. The state he's in, he might well blurt everything out.' She pointed to Charlie. 'Please stay up here with him until I get back.'

He looked confused. 'Shouldn't I go? Won't it make things worse leaving me here to look after the baby?'

'Possibly, but I haven't time to discuss it now. I need to get to Home Farm immediately. Will you tell everyone where I've gone?'

Downstairs she didn't stop to put on her coat, speak to her grandparents or her brothers, but raced across the yard and grabbed her bicycle. Alex was walking, and with any luck she would catch up with him before he got to the farm. He wasn't thinking straight; he would tell his parents their secret and cause a rift that might never be healed.

17

Barbara pedalled as if her life depended on it — which she supposed it did. She hurtled down the narrow lane, twice skidding and narrowly avoiding a head-first disaster into the hedge. About half a mile from Home Farm she saw the hunched figure of her husband walking head down in the middle of the road.

'Alex, Alex, wait for me! You shouldn't have dashed off like that. You don't understand.' Her voice carried between the high hedges and he swung round. He looked so old and tired, more forty-five than twenty-five. But he waited, although not looking especially thrilled to see her.

She braked hard, almost going over the handlebars, jumped off and dropped her bike. Without giving him the chance to step away she flung herself at him, putting her arms around his neck and dragging his head down so she could kiss him properly.

He briefly resisted, and then she was crushed against him and his lips were hard and demanding on hers. All her doubts, her worries, her grief vanished and passion consumed her. She wanted him to make love to her, and didn't care if they were in full view of anyone who came down the lane; she'd never wanted anything so much in her life. Even smelling and looking like a vagrant, he was the most desirable man in the world — he was her beloved Alex and he had come back to her.

Eventually he raised his head and gazed into her eyes, his own blazing with love. 'I don't understand. When I saw John in the kitchen as though he owns the place, I thought you'd done what I asked in my letter. I wouldn't have blamed you if you had — '

'Don't be ridiculous, Alex. I don't love John, and even if you had been dead I'd never have married him. It would be like marrying my brother.'

He laughed and suddenly looked like the man she remembered. He swung her around until she was giddy. 'Darling girl, I've thought about you every day. I didn't realise I'd been pronounced 'missing presumed dead' until I got back yesterday.'

'Do your parents know you're alive? Your sister had another baby last month, a little girl, and they called her Mary Jane.'

He kept his arm around her waist as he bent down and retrieved her bicycle. 'What do you want to do? Shall I come back with you, or shall we go to see my parents?'

'I don't want to share you with anyone at the moment. I told John that he's Charlie's natural father — he's going to tell his parents, but nobody else. I've told him our son can go and visit when he's older, when the war's over.'

They walked back linked together, Alex pushing the bicycle with his right hand whilst she brought him up to date with events at the Grove. 'It's been bloody awful for you, but I'll make it up to you,' he said. 'I overreacted when Charlie screamed, which was stupid and childish. Of course it's going to take him a few days, maybe weeks, to get to know me again.' He stopped and stared anxiously at her. 'Will John be staying much longer?'

'He's leaving tomorrow; he always was. Knowing him, I expect he'll want to return to the convalescent home immediately. He was devastated to think he'd upset us both. He's a lovely man; he has never tried to take your place and never would. If you don't mind, I'd much rather he stayed tonight and left as planned tomorrow.'

'Okay, the poor bloke can't help it if he loves you. Don't you want to know where I've been since last October?'

'Of course I do, but I think I can make a shrewd guess.' She smiled at him and his

371

expression made her heart flip. 'You were picked up by a French fishing boat and the Resistance moved you through France and into Spain, where you managed to get a ship back.'

'More or less right, but I went into Portugal first. I was damn near captured by the Nazis as I crossed the border, and had to hole up for weeks until it was safe to move again. That's why it's taken so long to return. They do a bloody amazing job, the Maquis; they risk their lives every day for British pilots. When this bloody war's over, I want to go back and thank the men who saved my life.'

'Of course you must. Maybe I can come with you, and use some of my trust fund to help the families if they need it.'

They were nearing the path that cut through the grounds and would save a mile of walking. 'If we go this way, darling, it's quicker, but you'll have to lift the bike over a couple of stiles.'

He chuckled. 'I might look like a scarecrow, sweetheart, but I'm quite capable of getting a bike over a fence if I have to. By the way, who's looking after our son at the moment?'

'Actually, John is. I didn't give him any choice; he came up to tell me you'd shot off, and I abandoned Charlie. Would you have told your parents?'

He half-shrugged. 'I wasn't thinking straight; I thought I'd lost you both. I don't know what I might have done. Thank God you came after me. I could have ruined everything.' He looked so miserable that she stretched up on her toes and kissed him.

'Even if you had let the cat out of the bag, we'd have managed somehow. Don't worry about it. Let's concentrate on the here and now and try to forget the past.' She ran her palm over his shaggy beard. 'If you shave, cut your hair and put on your uniform, I think Charlie will recognise you from the photograph. We look at it every day and I tell him that his daddy will be coming home soon.'

'Bloody hell! I was so keen to see you I didn't stop to think. Poor little chap, no wonder I terrified him. I had to ditch my uniform months ago and it was far easier to travel looking like I do.' He raised his arm and sniffed. 'Christ, I smell a bit ripe. I'll jump in a bath as soon as we get back and have a shave. Can you cut my hair for me?'

She shook her head. 'I'm hopeless at it. Mrs Brown cuts the boys' hair; I'm sure she'd be happy to do yours.'

The familiar outline of the grand Georgian house loomed through the trees. They were almost home. She stopped, making him halt beside her.

'I never gave up hope. I should have rung the War Office weeks ago and asked why your death certificate hadn't arrived, but I decided to put it off until after Easter.'

'Some sort of glitch in the office, I was told, but I'm bloody glad they didn't send it. I'm not going to be on the front line anymore. I'm taking over at Hornchurch — a desk job, and I don't have to report for another two weeks. I'm going to live here, but I won't get any petrol for the old jalopy so I'll have to use the bicycle.'

She rested her head on his shoulder, ignoring the strong smell of unwashed male, and for a moment she was silent, revelling in his return. He dropped a kiss on her head. 'Come on, your family will be having kittens if we don't get a move on.'

She didn't care what anybody thought. Life couldn't get any better. Never mind the war wasn't over; it was for those that mattered to her. Alex would remain safe behind a desk and John would become a police detective.

'It's the middle of the month, darling. I just know that we're going to start another baby tonight.'

His smile made her toes curl. 'We'll have a damn good try. But even if we never have any more children, we've got Charlie . . . and that will be enough for me.'